PRAISE FOR BRA
FINALIST MI

"Michael Laimo has the goods."

—*Hellnotes*

"Michael Laimo is a writer on the rise. He has a shrewd eye for macabre situations and knows how to draw the readers into the action."

—Tom Piccirilli, author of *A Lower Deep*

"Michael Laimo, in my mind, is the Alpha Male in the pack of new horror/dark suspense writers."

—P. D. Cacek, author of *Night Prayers*

"Laimo cranks up the fear quota several notches."

—Masters of Terror

"Michael Laimo's dark fiction creeps and cuts, calling as easily upon supernatural effects as psychological insights to disturb, startle, and just plain scare the living hell out of readers."

—Gerard Houarner, author of *The Beast That Was Max*

"Michael Laimo is able to draw out tension and suspense until it's almost unbearable."

—Edo van Belkom, author of *Teeth*

"Laimo is a delightfully twisted read. His work makes the dark scary and deliciously unforgettable."

—Linda Addison, author of *Animated Objects*

THE APPROACHING TERROR

Pilazzo straightened and stepped backward, across the sidewalk. He kept his eyes trained on the man, who wore jeans, a dirty white T-shirt, and a leather utility belt wrapped around his waist.

A construction worker.

Standing with his muscled arms at his sides, the worker opened his mouth and released a screeching howl on par with the sound a dog might make upon having its leg chopped off.

Pilazzo staggered along the length of the gate, then darted across the street. Heart pounding furiously, lungs pulling hopelessly for air, he continued racing away from the man, down the street toward Third Avenue.

Just ahead, another figure emerged from an apartment doorway.

Pilazzo gasped. He put his hands to his heart, but felt nothing.

Nothing but fear and the clear image of horror before him.

In the semidarkness, Pilazzo could see a figure—a man—was dragging a body....

Other *Leisure* books by Michael Laimo:

DEAD SOULS
THE DEMONOLOGIST
DEEP IN THE DARKNESS
ATMOSPHERE

MICHAEL LAIMO

FIRES RISING

LEISURE BOOKS NEW YORK CITY

A LEISURE BOOK®

March 2008

Published by

Dorchester Publishing Co., Inc.
200 Madison Avenue
New York, NY 10016

ISBN 10: 0-8439-6064-7
ISBN 13: 978-0-8439-6064-8

Printed in the United States of America.

10 9 8 7 6 5 4 3 2 1

Visit us on the web at www.dorchesterpub.com.

This book is for my parents, Stellario and Josephine Laimo

* * *

All my love to my family, and my friends.

Shout-outs to everyone who's ever bought or read any of my books. I truly appreciate all the support you have given me over the years.

To all my MySpace friends and supporters—you've made a difference.

To my dear friends: Brian Keene, Gord Rollo, and J. F. Gonzalez. You guys make all the hard work fun and interesting.

Special thanks goes out to Monsignor Thomas Sandi, who provided valuable feedback to me in the writing of this book. I hope I got it all right. Oh, and you're not allowed to read it. I still can't believe you read *The Demonologist*.

FIRES RISING

PROLOGUE

On the Upper East Side of Manhattan in 1892, twilight gathered.

The October sunset tossed its ruby rays across the hog farms and uncultivated lands. Small clusters of huts flanking Central Park stood firmly against the cold October winds. Their occupants, too poor to afford housing in the heavily populated downtown area, shivered and prayed for better days.

Twenty blocks to the south and a little farther east, the more fortunate settled into the new brownstones built alongside older wood-and-frame buildings. Sporadic gas lamps lined the curb, tossing gloomy circles of light upon the footpaths. Horse-drawn carriages meandered crookedly along hay-covered streets, people pacing silently along, men in long suits and derby hats, women in dresses and gossamer veils. The air reeked of coal smoke and horse manure.

It was here that nearly one hundred men had come down from the hovels and settled into a pocket of land, working endless days and nights building the church of their hopes and dreams.

Layer by layer, brick by brick, they constructed the framework from the ground up. Outside, beyond the walls that offered them security, children carried out menial tasks in exchange for fruit and water. The women wove tapestries, soon to adorn the walls of the church.

Three miles away at the seaport, two men who only hours earlier had toiled inside the newly built rectory, stood at the edge of an arched-brick warehouse that extended all the way to the wharf.

To the east of the pier stood the sailors' lodging houses. To the west, grog shops and marine cellars, their lanterns tossing garish red light onto the foggy streets. Many of the buildings here were of a neo-Gothic design, with stonework cornices and vaulted beams.

The ship the two men were told to locate loomed before them, looking not much different than the warehouse into which it had unloaded its cargo. Behind the men, the doors to the warehouse opened. A shop worker appeared whose mustache and beard were as unruly as the rats skittering about the docks.

He nodded to the two men.

The men saw a wooden sign over the door—PIER 13 it read in painted black lettering—and followed him inside.

A pair of electric bulbs encased in metal cages lit the entranceway, casting a dim glow onto the wood floor. The two men followed their bearded guide down a dusty corridor lined with dingy windows that looked out into an alley way. The corridor led to a small room, empty save for a wooden fruitwood crate that lay in the center of the room, waxed rope handles anchored into its sides.

The two men walked to the crate and examined the Latin phrase etched into its surface: *Castigo laudible, corpus meum* . . .

The man with the beard gave them a manifest, which they were told to sign. Although the monsignor had told them that the shipment was to have come from Italy—a gift from the pope himself—the manifest read *Origin Unknown*.

They questioned the accuracy of the manifest.

The bearded man told them to touch the crate.

They did so, and in seconds realized that the cargo was indeed meant for them, for their church. The men looked at each other in amazement, their hands still tingling from the warmth emanating from the polished wood. The bearded man handed one of the men a sealed document intended for the monsignor, which the man pocketed. This, the monsignor had told him, would be read at their next service, prior to bestowing the gift of the crate upon the parishioners.

Each man grabbed a roped handle and exited back out onto the pier.

They walked at an even pace, passing a multitude of shops, now closed as the sun began to set behind the river. They turned and walked north through the lower stretches of the Bowery. Their senses thrived to the sounds around them, to the clanking horseshoes, the yelling and shouting and distant singing, to the whinnying and snorting of horses. The air was charged with the foul stenches of barnacles and horse dung.

They walked farther uptown. Here the streets were filled with bobbing derby hats and crossing horse buggies. Pushcarts lurched down the center of the road like charging bulls. Peddlers lined the narrow sidewalks, selling their wares to those within earshot, be it pans or apples or steamers.

Each man gripped the rope handles tightly. The warmth from within somehow provided them with the strength and fortitude to continue unhindered by fatigue. They kept their gazes straight ahead, their minds focused solely on transporting the gift to their church.

They turned the corner. The elevated train platform towered over them, dark oil and slimy ash coating its underside. The train seemed to await their arrival. Black smoke unfurled from its stack, darkening the evening air. The men quickened their pace and climbed the steps to the platform, where they paid a two-cent fare and entered the train. The doors closed seconds later, the wheels squealed, and they were on their way uptown.

Around them, passengers chatted in clutches, undoubtedly wondering who the two ill-dressed men were and why they were holding such a fine-looking crate.

At Forty-second Street, the men disembarked and boarded a streetcar for a penny each, where they rode to Seventy-sixth Street, three blocks from their church.

Astoundingly, the final three blocks of their journey found them with more strength and vigor than they'd ever felt before. Their blood rushed furiously, hearts pounding to keep the pace. A wealth of sudden happiness washed over them, and they both understood that this crate and its contents were indeed an empowering gift from God, one that would allow their church to stand tall and powerful for many years to come.

They entered the church and walked down the center aisle, its plywood flooring soon to be covered with a donation of marble from a local factory owner. The men approached the altar, where the monsignor stood in prayer.

He smiled. "Bring the gift into the rectory."

The man with the sealed document handed it to the monsignor, and the pair moved into the rectory with the crate.

Everyone was gathered inside, many of the men who'd constructed the church, the women who'd painted the walls, the children who'd run errands. There were fifty people, perhaps more, standing around a pit that had been dug deep into the earth's foundation.

The men carried the crate to the edge of the hole. They placed it down before the waiting priests. Soon the monsignor entered and stood alongside the priests. He opened the sealed document and began reciting its contents, written in Latin.

A minute later, when he finished reading, he said, "We have been bestowed a gift of great importance. We will protect it and in turn it will bring our church great strength. Its contents shall never be revealed. It will remain buried here beneath our church for as long as it stands."

The monsignor walked to the men who had delivered the gift from downtown. "Do you feel its strength, its power?"

Indeed, the men did. They nodded.

"And so all here today shall benefit from its holy power."

Under the watchful guidance of the monsignor, each man, woman, and child took turns touching the crate. Everyone could feel its warmth, its gift of empowerment. They walked away, staring deeply at their flexing hands, utterly aware of the strength and spirit granted to them.

When all had taken their turn, the monsignor led the congregation in prayer. Afterward, he instructed a group of men to lower the crate into the ditch. A number of men jumped into the hole, while two others grabbed the rope handles and lifted it over the edge. . . .

One of the men holding the crate lost his footing and fell into the hole. The other man made every effort to hold on to the crate's handle, but it slid free of his grasp. The crate tumbled over the edge and hurtled to the bottom of the hole, landing with a loud crack. The lid broke open, and the crate's contents fell free for all to see. . . .

48 hours later

The boy, who'd turned twelve years old a week earlier, followed his mother through a dark corridor.

Both were crying.

They rushed into a small basement room that resembled a cell. A wooden table and a lone chair sat in the center of the pale stone floor. A pair of burning candles on the table cast flickering light against their frightened faces. The woman sat her son in the chair and kneeled down before him.

She swallowed hard and asked in a frantic whisper, "Do you see what is happening? What *will* happen to the rest of the world if you don't do what I ask?"

Trembling, the boy nodded.

The woman reached into the bosom of her dress and pulled out a string of large wooden beads. Separating the beads were a variety of tiny star-shaped charms, plus a sole three-inch crucifix that dangled like a Christmas tree ornament.

The woman handed it to the boy.

"What is it?" he asked.

She tucked it into the boy's hand and bunched his fist over it, holding his hand as she spoke. "It might be what people have been seeking for thousands of years. The Holy Grail, the one true name of God. Many men have sacrificed their lives for this. This is the creation of all life. It's now up to you to see it back to its rightful place."

The boy shook his head vehemently, panic twisting his dirty face. "I . . . I . . . can't." He looked at his mother's hand and saw a ruby ring of scars on her finger, swollen and bleeding, glowing beneath the golden candlelight.

"You *must!*" she insisted. Eyeing him tearfully, she released his hand and touched the glistening ring of scars on her finger. "You see this, don't you?"

He nodded.

"You are His son. You are the sinless one."

He knew the scars on her finger represented her marriage to Christ.

He looked at the crude rosary in his hand. Beneath the beads, in the center of his palm, deep red bruises emerged.

Soon they too would start bleeding.

She stood. "You've seen what evil does to men. You must use the goodness in your hands to restrain evil and put it back where it belongs."

He gazed up at her, disbelieving. *I am the sinless one. . . . I am the son of Christ.* "Why didn't you tell me this before?"

"If I'd known it would come to this—"

The door to the room burst open, and one of the church builders appeared.

Evil had him.

The builder stood bare-chested on the threshold, streaks of blood on his body and face. His scalp was in tatters, hunks of skin torn away to reveal white bone underneath. His eyes were rolled up into his head.

In his hand was a Civil War–era sword, its blade dripping with blood.

He stepped into the room.

The woman stood in front of her son, protecting him from the possessed man.

The man raised the sword . . . and lunged forward.

"Run! Now!" the woman shouted, shoving her son away with an arm behind her back. The boy screamed. He thrust the rosary into his pocket and stumbled around the table, past the builder. He tried not to look at his mother . . . but was unable to tear his gaze away from the blade slicing into her shoulder.

The builder yanked out the sword. Blood spouted from the wound. The builder raised the sword again. . . .

The boy fled the room. From behind he could hear the heavy grunts of the builder, the sound of the sword cutting into flesh and bone, his mother's agonizing screams of death.

Crying, he charged through the dark hallways. He passed into the church, which was nearly completed but utterly empty—a sight he never imagined possible. Five years of work and no one was there to embrace its otherworldly pleasures. He crossed the altar and went into the hallway toward the rectory.

He walked down the dark passage, slowly, quietly. At the entrance to the rectory, he paused, listening intently. Through the sound of his breathing, his ears picked up echoes of torture coming from the meeting room—the moans and screams of evil's victims, the guttural laughs of those caught in evil's grasp.

He clutched the rosary in his hand. It was warm and moved slightly, like a snake. He looked down and could see blood in his hands now, a jagged lesion in the center of each palm.

Stigmata . . .

He shuddered and moved into the rectory, knowing for certain now that he was the only one capable of saving the lives of those still alive.

I am the sinless one.

He walked down the hallway toward the meeting room, listening to the screams coming from inside.

In his mind, his mother's voice came: *The rosary will protect you. Heed its word and do your part to bring down the evil that promises man the end of days. . . .*

He recalled the moment the crate broke at the bottom of the pit. A sound like wind gusting in from a violent storm had emerged, and then from within the crate a black chalice floated into the air to a spot four feet above the edge of the pit.

All present had dropped to their knees and prayed to the miracle before them.

But not his mother. She had seen something else fall from the crate, and while everyone else's eyes were fixed upon the floating chalice, she climbed down into the pit and retrieved a set of rosary beads. She'd gripped the beads in her hand, seeing now for the first time what she'd been expecting all her virgin life: the ring of ruby scars around her finger. She'd shuddered, knowing she couldn't disclose this incredible discovery to anyone except her son, for he was the only one—the sinless one—meant to use the charm for its true intent.

The boy entered the room.

And saw the chalice.

It was floating over the center of the pit just as he'd first seen it, black and glossy, covered with blood and fire. Below it was a scene straight out of hell: the church builders standing at the edge of the pit, soaked with the blood of those they'd sacrificed—their wives, sons, and daughters.

In their hands were the tools used to build the church—the weapons used to slaughter their innocent families.

Piece by piece, limb by severed limb, the builders fed their victims into the pit. From an unseen point below, thin streams of blood arced up and splashed into the chalice. Within the chalice itself raged fires and wind, torturing the boy's ears.

The builders turned and looked at him. Their eyes were rolled back, faces bloody masks.

The boy held the rosary out before him.

The men cowered and screamed like burning witches. Then from within the bowels of the pit a wretched beast rose up, composed of blood and mud and the severed body parts of those slaughtered. Its head, formed of the heads of those recently decapitated, lolled on a twisted bundle of spinal cords. The mouths of the human heads screamed in unison.

The workers fled to the corners of the room in odd jerking motions. Those still not sacrificed or possessed by the beast screamed hysterically and scampered away through puddles of blood and gristle.

The beast roared—with failure, with expectation, with disorientation.

The boy stepped to the edge of the pit, just feet from the beast and reached for the chalice. . . .

Gather yourselves together, that I may tell you that which shall befall you in the end of days.

Genesis 49:1

Stigmata is a phenomenon observed in a number of Christian saints and mystics for which no satisfactory natural explanation has been offered yet. It consists of the appearance, on the body of a living person, wounds or scars corresponding to those of the crucified Christ.

Encyclopedia Britannica

CHAPTER ONE

In his dreams he witnessed the past, hundreds of faith-ful worshippers—men, women, and children—flocking to share their beliefs within the walls of the church where he now slept. They'd built the church by hand, working endless hours until they lay fatigued and bleeding. Ultimately, some men even perished be-neath the perfection they aimed to create, their bodies laid to rest in the cement foundation poured beneath the wooden floors.

And what colors! The statues, the altar, the tapes-tries, the pews, each erected with utter devotion for those waiting to worship. The columnar supports, artis-tically carved to portray the story of Jesus's birth; the vaulted ceilings, stained-glass windows, and arched doorways, constructed to inspire reflection of the heavens. Here was heaven on earth, a sanctuary that offered peace, solitude, and gratifying conformity to the appreciative masses.

Something is calling me. And I must follow.

But these were just dreams—dreams of a past more than a hundred years gone. He'd been having them ever since he forced his way into the abandoned church nearly two weeks before. He remembered how the grates leading from the subway tunnel to the church's ventilation ducts had been old and rusty, proving easy enough to remove; the ducts just wide enough to crawl through. He'd made every effort to keep his special place hidden from the others—there were actual beds on the second floor of the rectory! But soon word got around, and the church filled with his street brethren in a few days, all of them marking their territories upon the damp mattresses and carpets, like stray cats on a doorstep.

When Jyro had been a young boy and his mother was still alive and called him Jerry, she would tell him that *All good things must pass.* Time and time again the adage proved true. And here it was again: Just as things were already growing uncomfortably crowded in the rectory, the construction crews arrived to tear up the floor below.

Some of the vagrants fled back into the streets and subway tunnels, unable to cope with the round-the-clock clamor. Others found the beds good enough reason to keep their heads buried and suffer through the noise, so long as the crews remained downstairs. Jyro, on the other hand, was unaffected by the sound of the jackhammers and circular saws—years on the city's streets had made him immune to loud noises—and slept soundly.

And in his sleep, dreams of the mysterious past continued, seizing him like a fly in a spider's web.

Something is calling me. And I must follow.

After six days and nights of endless toiling, the workers stopped. As the sounds faded into the night, the dreams left Jyro, and sleep escaped him. He tossed and turned, the moans and snores of the others—Jyro had counted nine in all—driving him toward madness.

14

How is it that grinding machinery lulls me to sleep, but snoring hits my brain like a shot from a nail gun?

He sat up and gazed at the sleeping bodies lying side by side in the shadows. One of the squatters, a man named Larry who had one ear and two teeth, kept a collection of pilfered tools beside him as he slept. Jyro thought it strange that the workers below never saw Larry rummaging through their things. *It's also strange that the workers haven't come up here and found us.*

Unable to sleep, Jyro decided to investigate the quiet goings-on in the church below. Carefully he reached beneath Larry's blanket and "borrowed" a halogen flashlight. Then, while the others slept, he left the bedroom and padded down the dark hall, tailing the wide beam, looking left and right and turning around to make certain that none of the others saw him.

He went down the still-carpeted stairs, each creak like a firecracker beneath his footsteps. He reached the bottom and went into the rectory lobby.

The lobby was fairly large, and at one point perhaps had served as a living area for the priests and deacons. Cracks twisted up the walls and across the ceiling. A sole emergency beacon on the ceiling provided a dim light, revealing a desk, a sofa, and a number of metal folding chairs leaning against the wall.

Jyro stepped to the center of the room, swinging the flashlight back and forth. To his left he saw a hallway, ominous as it trailed away into darkness. He narrowed his eyes but didn't see any evidence of work being done here.

He moved into the dark hallway.

On his right he passed a doorway that led into a

small white-tiled lunchroom. A row of rusty combination lockers followed, lining the wall like soldiers. Ahead, piles of splintered wood came into view, burying the threadbare carpet.

Soon he came to a large double doorway. He crossed the threshold, facing what appeared to have once been the church's recreation center: a fifteen-hundred-square-foot gymnasium with a small stage running the entire length of the far wall. He shined the flashlight upon a lone basketball hoop anchored to the ceiling, then swung the beam downward, where he immediately beheld the hideous work of the construction crew.

In the hardwood floor was a hole so large that it swallowed nearly half the gymnasium, the edges jagged and splintered upward. Jyro could see a folding card table dangling precariously at the far edge.

He stepped forward. In the trembling beam of the flashlight, he could see a variety of tools shoved against the stage and wall. *Something is calling me, and I must follow.* The words surged through his mind again, grasping him and forcing him to press on.

His frayed boots crunched on bits of debris. A sudden flash of heat enveloped him, making it difficult to breathe. Encroaching grayness created a tunnel of vision, forcing him to focus solely on a lone dark spot in the hole. He stretched his arms toward the spot. *It's calling me. Something there . . .*

The uneven edge of the opening met his feet. For a moment he remained still, frozen in place. Then the floor dropped out from under him. He pinwheeled his arms for balance, but slipped down, the flashlight falling from his hand and clunking somewhere nearby. His tattered jacket got snagged and tore down the back. He thudded on the rock-hard bottom six feet below amidst a pile of talus, his breath escaping in a painful whoosh. He rolled over and something jabbed painfully into his ribs; he cried out and rolled back.

He opened his eyes.

And saw bones—*human* bones—jutting from the ground.

He skittered away in a panic, grabbing the flashlight. A cloud of dust rose around him. He aimed the flashlight around and saw in the wavering beam a long line of skeletons—complete rib cages, leg bones smattered with bits of gristle and rotted flesh, skulls with snarled clumps of hair still attached.

Decapitated.

I saw them being buried in my dreams. But . . . there are more here than what I saw. What is this?

He moved the beam away from the graveyard of bones and focused it ahead.

Here he saw a solid wall of fill, the lower strata of the church's foundation open like a wound: asphalt and cement layered over brick and soil. Here is where the workers would lay a new cement foundation. He shined the beam across the fill and saw what appeared to be a wooden crate protruding from the lower layer of soil. He shook his head, gathered his composure, and struggled to his feet. Taking a deep breath, he stepped toward the crate. The aged bones in the soil crunched beneath his weight.

Using just his fingers, he began to dig away at the hard earth packed around the crate. He worked gingerly at first, but then more furiously as his heart began to pound with inexplicable excitement.

Something is calling me, and I must follow.

He cleared more and more of the surrounding soil

away. The box seemed to grow warm . . . or maybe it was just his head playing with him. Regardless, he worked and worked until a chunk of earth below the crate broke off, allowing it to fall free.

He gripped the edge of the crate and jerked his hands away in pain. It was *hot*. He scratched the gruff on his face. Then, like a child cooling soup, he blew on the surface. Dust burst up in a cloud, assaulting his nose and making him cough.

He retrieved the flashlight and angled it at the top of the crate. The wood was branded with foreign words. He brushed away as much of the soil as he could, but couldn't make any sense of the writing.

He whispered as he read: *"Castigo laudible, corpus meum . . ."* An odd disquiet washed over him.

He wedged his fingers of one hand beneath the edge of the lid, which had come loose. With a grunt, he yanked it off. That was too easy, he thought.

He slid the lid off the crate, let it fall to the ground.

He aimed the flashlight's beam inside.

His heart leaped in his throat. *My God . . .* And yet there seemed to be no logical reason to be so frightened at what he saw inside the crate: two very ordinary-looking burlap cloths, stiff and tattered.

He reached for one of the cloths.

Laden with dry rot, it crumbled into pieces. A heady sea-salt odor rose up as a string of wooden beads slipped free of the cloth, into his hand.

He cleared bits of the rotten cloth away from the charms. Yes, he knew what this was. His mother used to carry one everywhere she went. *It's a string of rosary beads. But . . . it's different from the one my mother had: These beads are as big as marbles. The cross is almost*

*the size of my index finger. And what are these oddly
shaped trinkets that look like stars?*

He allowed the beads to cascade through his fingers. His body shuddered at their nearly tangible offer
of otherworldly comfort: They were warm to the touch,
human warm.

Quickly, he shoved the beads into his left pocket.

And peered back inside the crate.

The other burlap bag was moving, as though a
mouse or a large insect were fighting its way out from
beneath it.

Jyro reached for it. It stopped its undulations and he
jerked his hand away, gooseflesh rising across his back.

He stared at the bag for a few seconds. Then, ever so
slowly, reached for it again.

A splay of red light burst out from below the shred of
burlap. Jyro flinched back against the hard wall of the
ditch. He coughed, holding an arm up, wincing as
something heavy turned in his stomach.

A tiny flame burst from the burlap bag, swallowing it
up. Black ashes and glowing embers fluttered up like
moths, revealing what appeared to be a goblet inside
the crate.

Leaning forward, Jyro could see that it was perhaps
eight inches high, black and glossy, with a coat of
shiny, smoldering residue. Like a magician's assistant, it
floated up out of the crate into the air, emitting the
same soft red glow he'd seen beneath the burlap cloth
just moments earlier.

Unmoving, Jyro could only stare wide-eyed as it
climbed to a height of ten or twelve feet. On the outside of the chalice he could see etchings similar to
those of the surface of the crate.

The red light grew brighter around it, the chalice itself swelling before his eyes, like a great pupil focused solely on *him*.

The room grew hotter. Sweat gathered on his brow as fear and anxiety roiled in his blood. He shoved the flashlight into his pants, then with a gasp stepped onto the crate and gripped the sheared edge of the wooden floor. He hoisted himself up, feet scrambling against the exposed bricks, fingers digging into soil, face in the dirt, hands cramping as he pulled himself up out of the hole onto the dusty floor. Quickly, he climbed to his feet and scampered to the room's entrance, where he grabbed the doorjamb and peered over his shoulder to look at the chalice again.

It floated far above the hole: a widening spot in the aura of red light still aimed at him, *looking* at him.

From within the hole, a din of raging fires surfaced. It filled his ears with dense pressure that dulled his shouts. A wind sprang up, stinking of rot and sulfur, shoving him back into the hallway.

He looked around wildly and staggered away, following the flashlight's beam back to the dark lobby. When his breath returned, he released a sharp gasp and looked back down the hallway. Red light spilled out of the rec room, illuminating the hallway as though a fire were raging nearby.

He fled up the steps to the second-floor landing, where he collapsed breathlessly onto the threadbare carpet, trying to rid the image of the floating chalice from his head.

These will help me, he thought, seeking the rosary beads in his pocket. Hands trembling, he gripped them tightly, staring at them with awe and wonder.

They're beautiful, and they'll protect me like my mother's beads protected her until the day of her death.

He grasped them into a tight ball, thoughts focused solely on the calming magic they seemed to possess. Exhausted, he lay down on the carpet and stared into the darkness, listening to his heart pounding, feeling his skin tingle.

Soon, sleep took him, and in his dreams he could vaguely hear his own voice repeating the same phrase over and over: *"The evil that promises man the end of days."*

CHAPTER TWO

Blue skies.

Proud sun.

Warm breeze.

The weather in Manhattan could have been described as joyful. Traffic was flowing smoothly, devoid of impatient horn honking. In the branches of trees growing in square cutouts in the cement sidewalks, birds fluttered and chirped, seemingly jealous of those brave pigeons pecking at the feet of passing pedestrians.

Two middle-aged men met on Seventy-eighth Street before the entrance to the Church of St. Peter. One of them was a priest, the other a construction foreman. They were approximately the same age, of the same build and height and ethnic background. But that's where the similarities ended.

"This way, Father."

The construction foreman, wearing a yellow hard hat, held up the orange construction tape to allow Father Anthony Pilazzo to pass below. The priest leaned down, the bones in his forty-three-year-old body creaking. *Perhaps now would be a good time to start exercising again*, he thought, knowing that finding time for even a simple routine would be as hard as performing a service for a church full of satanists.

He leaned back and eyed the Church of St. Peter, its crumbling face somehow more obvious now that its demise was in order. The once-red bricks were faded and chipped. The public announcement board was shattered, the majority of its plastic letters lying on the sidewalk below like discarded cigarette butts. What had originally read *I once was lost, but now I'm found, was blind but now I see* now read *new stud slut* in a disconcerting stagger of letters: the simpleminded brainstorm of some moronic passerby.

Pilazzo shook his head and adjusted his priest's collar as perspiration trickled its way beneath. He took a deep breath and tasted the grit of cement and sawdust, then buried his hands in the pockets of his black trousers. "One hundred and fifteen years. What a crying shame."

The foreman flattened his lips and narrowed his eyes to feign compassion. He slid the hard hat back on his head, revealing a sweaty brow.

He looks nervous, Pilazzo thought. *Why? All he has to do is tear the church down, then build it back up.*

"I've never been the religious type, Father, but I can certainly relate to your disappointment. My wife and I had to give up our home after her company transferred her to New York last year. Toughest thing we ever had to do, especially with the kids going to a new school and all. We're only starting now to feel comfortable in the new home."

In the tree immediately behind Pilazzo, a flock of sparrows tossed their tuneful song into the air. "It's much harder than you think," Pilazzo said. "It's like watching my own mother being led into the gas chamber, as morbid as that sounds."

Michael Laimo

The foreman smirked, no longer making an effort to suppress his lack of compassion.

Pilazzo shook his head. "With all due respect, Mr. . . . I'm sorry, what was your name again?"

"Henry. Henry Miller."

"Yes, Mr. Miller." He pointed to the church. "This church has been here since the turn of the century. It was built by our grandfathers, the priests and parishioners themselves, back in 1892. Every column, every pew, every sliver of stained glass paid for, manufactured, and erected by the hands of those who worshipped and lived in its walls. There's a history here that could never be duplicated. And now corporate America has brought its fist down hard on one of the few truly historical Catholic churches this city still has to offer. It's a terrible disgrace, Mr. Miller, an injustice to the Catholic religion."

Miller's eyebrows furrowed. "I don't disagree with you, Father. But I have a job to do here, ya know?"

Pilazzo continued, "What took our forefathers years to build will take your crew a couple of days to tear down. A few months from now, in this space between office building number one and office building number two, office building number three will stand, with money-hungry lawyers on the top floor overseeing contracts between landlords and their kennel of lessees. It's all about the money and nothing more." He paused, swallowed past the grit in his throat, and added, "No one cares about God anymore."

Miller lowered his dark eyes toward the sidewalk. Lunch-hour pedestrians walked busily along the curb, clear of the construction tape, oblivious to the fact—and not really caring—that a hundred-and-fifteen-year-old church was about to be torn down.

Pilazzo brushed by him and strode across the sidewalk toward the five steps leading up to the church entrance. He placed one foot on the bottom step and stared into the darkness beyond the open half of the twin doors.

A breeze sprang up, carrying with it a cloud of dust that circled into the church's gloomy depths. It doubled back, tossing bits of debris onto Pilazzo's face. He closed his eyes and coughed. Behind him, the lone tree's leaves rustled. When he opened his eyes, the afternoon sun caught the metal edge of the closed left door, causing a pinpoint glare to pierce his eyes. As he moved aside, he realized that all the sparrows in the tree had ceased their tuneful chirping.

"The actual demolition won't start until next week," Miller said. "At this point the crews are disassembling the pews and some of the other items on the donation list. As we discussed, we'll need you to approve the new applications before we can move them all out."

Pilazzo nodded. He looked at the tree and noticed the sparrows had taken flight. *The tree looks empty without them. Like the church does now, without parishioners.*

"And the statues and the crucifix behind the altar . . ." Miller added.

"What about them?" Pilazzo turned his attention back to the foreman. His heart began to pound. He massaged his chest with a closed fist. "They haven't been damaged, have they?"

Miller hesitated. His face paled and his Adam's apple bobbed up and down. "No, they haven't," he answered weakly.

Pilazzo said, "I've performed thousands of Masses

under the watchful eyes of those statues. I hope noth-ing bad has happened to them."

"As you know, our . . . our crews aren't insured for moving valuables. Again, I strongly suggest you hire a moving company to handle them. We won't be able to move them out unless you sign a damage waiver . . . but I advise against that. Our men aren't trained to be delicate, ya know what I mean?"

If it weren't considered an act defiant of the graces of God, Pilazzo would have cursed the man out, and Lord, it probably would have felt darn good using those words he'd only heard others say during confes-sion or in the movies.

"I'll see to it, then," he muttered, eyeing Miller suspiciously. Something about the foreman bothered Pilazzo. *It's his eyes,* he thought. They're cold and dark. Then he wondered if Miller's men had damaged the statues after all.

Dear God, no . . .

Again Pilazzo stared into the darkness beyond the open door of the church.

The breeze emerged once more, as if attempting to send a message to the priest. This time it created a spiral of dust at the jamb that for a moment resembled a tiny tornado. Pilazzo felt himself being drawn toward the windswept debris, toward the door and the waiting dark-ness beyond, wanting to enter the church one last time and bless its walls before they came tumbling down.

Something is calling me, and I must follow.

"Father?"

Pilazzo turned and looked at Miller. The foreman had removed his yellow hard hat, exposing a hairless, sweaty, sunburned head. There was a patchwork of dark lumpy freckles, suggesting too much time in the sun and not enough concern for skin cancer. "Yes . . . Mr. Miller, what is it?"

"It's lunchtime now." A cocky grin cut into his stone face. "The guys are on break for the next hour. If they ask you for ID when they get back, just show them this." He handed Pilazzo a plastic card with the word VISITOR in big bold letters on the front. Along the top in smaller letters was the name of the construction company: *Pale Horse Industrial*.

Pilazzo grinned, despite the upsetting state of affairs. "Thank you, Mr. Miller."

Miller nodded. "You're welcome, Father."

"If I sounded crass, please know it's because I've been living in this rectory for seventeen years. After getting evicted . . . well, let's just say that the last two months of my life have been less than comfortable."

"I understand," Miller said unconvincingly, seemingly impatient with the priest.

Pilazzo shook his head, suddenly and quite inexplicably assaulted by anger and resentment. "No, I don't think you do, Mr. Miller. Imagine this: One day you wake up, and there are city employees knocking on your door, telling you that one of their attorneys has just found a loophole in your sixty-year-old contract and that now they own your property, and 'thank you for your business sir, but you now have exactly one week to gather your things and get out.' Think about it, Mr. Miller. How would that make you feel?"

Miller nodded, dark eyes again aimed toward the ground. He looked like a scolded child—one with a hidden weapon up his sleeve. "Not too good, I suppose . . ." He hesitated, adding as Pilazzo gazed at the open door, "If you don't mind, Father—" He pointed up the street, signaling his exit. "I'm on union hours."

Pilazzo brushed him away with one hand. "Go, then. I'll be fine."

"There's some protective gear on the table to the right, as soon as you walk in. There's also a yellow envelope in there with the documents for you to sign. The ones on top are for the donations, and the others are damage waivers. But again, I gotta tell you we'd rather not have to move—"

"I'll hire a mover," the priest blurted. "But I won't sign anything until I do. I have to sit in the confessional this afternoon and really can't afford any distractions."

Let the foreman wait.

Miller grinned smugly. "Tomorrow, then. But I'd prefer you came at noon, so there won't be any work going on while you're inside. For your safety." He tossed his hard hat into a truck and bustled away, the sun beating down against his spotted baldness.

Father Anthony Pilazzo remained standing on the cordoned-off sidewalk for what seemed an eternity, staring into the stark blackness beyond the doors.

This time, no whirling dust . . . but still, it calls me. I can feel it. . . . He took a deep breath, then walked away from the place he'd called home for nearly twenty years.

CHAPTER THREE

Again Jyro dreamed of the church fathers who'd labored so hard to erect its walls and adorn its interior. Like a fly on the wall, he witnessed the men of the past digging a hole similar to the one he'd found in the rec room. He watched as they threw their shovels down and lowered the crate with the odd lettering into its hidden depths.

A crowd of people looked on from the perimeter of the hole. They were crying and praying with their eyes closed and their heads shaking back and forth, tears glistening in the flickering candlelight.

The men standing in the hole began to shovel dirt back on top of the crate. An odd wash of red light spilled out of the crate and spread across the entire hole. Now Jyro could see dead, naked bodies lying in the hole, dozens of them, men, women, and children, bleeding out onto the dark soil. They'd been quartered, their arms and legs positioned across their torsos like logs on a flatbed, drawn bowels exposed to the elements. Blood streamed from their eviscerated abdomens into the ditch.

Jyro tried to move closer. He wanted to confirm that what he was seeing was real, that there were in fact murdered . . . no *sacrificed* people being buried in the hole, that their blood was actually *flowing* across the bottom of the ditch. He felt himself floating down from his place of safety into the crowd of onlookers. When he reached the ground, he staggered through the people gathered around the hole until he broke through the front. Here he was confronted by the waiting gazes of the men in the hole, each of them staring up at him as if he were an intruding enemy. One of the men appeared beside him and grasped his arm, brandishing a knife, its twelve-inch blade coated in blood. Jyro tried to scream, but like in many other nightmares, was unable to find his voice.

The man's eyes rolled up into his head . . . and with a single thrust, he plunged the bloody knife into Jyro's gut. . . .

Jyro startled awake, the horrific nightmare giving way to the snores of the sleeping vagrants in the bedroom.

He rubbed his eyes, then his stomach; he could feel the ghostly ache of the knife from his dream. As the images of his dream faded, he wondered if the chalice he saw floating in the air had indeed been real.

And if so, was it still there now?

The rosary!

Heart pounding, he clawed into his right pocket and for a moment panicked because all he felt was a torn hole giving way to the rough bare skin of his thigh. But then he realized he was fishing in the wrong pocket. When he checked, he was relieved to find the rosary still in his left pocket.

This means the chalice I saw was *real*. . . .

He struggled to his knees and looked around for a good place to hide. He wanted—needed—to remain alone with the rosary. After all, it had called to *him* and perhaps even had a message for him. As he climbed to his feet, a number of tender places on his body reminded him of his fall into the hole: his back, hips, and legs all throbbing with sharp aches and pains. Grimacing, he bent over to massage his right thigh and saw the halogen flashlight he'd taken from Larry on the floor along the wall.

He retrieved the flashlight and plodded away from the carpeted landing, his laceless boots leaving a dusty trail on the hallway's hardwood floor. He passed the bedroom and peeked inside. It was still packed with sprawled bodies, many of them snoring loudly or mumbling in their sleep. Beams of dim light played in through the room's only window, illuminating the dust motes floating lazily over the sleeping men.

It's daytime now . . . how long have I been sleeping?

He looked down the hall toward the rectory's only bathroom, its door slightly ajar.

He limped to it, hesitated at the threshold . . . and went inside.

Something is calling me. And I must follow.

The bathroom stunk to high heaven. He switched on the flashlight and shined it around. He glimpsed the toilet, backed up and overflowing with thick, dark sewage. Gagging, he turned, thought about leaving but ended up closing the door behind him, fighting back the stink with a nausea-filled gulp. He took a step forward, placed the flashlight on the edge of the sink and aimed it toward himself, then cocked an ear against the door.

Certain that no one else was around, he dug a hand into his pocket and took out the rosary.

It's beautiful. . . .

Like an entomologist studying an insect, he contemplated it with heart-pounding fascination, with awe. He touched every marble-sized bead, the crucifix, its star-shaped charms carved in ancient wood.

It's mine. It called to me. . . .

One thing was certain: He wouldn't let anyone else see it. If they did, they would most certainly fight him for it, because a charm like this would fetch a pretty penny at the pawnshop on Eighth Avenue and Forty-fourth Street—enough, at least, to buy a good bottle of liquor or a meal at Tad's Steakhouse.

He closed his eyes and let the rosary slip through his fingers. It seemed to press up against his skin, like a cat looking to be petted. *Must be my imagination,* he thought, feeling the weighty beads as they released *warmth* into the center of his palms.

Time seemed to slow. He felt rejuvenated, stronger perhaps. When he moved his arms, he could feel his biceps flexing. The aches and pains from his fall last night were no longer there. *It's as if it's . . . healing me.*

His fingers moved along the beads more fervently now. Out of the blue, fond memories of his mother returned to him. She was doting on him when he was a smart young boy, watching over him every second of the day with her strict and God-fearing eye to protect her only son from the evils of the world. As a young boy, Jerry Roberts saw no choice but to gratefully accept his mother's vigilance, and follow God's path for him.

He saw images of his father and how the man had given him a harsh and drunken demand to "ignore your nut job of a mother," had told him to find some work other than his after-school duties as an altar boy at the Church of Holy Innocents. His father would shout, time and time again: "We need you to help support the family. We earn barely enough money to pay the rent on this hell-forsaken rat hole we call home. You earn straight A's in school—put some of those smarts to work and help us pay the goddamned bills!"

Jyro realized that his father had been justified in his demands, but the old man was unable to win the losing battle and in frustration had chosen to drink away his sorrows. In the end, his father had surrendered his liver to the devil, who, as his mother once said, was more than willing to take it from him.

Jerry had been sixteen when his father died. Three days later, as they walked home from the funeral, his mother was killed by a hit-and-run driver, snatched away from him as he held her hand, the rosary in her fingers torn apart, its beads scattered in the street like seeds.

Soon thereafter, he'd quit school—much to the dismay of his teachers, who were all quite smitten with their attentive honor student—and started attending church every day; it was the only thing that helped erase the haunting image of his mother's body lying bloody and mangled in the street, her eyes fluttering as they took one final glance at him. He'd prayed daily for the strength to carry on. But with no inheritance to claim—and no living relatives to take care of him—the rent on the "rat hole" came due.

Despite his prayers, Jerry Roberts had no money left after feeding his inherited propensity for drink.

With nothing more than the clothes in his closet, Jerry Roberts soon found himself among the wanderers in the streets of New York City.

He shook the memories from his head, squeezed the rosary tightly, and prayed for them to lead him away from the fourteen years of pain and sickness he'd suffered while living on Manhattan's streets and in its shelters.

The rosary will protect me, guide me. I never lost faith in God. My mother introduced Him to me, and I lived with Him in my heart ever since I was an altar boy. Now, he's called on me to perform a service, just like He did when I was a boy, after my mother died. Yes, I can see it now . . . the beads. I have to listen to them.

He opened his eyes and met the light from the flashlight. The shadow it created upon the soiled wall was that of a praying Virgin Mary, her innocent image shattered by water stains mimicking the blood of an unbound period. He sucked in a long breath and shut his eyes. He squeezed the rosary more tightly, the warmth emanating from it both certain and disconcerting.

"Find him. . . ."

The whisper in the room was as real as the beads were warm. His hand went to his mouth, and his eyes shot open. The hair on his arms stood on end, his gaze fixed upon the wavering silhouette, the stains on the wall darkening.

"Who?" he managed to ask, eyes still fixed on the shadow. It appeared for a daunting moment to have moved, the dark outline twisting toward him, eyeing the rosary in his hand. *Wanting* it.

There was a surge of light as the flashlight's beam brightened. Then it faded and died with a pop.

From the darkness that now surrounded him, the icy-cold grasp of a hand seized the back of his neck.

He cried out and swatted himself, writhing against it. He leaped forward and banged into the closed door, fumbling blindly at the knob and listening to the whispering voice of the unseen shadow behind him as it filled his mind: *"Find him."*

He cried out until the knob turned beneath his slipping grip. He burst free of the bathroom like a tiger from a cage, clutching the rosary against his chest as he shambled down the hall, away from the tainted darkness.

And into someone he'd never seen before.

CHAPTER FOUR

One block away from the Church of St. Peter, Father Anthony Pilazzo entered the subway station at Seventy-seventh and Lexington, tackling the steps as the heated stench of urine seeped into his nose. People of all denominations scurried to and fro, some more quickly than others, having to sidestep a pair of homeless men sitting in front of the turnstiles, tin cans in their shaking hands. Pilazzo had read somewhere that the average Manhattan panhandler netted approximately forty grand a year. Considering that the Church of St. Peter brought in roughly a hundred thousand a year, panhandling didn't seem like such a bad racket after all. Pilazzo once jokingly told his fellow priests that he might dress them up as panhandlers and have them cruise the subways in between Masses.

He waited on the platform, watching no one in particular but noticing two construction workers engaged in conversation near a cement support beam. They wore soiled jeans and tees with leather tool belts draped around their bulging waists.

An attractive young woman in high heels and a navy business suit walked past them, becoming an immediate target of their distasteful comments. She paid their catcalls no attention, hurrying along the platform with her leather briefcase clutched tightly in her right hand, her blond hair blowing in the breeze escaping the tunnel. The men laughed and shamelessly resumed their discussion.

The train pulled into the station. Pilazzo stepped to the edge of the platform, a few feet in front of the construction workers . . .

. . . *and shuddered as he imagined, for the briefest moment, both men leaping forward and pushing him onto the tracks before the oncoming train.*

He turned and looked back at the workers. The two men had stopped their conversation. They were staring at the priest, their eyes boring imaginary holes into him.

Pilazzo's face tightened as uneasiness overcame him. He offered the men a weak grin and turned away.

The two men seemed to contemplate him as though he were a curiosity at the zoo. *It's as if they're scared of me,* Pilazzo thought.

Pilazzo stepped back.

He looked at the men again.

The man on the right, thirty something and in need of a shave, clutched his stomach with both hands, as though stricken with cramps. His cohort remained motionless with his hands at his sides, eyes still glued to the priest.

The train's brakes squealed as it came to a grinding halt. Pilazzo nodded toward the two men as the doors opened, then turned nervously and entered the subway car.

Three plastic blue seats offered him a view of the platform. He sat in one and peered back out through the open doors.

The two workers were still there, seemingly unwilling to board the train they'd been waiting for. The doors shut, the train pulled away, and Pilazzo watched with consternation as the two men craned their necks to look at him through the soiled windows.

"Spare some change, Father?"

A ripple of gooseflesh sprinted down Pilazzo's spine. He twisted his head around and locked gazes with a grubby homeless man. Hunched and scowling, the man pushed out a calloused hand that trembled as if with Parkinson's. He stared into Pilazzo's eyes.

"My uncle was a monsignor, Father."

Automatically Pilazzo nodded, shuddering beneath the pungent shadow of the man. The train shifted and shook as it raced through the tunnel. The homeless man's body wavered forward, but didn't tip; he had the balancing act down to a science.

Grinning congenially Pilazzo looked at the floor, focusing on a spot of gum, trampled into a dark gray circle. Ignoring beggars in the subways and streets of New York City was the universal way of letting them know that they should shuffle along.

But the homeless man remained unmoving.

Seconds passed. Again the priest shuddered, his mind now fraught with anxiety: *There's more to this man than a simple request for loose change.*

Pilazzo looked back up at the homeless man, and saw a glow in his previously dead-to-the-world eyes that wasn't there before. His eyes, once black, now brimmed with intellect and an inexplicable bond, which for the moment was unbreakable.

The vagrant reached forward and grasped the priest's shoulder . . .

. . . and in that moment Father Anthony Pilazzo saw

in his mind blackened skies and an army of tattered men facing a great evil rising up before a wall of raging fires and billowing smoke. . . .

The sound of the train doors opening shook Pilazzo from his nightmare. He slid out from beneath the grasp of the homeless man and staggered away through the open doors onto the subway platform, uncaring which stop it was.

He leaned against the arm of a battered bench and turned to look at the homeless man, now pleading for the generosity of an indifferent young woman seated with her head faced down.

Slowly, the train began to pull away, and the homeless man rolled his eyes up and pinned Pilazzo through the cloudy window. The priest's breath escaped him in a single gasp, leaving him confused and afraid as the clear, daunting image of destruction continued to burn in his mind.

A wall of raging fire and rising smoke . . .

He rubbed his eyes, wishing it all away. Soon the train disappeared into the tunnel, and the image of the homeless man faded . . . but in his mind, the nightmare fires continued to burn as he made his way back out onto the streets of Manhattan.

CHAPTER FIVE

Before Jyro stood a pale, dirty-faced boy who, despite being nearly six feet tall, looked maybe sixteen years of age. He wore jeans and a stained yellow T-shirt that hung slackly over his thin frame. His blue eyes, bloodshot and swollen with tears, stared inquisitively at Jyro.

"What are you doing here?" he said, his voice weak and hoarse.

Jyro remained silent, fingers trembling as he covertly tucked the rosary into his palm. His heart raced. The rosary was strangely warm against his skin, as though it were a living, breathing creature. He swallowed past a nervous lump in his throat, and in an attempt to distract the boy from the rosary, motioned toward the bedroom, which was still packed with lazing vagrants.

The boy shoved past Jyro and looked into the bedroom. The expression on his face was one of shock and disbelief. "How long have you all been here?"

"About two weeks," Jyro responded, both hands now clenched around the rosary to keep it hidden and safe.

It's mine . . . all mine. . . .

The boy paced a tight circle in the hall. Jyro noticed a patch of blisters on his hands, wet and red as if recent. "It's only been two months since we last performed Mass here," the boy said, "and now just look at the place. . . ."

"The construction crews," Jyro replied, as if to say, *Don't worry, we won't be here for long.* He added, "The rec area . . . didn't you see it? It's destroyed." His thoughts flickered back to his midnight walk: *Strange that the construction crews aren't tearing the place down as they should be. They've been here nearly a week. And all they've really done is dig a big hole in the ground.*

That's because they are looking for something. . . .

The boy gazed about the hall, clearly distraught. He looked at Jyro and said, "I saw it." Fear and pain seeped into the boy's face, and he looked down at his burned hands.

"The hole? You saw it?"

The boy nodded. Tears flooded back into his eyes. He shuddered hard and wrapped his arms around his waist.

Jyro stared at the boy and wondered if there was any connection between him and the chalice.

"Did you notice anything *odd* about the hole?"

The boy's eyes darted back and forth between Jyro and the entrance to the bedroom. "I came back here because I'd forgotten to empty my locker. And that was when I saw the hole." He shook his head. "It broke my heart to see that—do you know how many games of basketball we played down there? How many times we sang on that stage?" He paused and seemed to gather his thoughts. "I . . . I don't know how long I was down there, but at some point I got real scared and ran out of the room and came up here . . . and . . ." He trailed off, rubbing his wet eyes. "I think you need to leave now. All of you. The construction workers are going to come up here next."

The workers, Jyro thought. *They* must've *seen the floating chalice. One of them probably grabbed it, just like I took the rosary.*

Jyro asked, more sternly now, "Did you see anything unusual in the hole?"

The boy began to fidget uncomfortably and seemed eager to leave. "Unusual?"

Yeah, like a floating chalice filled with fire? Is that why your hands are burned? Because you tried to grab it?

Jyro worried that maybe he really shouldn't have brought up the chalice at all—what he had witnessed was a mystical occurrence, one that may have been meant for his eyes only. But he found it odd that a boy would have remained here at all, carrying on a conversation with a vagrant. *Is he meant to be a part of it all, too?* he wondered. *A floating chalice. A strange rosary. A whispering shadow. It all must mean something.*

And on top of that revelation, he thought: *My God . . . the boy came for the rosary. His tiredness and blisters are his battle wounds from trying to find the rosary.*

As surreptitiously as possible, Jyro shoved the beads into his pocket.

The one with the hole.

It dropped down his leg, past his torn cuff, and onto the floor.

Jyro cried out, clawing at the burning pain the rosary left behind on his thigh. He looked down and saw the beads lying on the floor like the shed skin of a snake, free for anyone's taking.

No!

He scrabbled down on his knees and quickly retrieved the rosary, kissed it and rubbed it all over his face, whispering tearfully as he relished its warmth, "I'm sorry, I'm sorry . . ." An odd feeling of mourning prevailed over him, his heart and blood tingling with waves of despair. *Don't leave me, ever again. . . .*

"Are you a religious man?" the boy asked, puffy eyes narrowing.

Jyro nodded emphatically without looking up, tears filling his eyes. "I used to be an altar boy, just like you."

A few seconds passed as a deafening silence pervaded the room. The boy cocked his head and replied, "I never said anything about being an altar boy."

Uncertainty filled Jyro's mind. He pulled the rosary away from his face and stared at it—had it revealed to him that the boy had served as an altar boy here at the Church of St. Peter? Or did he guess it from what the boy had said about performing Mass here?

It didn't seem to matter because somehow he also knew the boy's name.

"Timothy," he whispered, wholly aware of an undeniable—and inexplicable—connection with the boy.

The boy's mouth fell open, eyes wide. "How . . ."

But Jyro ignored him, feeling the need to gaze upon the rosary between his fingers. He marveled at its carved detail . . . and the power buried deep within it. At the irrefutable message it seemed to convey.

"That rosary," Timothy said. "It *is* beautiful . . ."

Find him. . . .

The boy?

Jyro looked up, shuddering now with dismay. Like an animal eyeing its prey, Timothy was staring at the rosary. A moment of grave silence passed.

Stirring, the boy shook his head. He closed his eyes for a second, then gazed back at the rosary. "Where did you get it?" he asked calmly, after taking a deep breath.

"It's mine. . . ." Jyro said, the instinct to protect the rosary burning in his blood. He climbed to his feet and took a step backward. He jerked his hands to his side, keeping the beads close. "My mother gave it to me, years ago."

Timothy's brow creased, blue eyes slicing through Jyro's lie. "You stole it, didn't you? It belongs to the church."

Two vagrants emerged from the bedroom, presumably to see what was going on. Jyro had become acquainted with these two during his stay here at St. Peter's. The first was a heavyset man named Rollo who toted a Bible around like a child would a teddy bear. He had a high-pitched voice and spoke primarily in biblical phrases. His thinner counterpart, Marcus, was a man only recently on the streets after he'd lost his job and apartment. His dress shirt wasn't even that soiled yet. He chain smoked and had a deep, raspy voice that corroborated his bad habit. With great interest, both vagrants watched the exchange between Jyro and the boy, but said nothing.

The beads grew very warm in Jyro's hands. He tightened his grip and took another step back, looking at Timothy, Rollo, and Marcus, feeling strangely threatened by them all. Was it possible that they all wanted the rosary? "No . . . they're mine. Mine . . ."

"Like hell they are!"

The voice had come from behind Rollo and Marcus.

The three vagrants and Timothy looked toward the bedroom and saw one-eared Larry, thief of tools, standing in the threshold. His hair was mussed, and his eyes were wild. His two teeth jabbed out in a mad grimace.

In a crooked yet hefty stagger, Larry dodged across the hall. He threw his arms out and slammed into Jyro like a linebacker would a quarterback. They toppled sideways and struck the wall with a crunch. Plaster rained down from the ceiling as both men locked their arms in a slow, pathetic brawl. Jyro saw a frightening level of brute determination in Larry's dirty face: eyes bulging, lips scowling. Clearly the madman wanted the rosary and would kill to get it.

Larry gripped Jyro's arm by the elbow and with surprising strength, yanked his hand out of his pocket. Jyro roared and thrashed, making every effort to defend his prize, but he was unable to twist himself loose. Suddenly he was convinced that everyone in the room had turned on him.

The rosary grew very hot. Screaming in pain, Jyro opened his fist and shook it . . . but the wooden beads remained clinging to his fingers like a praying mantis clutching a twig.

Larry snarled and lunged again for the rosary.

Timothy yelled, "Stop!" from his position on the landing, where he remained safely poised to flee the fracas should it get out of hand. The other vagrants had emerged from the bedroom to check out all the excitement and were now lined up in the hall, wide-eyed and gaping. One vagrant, a lanky albino, clutched the threshold and trembled like a frightened puppy.

There was a smash of breaking glass, and in the next moment Jyro could see the neck of a shattered amber whiskey bottle in Larry's fist. He lashed out with the makeshift weapon at Jyro's face.

Jyro dodged sideways, avoiding Larry's assault. The bottle ripped into the plaster wall where Jyro's face had been, giving him enough time to whip his head forward in a desperate, do-or-die move.

His forehead connected full-force with the crazed bum's nose. The collision produced an abrupt, wet cracking sound, followed by a shocking flare of blood that spattered the wall like a burst water balloon.

Larry staggered back against the opposite wall. His mouth fell open, taking in the blood pouring from his nose. His hands swung blindly through the air, and he dropped the bottle into the growing puddle of blood on the floor.

Jyro stood paralyzed as a harsh bolt of pain ripped through his head, echoing the raw burn of the rosary in his hands.

Screaming, he broke his paralysis and shook his hand hard. The rosary at last separated from his skin and dropped to the floor. Tiny patches of his flesh smoldered on its dark surface like embers.

Dizzy and nauseated, Jyro faltered along the length of the wall toward the bathroom, flexing his hand in agony. His vision blurred, obstructing his view of the rosary, which appeared to be writhing on the hardwood floor like a worm. He fell to his knees, leaned forward to grab it . . . but it was too far away.

He looked up and saw Larry, running blood coating his mouth and neck like a scarf. Larry attempted to shout, but only guttural, throaty gurgles emerged. Then he slipped into unconsciousness and collapsed to the floor.

Shaky and confused, Jyro struggled to stand. He

made it to one knee and almost fell back down, but was immediately aided by a pair of helping hands. On his feet, he leaned against the wall, head spinning, listening to his labored breathing and the chatter filling the hallway.

Blurry faces stared at him, so many of them. No one spoke except Rollo, who had his Bible open and was reciting from the Book of John.

He twisted his neck to look at the man who had helped him to his feet. He was in his thirties, gawky, going bald, wearing glasses with the frames taped at both corners. He stared not at Jyro, but at the floor, eyes dark behind his clouded lenses.

"What is it?" Jyro asked him.

The man's eyes stayed pinned to the floor. "You . . . gotta . . . be . . . shitting . . . me."

Jyro traced his line of sight. In silence, all the others in the hallway did the same: nine homeless men—not including the unconscious Larry—and Timothy, who had meandered back into the hallway.

At first Jyro had assumed that everyone was looking at the rosary—after all, just moments earlier he thought he'd seen it moving on the floor—but that wasn't the case at all. It remained just as he'd left it, bunched into a small pile. No . . . what he saw on the floor was something much more unsettling, and it made him realize that, indeed, something dark and foul was present within the tattered walls of the Church of St. Peter.

Larry's injury had left a pancake-size puddle of blood on the hardwood floor in the center of the hallway. It was *moving* . . . rippling along the edges as though a rock had been dropped into its impossible depths. Jyro found himself stiff with fear. His mind's eye flickered back to his dream, how the blood had flowed of its own accord across the bottom of the pit into the ditch the men had lowered the crate into. *Just like this blood . . .*

Everyone watched incredulously as each drop of blood in the hallway was drawn into the puddle—the spots on the wall, the stream on Larry's face, even the blood on Jyro's clothes and beard. Every last bead, skittering and hopping like water in a hot frying pan toward the rippling puddle.

The room plunged into silence as everyone struggled to make sense of what they were seeing. Movement was everywhere as all around them tiny drops and thicker streams of red crawled snakelike on the floor and walls, leaching out of their clothes and skin. It was an unreal picture. And yet there they all stood, witnessing it.

As the reality of the situation struck, the albino vagrant cried out and slipped back into the bedroom, looking not at all well. Everyone else stood and watched as the puddle, widening and now nearly a foot across, started to seep across the floor, moving slowly and in stages like a jellyfish in saltwater, producing a wet slurping sound as it went. Streaks of blood, like rivulets of rainwater on a windshield, wandered across the floor and bled back into the puddle, causing it to grow thicker and larger. All eyes watched in silence as the blood seeped across the threshold of the bathroom and disappeared into the darkness beyond.

The thin man with broken glasses held Jyro's arm in a tight grip. Jyro jerked away and eyed him fearfully, as if he'd been the cause of the blood moving.

Then he looked around at all the men. They were terrified. He turned back toward the bathroom, then stepped down the hall and stood before the open door.

The air felt thick, greasy. As he gazed into the darkness beyond, his mind reeled and he could hear his heartbeat in his head.

"Here."

Jyro spun around, startled.

The vagrant with the taped glasses stood behind him, offering a penlight. "I found it in the bedroom, along with a bunch of tools." He licked his lips and added soberly, "In case you're thinking of going in."

The rosary!

Jyro panicked. He jerked his gaze to the bathroom, the vagrant with the glasses, and the floor. In an instant of terror, he saw that someone had lifted the wooden beads—*my God it's gone no no no*—but was immediately relieved to see Timothy approaching, clutching the rosary in his right hand.

Find him. . . .

He held it out toward Jyro. "Maybe we can use this to protect us."

Jyro nodded in silence, wondering again if the rosary was meant for Timothy. Could it be that the altar boy was the one Jyro was supposed to find, and that he would help protect them from the evils unleashed here?

He looked around. The small group of homeless men had formed a distant semicircle near the bedroom door; the thin, lip-licking man with broken glasses; the scrawny elderly man with long straggly hair and faded tattoos covering his arms; the bearded man in his late twenties with dreadlocks down to his waist and tiny bones piercing his earlobes; the tall, bald, muscular black man with eyes that penetrated

Jyro like lasers; Rollo with his Bible clutched tightly against his chest, standing alongside Marcus, who was nervously smoking a cigarette; and finally, the heavy-set vagrant with a mane of blond hair, blue eyes, and an endlessly nodding head who in a mindless ramble yesterday had introduced himself as Weston.

Jyro looked back to the bedroom. The albino was now perched at the door, hair wispy thin and snow white, hanging over eyes as red as rubies.

All the men stared at Jyro pleadingly, as if he by default had become some sort of leader. Jyro locked gazes with Timothy, hoping for a partner in crime. The boy remained silent as he rubbed the rosary in his hands—hands that didn't appear as burned as they had been just minutes earlier.

"Do we have a choice?" Jyro asked, peering into the dark bathroom.

"I don't know . . . I mean, all I really came here for was my duffel bag," Timothy said.

Jyro paused, looked back at Timothy. "So why then, after two months, did you decide to come for it today?"

The boy shrugged. "I . . . don't . . . know."

Disconcerted, Jyro peered back into the looming darkness of the bathroom, its stench stronger than ever. "You do now," he said. When Timothy didn't question him, he aimed the penlight inside. "C'mon . . . let's go find out why we were called here."

CHAPTER SIX

To keep himself from falling, Father Anthony Pilazzo brushed his fingertips against the facing of the storefronts he passed, pulling away only when an oncoming pedestrian got in his way. He'd walked this way for seventeen blocks to 103rd Street, where the Church of Holy Innocents stood waiting like an oasis in the desert.

When Pilazzo had been forced to leave St. Peter's two months earlier, Monsignor Thomas Sanchez at Holy Innocents had enthusiastically offered him residency at his parish. They'd been childhood friends, having attended Catholic school together in the Bronx, where they obeyed the orders of the teachers, all of whom were ready, willing, and able to wield their mighty wooden rulers should any shenanigans occur in their classrooms. The boys spent weekdays playing stickball in the streets until their mothers called them in for dinner at six, and on Sundays, they would fritter away their afternoons at each other's homes, discussing religion and arguing about whose mother made better meatballs and sauce.

Unlike the Church of St. Peter—one of the last remaining churches in Manhattan that had offered all-day Masses—Holy Innocents provided services only once an evening Monday through Saturday, then all day on Sunday. Pilazzo found it odd to walk into an empty church in the middle of the day. Having performed two Masses daily at St. Peter's, he'd wondered what he might do with his free time, knowing that he'd probably end up hearing confessions. Here in the city, those seeking forgiveness of their sins were more than willing to cough up every detail of their indiscretions, something Pilazzo, despite his pledge to society, hated having to listen to. *I'm a priest, not a psychologist.*

Today Holy Innocents offered much of what he'd become used to: emptiness. Like most days, not a single person stopped to pray, leaving the pews bare and vacant in spirit. The lamps overhead were dimmed, coating everything in dull, amber light. The brightly painted walls lay drab and ghostlike in the gloomy atmosphere. Candles flickered from the pulpits assembled on each side of the altar, their crimson casings casting a reddish glow against the statues of Jesus and Mary peering remorsefully at the communion rail.

Pilazzo's footsteps echoed in the tomblike silence, the faint smell of incense hanging in the air. He reached the transept, directly before the altar, knelt, and performed the sign of the cross. After a moment of prayer, he stood and walked to the far right corner of the church, where the two confessional booths stood, their black curtains showing signs of wear and tear—a consequence of the eager hands of those anxiously seeking solace behind them.

He unlocked the first confessional, reached up and turned on the light. Two bulbs ignited beneath faux brass shades, a white one in the compartment he entered and a green one opposite the sliding plastic grate, where the open curtain offered comfort.

Closing the door, he sat in silence on the cushioned bench, his thoughts racing with the events of the day.

An army of tattered men facing a great evil rising up before a wall of raging fires and blackened smoke . . .

The sound of the curtain sliding in the attached booth jarred Pilazzo. He gazed at the opaque plastic partition, strangely hesitant. He peeked down at his watch and was startled to see that almost thirty minutes had passed since he sat down. His hands trembled, as baleful images filled his mind.

Visions of apocalypse.

Tears welled in his eyes. He shook his head, cracked his knuckles, and slowly slid the plastic divider open.

At once he could hear deep, raspy breathing. A moment of uncomfortable silence passed, and he briefly thought of all the confessors he'd encountered over the years seeking God at the eleventh hour due to some life-threatening operation or diagnosis of cancer. Finally, Pilazzo asked, "What is it that ails you, my son?" He felt no need or desire to commence with a prayer.

"We are brothers," the man croaked. "Brothers in arms."

The stench of something rancid seeped through the plastic partition. Pilazzo grimaced, realizing at once that in the attached booth sat a down-and-out veteran of the street: a homeless man.

"Then brothers we shall be," Pilazzo replied hesitantly.

"And as brothers, God's lambs, we shall fight evil hand in hand until death comes pounding on our doors. There is no promise of sanctuary in this world we exist in. Evil has arisen. And it awaits us . . . brother."

Pilazzo grinned pitifully . . . and then a bit uncomfortably. Having heard some unusual confessions in the past, he thought little of this somewhat disconcerting display: a homeless man near death, in fear of the devil due to a life of iniquity and sin.

Is it that . . . or is it something else that drives this man?

"God forgives all those who've sinned in their lives, regardless of whether their failings amount to one or many. You are His child, and you shall be forgiven. All you need to do is ask for His forgiveness through penance."

Silence, save for the man's labored breathing.

"Your guide into heaven lies—"

"We must fight evil hand in hand," the man whispered hoarsely. "As brothers. As God's lambs."

Lambs to the slaughter . . .

Pilazzo blew out a long breath—frustration worsening his already enfeebled state. "God asks that you face your fears—"

"No!"

The man's bellow ricocheted through the church like a gunshot. Pilazzo started, clutching the brass cross dangling from the chain around his neck. His heart rate sped, like it had when the vagrant on the subway grabbed his shoulder. He turned the latch on the door to his compartment, locking himself in as a precaution. Four years earlier, a priest at St. Joseph's in Harlem had been murdered in the confessional, slashed repeatedly in the empty church while people lined the streets not two hundred feet away. Since then, a number of parishes had locks installed in the booths.

Pilazzo peered at his watch again. Somewhere in the attached rectory a hundred feet away, his fellow priests and deacons were studying, playing cards, watching television. Surely they heard the man's shout and would investigate? He glanced around the booth, hearing only the labored breathing from the opposite side of the partition.

The homeless man scratched his fingernails against the plastic partition, the sound sending shudders through the priest's tightening chest. In a strange monotone, the vagrant declared, "Evil has dug its way out from the grave, brother."

Pilazzo replied gruffly, "And just what is this evil you speak of?"

There was a pause, the seconds ticking like hours. Eventually, the man answered, "The evil that promises man the end of days."

At once fear doused Pilazzo. His mind assailed him again with the now familiar, haunting images of fire and smoke rising to the heavens before an army of tattered men.

Men who were suddenly coming into focus.

Oh my dear God . . .

He could see them now. The tattered. The torn.

The homeless.

Bewildered, Pilazzo squeezed the cross in his hand, the images in his mind as real as the words seeping through the plastic divider from the unseen vagrant. He'd never experienced such a hallucination before, a vision that he could see, *smell.* He tried to speak, but his tongue was coated, the words crawling from his mouth in a harsh whisper. "What is this evil you speak of? Is it . . . is it an army of men?"

Light, throaty laughter emerged. "Now you see, brother."

Pilazzo nodded in the darkness, inhaling deeply the man's penetrating stench. The muscles in his neck tightened, delivering jolts of pain into his head. "I see the army . . . and behind them, fire and smoke."

"It is an image, brother, that will stay with you until *we* bring evil down."

"We . . ."

"You and I. As brothers, we will fight to the death against evil."

Pilazzo searched for a fitting response. As he started to speak, the sound of the curtain's hooks sliding on the bar sifted through the partition. Racing footsteps followed, their echoes fading quickly. He leaped up and twisted sharply at the latch. Forgetting it was locked, he caught his index finger between it and the wooden door. He cried out, shook his hand with frustration, then unlocked the door and threw it open.

Ahead, the dark shadow of a figure sped out of the church, an invading beam of sunlight blinding Pilazzo before thinning and vanishing behind the church's closing door.

Pilazzo sprinted from the booth to the nave. He stopped with his hands on his knees, gasping, his mind racing in circles. As mad as it seemed, the coincidence of two homeless men delivering messages of destruction—of apocalypse—could not be ignored.

He slumped down in the pew closest to him. He sat in restless silence, unable to turn his thoughts from the strange events of the day.

The evil that promises man the end of days . . .

And as he managed for a moment to reflect upon the empty church, he couldn't help but lament again the demise of his former home, the Church of St. Peter, once bustling daily with parishioners, now dead and being eviscerated by Henry Miller's construction workers.

CHAPTER SEVEN

The beam from the penlight in Jyro's hand somehow only further defined the odd shadow on the wall, its tall shape still that of a praying Virgin Mary, the stains near her womb nearly black now. Behind him he could feel the presence of Timothy, the tall boy peering closely over his shoulder.

"Jesus, it stinks in here."

Jyro grunted, his mind suddenly filled with memories of the past—of the devout Catholic belief he'd lost years ago while living on the streets. How on his first night sleeping beneath the clouded moon he had sought the shelter of a Dumpster in an alley, only to encounter an older resident who took exception to his territory being invaded. The two men, both drunk, had argued, then fought, the conflict coming to an abrupt end when the crazed bum flashed a switchblade at Jyro. Jyro had fled into the night, coming away from the experience with a slashed lip and the lasting fear of entering some other drifter's domain. From that point forward, he knew it would take much time to learn the unwritten laws of the street, so he reached out and sought the shelter of the local churches, praying to God daily for some miracle to deliver him from the evils of the cruel world. But as his appearance and cleanliness sunk to repellent levels, even the usually accepting hand of the church rejected him, forcing him to remain on the streets, bitter and resentful of the path God had chosen for him.

"Reeks of evil," he replied, staring at the shadow, thinking for a moment that it had moved slightly. *Like before.*

He entered the bathroom and stepped to the left, allowing Timothy to squeeze in beside him. He moved the penlight's beam across the cracked tiled floor.

No sign of the moving blood puddle.

"Did we really see it come in here?" Timothy asked, massaging the rosary. "Or am I crazy?"

Jyro took a step forward. The edge of the porcelain sink dug into his bruised hip. A burst of pain shot across his midsection and he grunted. The dead flashlight he'd left there toppled in with a clunk.

"You all right?"

Breathing deeply despite the stench, Jyro angled the penlight's beam toward the backed-up toilet. Motioning with his head, he replied, "No. Not at all."

Timothy's eyes traced the beam. After a deadly pause, he whimpered, "Oh my God . . ."

Beneath the diffused glow of the penlight was the puddle of blood. It was pooled around the base of the toilet, a foul moat welling and rippling like dark lava. Thin streaks of it flowed up along the porcelain like veins, glistening as they vanished over the soiled rim into the sludge.

In a sudden sweat, Jyro muttered crazily, "Drink this, for this is my blood."

As if in response, the sludge in the toilet gurgled. Once, then twice. Then, like a science experiment gone bad, the horrid stuff erupted over the brim of the toilet onto the floor, soaking up what remained of the stirring blood.

Timothy thrust out the rosary. Its small charms dangled in his shaking hand. Jyro heard him mumble something, but couldn't make it out over the bubbling sounds the sludge was making. He stepped back and hit the doorjamb, unable to peel his eyes away from the erupting sewage.

Timothy leaned forward, arm still outstretched, fear and curiosity evident on his face. He shook his head back and forth.

"What's happening?" Jyro asked. His eyes darted between the boy and the toilet.

Timothy didn't reply. Jyro pressed him, more urgently now. "What do you see, kid?"

"I *don't know*," he answered sharply.

And then the toilet exploded, spraying them with shards of porcelain and thick brown sludge.

Jyro screamed so loudly it hurt his throat. Both he and Timothy cowered and tried to cover themselves with their arms. Shouts erupted from the hallway. Jyro heard someone call out, "What the hell's going on in there?" but no one ventured in to investigate.

"Kid, c'mon!" Jyro grabbed Timothy by the arm. The slanted beam of the penlight bobbed and weaved across the bathroom walls. "We need to get out of here!"

Timothy didn't move. Terror had him. His eyes were bulging, body trembling like a bundle of charged wires.

Jyro shook him. The boy remained unresponsive. A whisper fell from his lips, "Oh my God . . ."

There was a dull sound, an odd shaking thump that

Jyro felt in his feet. He looked toward the toilet . . . and saw something rising from its shattered remains: a hideous bulk of malformed legs—vestiges of some freshly slaughtered carcass bound together like a hunter's bounty. The thing was moving, shaking loose its foul coating of waste . . . and then the animal legs— those of a deer perhaps—pulled apart with brutal tearing sounds: *Phrrrrak! Phrrrrak!* Huge lizardlike claws burst out of the thing. They latched on to the edge of the shattered porcelain and pushed upward. Jyro gasped as the massive thing rose to the ceiling, a misshapen lump of feces wrenching back and forth like a birthing animal, black craggy slabs of sewage sliding from its splitting surface, leaving behind slick patches of blood.

He spun away from the thing, a silent scream snared in his throat. He lunged for the exit, but the door slammed shut in his face with a deafening crash, closing out the weak splay of light seeping in from the hallway and his ability to see the creature.

Timothy, having remained impossibly quiet to this moment, screamed bloody terror in the dark. He turned and began kicking and flailing against the wall. Jyro pointed the penlight at him, and the boy shrieked, *"Get me out of here!"*

"Over here!" Jyro aimed the penlight at the door. He managed to grab hold of the knob, but it wouldn't budge. He banged on the door. Timothy stumbled over and did the same, their arms and fists colliding. Jyro could hear the shouts of the others in the hallway. Someone outside was trying the doorknob, to no use.

The thing behind them let out a monstrous croak, startling them into immediate silence. They stopped pounding on the door and cowered against it, listening helplessly to the squelching noises the thing made.

Jyro looked over his shoulder. He threw the penlight's beam at the thing. The shadows it made melted and moved behind it, seven feet of writhing, sputtering feces anchored from floor to ceiling, its surface roiling and shifting as various shapes took hold of it, deformed human hands, animal legs and claws, bestial faces emerging to scream only to melt back into its dark, jagged bulk. It seemed not formed of anything wholly solid, but vacillated amoeba-like, spitting hunks of itself onto the walls and floor that swiftly surged back into its massive collective.

"What is it!" Timothy screamed, shoving back against the door, tears bursting from his eyes. Jyro felt the boy trembling alongside him, offering his own terror no comfort at all.

As if responding to the boy's voice, the thing jerked toward him, its midsection bending sideways and showing signs of an apelike face within. From somewhere deep inside its churning mass, a series of bellowing snorts surfaced, like those of an angry bull.

Jyro and Timothy huddled against one another, wobbly with terror.

"*You're not real!*" Timothy shrieked. "*You . . . can't . . . be!*" The thing swayed back and forth and coughed a storm of foul matter across the small, tiled room. The severed pieces throbbed and rolled back into the bulk like drops of mercury returning to a silver pool.

Jyro yelled, "Go back to the hell you came from!"

From above came a ghastly sucking sound. Jyro pointed the penlight overhead and saw rootlike tentacles of sludge writhing and twisting across the ceiling.

They moved to a point just above their heads, then separated from the ceiling and wriggled down toward them. Jyro could see ridges on the pale underbelly of one, like those on a snake.

Jyro and Timothy screamed, *"No! No!"* They hunkered down, jerking their gazes about the dark room in an attempt to defy what they had already come to know: that unless they got the door open, there'd be no getting out of there.

Again they slammed the door with their fists, crying in desperation, *"Help us please! Help! Get us out of here!"* The doorknob shook back and forth, but the door itself remained impenetrable.

The tentacles continued downward. Timothy tore away from Jyro and slid on his knees across the wet tiles. Jyro shouted, "No!" and fell to his knees and grabbed the boy's belt.

A tentacle slithered around Timothy's waist. The tip of it brushed against Jyro's hand. He screamed and let go of the boy.

Dear God, help us . . .

Timothy looked down and saw what had him. His eyes bulged. He kicked and flailed. "Ahhh! Get it off! Get it off!"

"Oh Jesus, no," Jyro cried.

They fell from the ceiling like vines—a forest of winding ropelike things ringing around Timothy's arms and legs, leaving dirty wet trails on his clothing. The boy shrieked and clawed, whipped his head back and forth, but couldn't free himself. "Help me, please, help me!"

One tentacle channeled out of the darkness and latched on to Jyro's biceps. Jyro pointed the penlight's beam at it and saw two amphibious eyes glaring back at him, black and wet and multifaceted. They blinked and rolled in and out of its mucky body, as if attempting to focus.

Jyro screamed and swatted at it.

The tentacle coiled around his biceps and traveled to the nape of his neck, leaving a trail of sludge on his arm.

He dropped the penlight and clawed at the tentacle, burying his fingernails into its soft pulpy skin. The thing hissed at him. A chunk of writhing flesh tore away, and Jyro watched incredulously as it slithered away into the darkness. All the other tentacles started hissing at this moment, as if they had just now formed throats. They floated across the floor and curled around Jyro's and Timothy's ankles, thighs, wrists, waists, little puckering mouths taking bites out of them.

Timothy kept kicking and flailing wildly. Jyro could see his efforts waning. The tentacles swelled and bulged, pulling the boy across the floor toward the massive bulk.

Jyro spotted the penlight on the floor and with his free hand snatched it up. The light swam across the wall to where the Virgin Mary shadow had been. He noticed it was gone now—dark water stains included. He banged on the door and cried out, "Help me!" Again the door shuddered back and forth, but to no avail.

He spun and pointed the light past his feet, toward the bulk. He saw a dark trench in its side. *A mouth,* he thought with sick horror, and at that moment an oily, forked tongue slid out and whipped back and forth.

Timothy kept screaming, fingernails scraping madly at the tiles. He jerked his head back and forth. The tentacles drew him closer . . . closer to the massive flickering tongue and gaping mouth.

Jyro screamed *"No!"* realizing all too suddenly that he too was being dragged toward the bulk. The banging on the door went on and on. Ahead, one of Timothy's feet was off the ground. The monstrous black tongue was wrapped around his foot. By accident, the penlight's beam fell upon the rosary, still gripped tightly in Timothy's hand.

The boy, out of fear or pain or shock, had forgotten he still held it.

Oh my God . . .

It wasn't the rosary itself that gave Jyro the sudden hope; it was the sludge and liquid *around* it that made him realize they could actually come out of this alive.

He yelled, "Timothy! The rosary!"

Timothy, his foot now inches from the bulk's mouth, twisted his neck around and saw the rosary dangling from his hand.

And around it, eighteen inches of dry, clean floor.

The waste was unable to come into contact with the rosary.

The two former altar boys locked gazes, and at that moment they seemed to connect on a deeper, mental level—they came to a full understanding of each other, and what needed to be done.

More tentacles wound down from the ceiling and wrapped around their arms and legs. One closed around the toilet-paper dispenser and yanked it off the wall. The paper roll landed in a puddle of sludge, rolled a few inches before it was snatched up and pulled into the bulk.

Timothy, eyes suddenly bright and alert in the darkness, tightened his grip on the rosary . . .

. . . and in that moment Jyro recalled Timothy's words moments before they had entered the bathroom: *Maybe we can use this to protect us . . .*

. . . and Timothy lashed it into the gaping mouth of the devouring bulk.

A sound that rivaled the cries of the slaves of Hell ripped through the room, a thousand throats screaming out, deep guttural grunts along with the high-pitched screeches of women and children in agony. The tentacles whipped away, writhed frantically, then turned black and melted into runny sewage that spread across the floor in a deluge of gunk. From above, the liquefying appendages rained down on them. The massive bulk in the middle flopped back and forth like a salted slug before melting into a massive heap of waste.

For a moment there was no sound other than Timothy crying alongside the huge pile of gunk. Jyro turned the penlight to him and could see him lying on his side with his arm still outstretched, still clutching the rosary.

Jyro was about to say something when a loud slam shocked them both out of their skins: the door bursting open. Light filtered into the room, offering a shocking sight to those peering in upon the aftermath of the war that had taken place inside.

Over the sounds of Timothy throwing up alongside him, Jyro cried, "Get us the hell out of here."

CHAPTER EIGHT

The silence is deafening, Pilazzo thought, peering about the church. He remained seated in the pew, staring at the altar, vaulted ceiling, and walls—all dimly lit by the flickering glow of the prayer candles and lamps. No one else had come in for confession, leaving him time to think. He again found himself pre-occupied with the demise of his former church.

How will I feel when I see the walls being torn down, the pews being dismantled, the statues being moved out? He likened it to having to sit beside a loved one during their final painful minutes of life, something anyone would find difficult.

His thoughts drifted back to his mother's dying days: of how he had no alternative but to put her in a city-run home for the elderly because he couldn't afford a private facility on Long Island. He recalled how she had lambasted him from the discomfort of her soiled linens for his decision to become a priest, how in her illness she couldn't have cared less about his faith and wanted only to be comfortable, not saved, in her dying moments. How she had cried to him about how the screams from the other patients at night were driving her crazy—even more so than the lashing periods of dementia and delusions of ruby scars around her fingers. And then, how she never had said good-bye to him before the night she snuck out of her room while the nurse was making rounds, climbed out onto the roof of the old building, and hurled herself into the path of an oncoming cab four stories down. . . .

I'm sorry, Mother. . . .

The afternoon grew late, and the time had finally come for Pilazzo to retire to his quarters for the evening. Outside the shuttered doors of the Church of Holy Innocents, rush hour prevailed: the hustle and bustle of Manhattan's workers going home; cabs fighting one another for precious road space. The city's lifeblood coursing through its concrete veins.

Despite it all, deep silence dominated the church's interior, and for some reason it frazzled Pilazzo. *What was once comforting,* he thought irrationally, *is now just the calm before the storm.*

The war . . .

He took a long, deep breath. He smelled the faint odor of incense from Masses past, which under normal circumstances always brought a small sense of comfort, of solace.

Today, however, darker feelings prevailed.

He couldn't help being concerned by the images of devastation he'd seen in his mind's eye; it had been no dream. The homeless man had *touched* him, delivering a message that was clear-cut and tangible, undeniable. He'd been able to *smell* the charred remains, *feel* the hot wind on his skin as the distant flames raged and burned, *hear* the tortuous roar of the army as they gathered like bats in a cave at dusk.

Homeless men . . . thousands of them . . .

He'd never experienced anything even remotely like

it. And he knew it would continue to haunt him until he could unearth some rationale.

He stood and grimaced as his joints cracked. He walked around the altar to the rectory entrance, noticing suddenly how unusually hot it was in the church. The door to the rectory, eight feet tall, matched perfectly the wall on either side of it, making it nearly invisible in the church's dim lighting. He turned a recessed brass doorknob. The door moved, hinges squeaking as he crossed the threshold.

From the darkness behind, something cold and bone-dry touched the back of his neck.

He shuddered as every hair on his body stood on end. A rancid odor arose, like that of human waste, and he whipped a hand around to swat away the terrible sensation against his skin.

He turned around and saw only the door as it slowly closed and sealed out the calm of the church.

He stood still for a moment, listening to the blood rushing in his head, his heartbeat filling his ears. He took a few deep breaths, then entered the rectory's meeting room.

Must be the anxiety of the move catching up with me. There's nothing to be afraid of.

But as he entered the rectory, he realized he might be wrong.

Typically alive at this time of day, the rectory's meeting room lay in bitter emptiness, a no-man's land devoid of life. The card table and counters had already been wiped clean, a task customarily carried out before the priests went to bed around ten, still four and a half hours from now. The television was turned off. The room's lone window, looking out past a set of iron bars into a small alley, lay dark beneath its partially drawn shade. The kitchen, which should have been tossing its hearty aromas into the air (thank goodness for Father Keene, Holy Innocents's resident chef), looked oddly barren with no pots or pans on the stove.

Pilazzo looked around suspiciously. He called out, "Hello?"

No answer.

Leading away from the kitchen, past the gas oven, was the rectory's lifeline: a twenty-five-foot hallway that angled to the right and ran the entire back length of the church. Fondly referred to as Heaven's Walk, it was from here that the bedrooms branched off, each priest and deacon having the luxury of his own quarters—one of the few extravagances Holy Innocents claimed over St. Peter's, which housed only one stark barrackslike room for the five priests in residence.

Pilazzo stepped down the hall, which was lit only by nightlights plugged into the four wall sockets. Again he called, "Hello?"

Again no reply.

The first bedroom on the left belonged to Monsignor Sanchez. It was the largest of the rooms, fitting a double bed, an easy chair, and a private bathroom that always reeked of lavender.

The door to the room was ajar.

Pilazzo grabbed the doorjamb and quietly peeked inside.

He saw the monsignor kneeling on the floor before the carved wooden cross on the wall, a set of black rosary beads gripped in his trembling hands. He was dressed in his violet robe and cloak, odd to Pilazzo because he wasn't scheduled to perform Mass tonight. Pilazzo's gaze fell upon Sanchez's shadow on the wall, elongated and ominous in the dim light seeping in from the bathroom.

"Tom?" Pilazzo whispered weakly—it was the best he could do as he stepped into the room. A whiff of something foul hit his nose—the same odor he had smelled in the rectory moments earlier. He peered curiously toward the bathroom.

"Tom," he said, more forcefully now. "What's going on here? Where is everyone?"

Monsignor Sanchez turned to face Pilazzo. The man had been crying. His eyes were watery and red, their usual spark of kindness lost in a sea of misery and confusion. His hair jutted at untidy angles, as though he'd been running his hands through it. His face was drawn.

Pilazzo had never seen his friend like this. He stepped forward, wanting to help but hesitant to do so. Something wasn't right here.

"Tom . . . please, what's going on?"

"Anthony . . ." Sanchez finally whimpered. His eyes fluttered, releasing fresh tears. Voice trembling, he said: "We . . . are . . . being . . . summoned . . ." Then he closed his eyes and returned to his prayers.

After a few moments, Pilazzo found the strength to place a reassuring hand on Sanchez's shoulder.

The man was hot to the touch. Drenched in sweat. Pilazzo felt a vibration under his fingertips—not a trembling, but a *vibration*—and it made him jerk his hand away, as if a bug had skittered across his knuckles.

"Tom—"

"Do not tend to me, Anthony," Sanchez murmured, head still facing forward, eyes still closed. "Follow the message that God delivers to you. Heed His word and do your part to bring down the evil that promises man the end of days. . . ."

The evil that promises man the end of days . . .

Pilazzo staggered. Dizziness rushed through his head, and he had to grip the dresser for support. All he knew of life, the miracles of God and the studies he'd devoted his life's work to, the sacrifices he'd made, the vow of celibacy he'd adhered to instantly seemed not to matter anymore. All he could concern himself with was this specific moment in time, in which his lifelong friend had spoken the *same exact words* as the vagrant in the confessional.

Pilazzo stared at his friend, fear running through his body. Something terrible was happening.

This was a warning from God.

Follow the message that God delivers to you. Heed His word and do your part to bring down the evil that promises man the end of days. . . .

Pilazzo took one last glance around the room before leaving. In the hallway, he leaned against the wall, contemplating for a moment the state of depression Monsignor Sanchez was in. *All our lives we've waited for God to show Himself to us, to show us a sign of His existence. Well, here it is, and it's not the one we've been hoping for. What made us think that He would arrive on some silver-lined cloud to end disease, war, and famine? Instead, God has finally come after all these millennia to let us know we're knee-deep in some kind of mess that promises to bring man the end of days.*

He moved slowly and painstakingly, palms against the wall for balance. He peered into every dark room as he went by, watching the priests and deacons in their quarters, kneeling on the floor before the crosses hanging on their walls, whispering to God for answers.

And Pilazzo thought: *Messengers have come to*

me . . . but here I am, still riddled with doubt. Clearly something terrible's happening. Am I supposed to play a role in it? What should I do now? Pray?

He walked to the end of the hall, deciding to allow events to unfold around him while he waited for direction to come.

If one came.

He stared at the door to his room, the only one in the hallway that was closed. He gripped the knob. A static shock tickled his sweaty fist. He swallowed a soft lump in his throat and went inside.

Everything appeared as it should: the bed, the dresser, the television, the desk, and computer. He turned to close the door, but then thought better of it, as all the other bedroom doors in the rectory had been left open.

He'd noticed that all his brothers had been dressed in their robes, so he straightened his collar, removed a clean robe from the closet, and put it on. Gooseflesh appeared on his arms as he did so.

He turned and peered in the mirror.

His eyes widened.

One hand went to his mouth.

Oh my God . . .

Here was his message from God.

He stepped to the mirror and placed his fingertips against the warm glass, thinking for a moment that he might be able to reach through the reflection and touch it. A vibration rushed through him as he came in contact with the mirror's surface, not unlike the one he felt touching Sanchez's shoulder. For endless seconds he stared into the mirror.

Scrawled in black ash on the wall behind him was

his message, written in reverse so it could be read in the mirror's reflection:

Your Church Awaits You

He turned to the wall but saw nothing. No evidence that the words he saw in the mirror had ever been there. He thought it might be some sort of optical illusion, that the words had been drawn on the mirror itself. But when he looked back to the mirror and again saw the sprawling, jagged letters on the wall above his bed, he knew this could not be.

Frightened, he wondered for a fleeting moment what messages his brothers had found in their rooms. Specific messages that drew them away from their duties (were there parishioners sitting in the church at this very moment, waiting for the six-o'clock Mass?) and into prayer.

Prayer . . . is that what I'm supposed to do next?

He gazed down at his hands and all but fainted.

Like the words in the mirror, his mind insisted it had to be an illusion. A hallucination.

There was blood on his hands . . . seeping out from what appeared to be wounds in his palms.

Stigmata. The sacred wounds of the Lord. His calling to those free of sin.

Free of sin . . .

He dropped to his knees and held his hands up before his face, staring fearfully at the blood as it dripped down his wrists, beneath the sleeves of his robe. His jaw clenched at the sudden pain striking his feet, his chest. A perfumed aroma came from the blood, that of roses and sandalwood. *The odor of sanctity.*

He glanced into the mirror and saw that the scrawled message had vanished.

My message has been delivered.

His eyes bulged, wet with tears. He fixed his gaze upon the pain-filled eyes of Jesus on the cross above his door. A shudder went through him as he found himself instantly drawn to the cross, his terror diluted by a need to pray, a burning desire to beg God for His guidance in the difficult time to follow. His breathing quickened. He knew he was being called upon to allow Christ to suffer through him and guide him in reducing the suffering in the world.

Dear God, help me. . . .

Black clouds filled his vision, blurring the blood on his hands. Only the cross on the wall remained in view, and he crawled toward it, feeling his mind drifting . . . drifting away from all that he knew and understood. Nothing else mattered but the cross and the power and strength it gave him. Little by little, drop by drop, he could feel it filling his veins, his mind, his soul . . . a power he'd never felt before, charging his blood and body through the punctures in his hands, his feet. *Stigmata!* He remained motionless, unable to move or hear or see anything other than the figure of Jesus and its power, a power that ever so slowly descended upon him, granting him the fortitude to face the dark road ahead.

The road soon to be illuminated by a wall of raging fire and rising smoke.

CHAPTER NINE

The group of vagrants rushed Jyro and Timothy into the bedroom. Jyro staggered forward and collapsed onto one of the beds. His clothes were soaked with sludge, which spread over the bare mattress as he skittered back against the iron headboard. Gazing at the footprints he left on the floor, he screamed hoarsely, "Shut the goddamned door! Don't let it in here!" He was afraid the sludge on him would begin moving like it had in the bathroom. It didn't.

The old, tattooed vagrant slammed the door, closing them inside the bedroom. A dreadful silence consumed the room. The only sound was the labored breathing of the vagrants as they stared at the closed door.

"Is everyone here?" Jyro shouted. The men looked around frantically. Jyro counted ten total, including Timothy.

"Got us ten men," Weston blurted breathlessly, head bobbing up and down. The burly man's eyes were bloodshot and scared, his blond hair matted across his forehead in greasy strands. He lowered his head near Jyro's. Weston whispered, "We're dead meat, ain't we?"

Jyro looked across the room. The man with the dread-locks was setting Timothy on a bed. The boy was covered in waste from head to toe. His eyes bulged whitely beneath the dark mask of filth on his face. He jittered and twitched like a tangled marionette. Rollo stood at the edge of the bed with his Bible open, the Lord's Prayer spilling from his lips in wavering stammers.

Weston snapped his fingers in front of Jyro's face, then jerked a swollen red thumb over his shoulder toward the big black man behind him. "This here's Wrath. He—"

"What went on in there?" Wrath's voice was deep and booming. "You were in there for hours."

"Hours?" To Jyro it seemed only twenty minutes had passed since he'd first gone into the bathroom.

Weston nodded interminably, up and down, up and down, as he spoke. "We waited for you to come out. Both me and Wrath banged and kicked the door, but it was no good. Even tried to break it down with a hammer from the crazy guy's stash." He motioned toward the hallway where one-eared Larry still lay unconscious. "But the *flames—*"

"Flames?" Jyro looked at Wrath, then back at Weston. Jyro noticed a small patch of dried blood on the man's chin, and there was a faint yellow bruise beginning to form on his cheek. He wondered if he'd recently been in a fight.

Weston kept nodding, and Jyro figured it was a nervous tic. "Every time one of us touched the door these blue flames shot out of it. The doorknob . . . it was . . . on fire. Burning up everyone's hands. When Wrath kicked the door, it burned his leg. There was no way we could get you out of there. Look at my hands. . . ." He spread his scorched fingers, then grimaced.

Jyro looked at the big man's pants. They were worn at the knees, charred at the edges, and displaying blistered skin beneath. Recalling that the boy's hands had been burned as well, he glanced at Timothy and saw him staring at his palms with fascination, mouth hanging open, snot carving a swath through the filth on his face. He looked far gone, as though dreaming while awake.

Jyro muttered, "Christ . . . what kind of mess are we in?"

Voices rose as the men shouted and gestured maniacally, much to the dismay of Jyro, who thought it might be best to keep things quiet. Weston and Wrath talked about the mysterious flames and examined their wounds uneasily. The albino, beside the closed door, studied Jyro for a moment, then looked away, keeping as still as an ash tree on a cold winter's day.

Jyro closed his eyes, vainly trying to close out the clamor. He wondered if they would survive much longer. He placed a hand over his mouth, hoping to restrain the screams threatening to make their way out. He'd never been so scared in his life, in spite of all his years on the streets among drug dealers, muggers, and addicts.

He had a feeling things were going to get worse.

The elderly man with the tattoos began shuffling back and forth, eyes wide, tufted hair waving like spiderwebs in the wind. He spread his arms, looking at no one in particular as he shouted, "I tried to leave, but the door to the church burned my hands!" Spittle sprayed from his cracked lips, hitting anyone within five feet of him. He marched toward Jyro and displayed a map of smooth, red patches peppered with white blisters on his palms. "See?" He looked at Wrath

77

and Weston, then back at Jyro. "Something ain't right here, man," he whispered, lips wrinkling back to show yellowed teeth. "They don't want us to leave."

They.

Jyro nodded, thinking of the tentacles, wet and marauding, grabbing him, trying to feed him to the thrashing tree trunk of sewage. He peered toward the door and saw the albino man still staring at him with those creepy red eyes. Something about the pale man bothered Jyro. He said, "After what I just saw in there . . . I'd believe anything." The albino looked away.

Strangely, no one asked what he had seen in the bathroom. Instead, an uncomfortable silence filled the room. The men just stood looking at one another, no doubt wondering if they were going to die in the next few minutes. Clearly, they were all just trying to cope.

The dreadlocked vagrant began pacing erratically, glaring at Weston and Wrath. "So what are we gonna do, man? Huh? How the hell are we gonna get outta here?"

Timothy stood up. Pieces of waste fell from his body and plopped on the floor. He marched into the uneven circle that had formed and eyed the dreadlocked man. "We're gonna get out of here. We just need to work on this together." A promise as empty as the church below.

Weston spread his huge arms, the white of his skin seeming to shed some light into the shadowy room. "How?" He pointed a scorched finger toward the door. "If we try to leave, we're just gonna get burned again!"

"Well, we can't just sit here." Jyro struggled to his feet. He sidled up alongside Timothy. "Me and the kid were almost eaten by a goddamned monster in there!"

From the corner of the room, Rollo held his Bible

high over his head and lamented, "The end of the world is nigh! The devil has risen and disgorged its atrocities upon us all!"

"Shut up, dude," the dreadlocked man shouted. "We don't need that kinda crap right now."

Rollo waved the Bible back and forth. "The scourges of Hell are upon us. What do you think it was they battled inside that bathroom?"

"Enough!" Jyro shouted, silencing the room.

Rollo looked at Jyro, eyes piercing him balefully. "Are you afraid to confront the truth?"

"I've seen the truth, and it ain't pretty," Jyro replied loudly, sounding mostly frustrated and scared. He shambled past the man with the taped-up glasses, knowing that they couldn't just stay put; they'd all end up killing one another out of fear. He stopped by the door, ignoring the albino's creepy glare. He grabbed the doorknob; it felt warm, almost hot, but there was no fire as the others had claimed.

He opened the door and went back out into the hallway, the image of the monster in the bathroom now playing out in his mind like a video in frame-by-frame. *Are there more monsters here?*

Then he wondered: *Did it appear because of what I did? The chalice? The rosary?*

The rosary!

He took a deep breath, held it in his lungs.

He looked toward the bathroom.

Larry, thief of tools, was kneeling on the floor just inside the bathroom. Like Jyro, he was covered in sewage from head to toe. His pulverized face was seeping fresh blood, in utter contradiction to the grin he wore, gray teeth bared as if entertained by some amusing story.

In his hand was the rosary, swinging like a hypnotist's timepiece.

Jyro stepped toward him, gazing intently at the rosary, watching it go back and forth, back and forth. The blessed beads seemed so unreal in the hands of such a thief, a monster, a *sinner.*

It does not belong with him.

Larry's arm twitched and quivered, as though charged with volts. The rosary continued moving back and forth, left and right. Jyro could do nothing but stare at it. He felt a sudden *longing*—not for the rosary itself, but for the message buried deep within it.

Timothy appeared at the bedroom door like a shadow. So did Weston. Behind them, Wrath loomed.

Weston made a move toward the bathroom. Jyro held out a stiff arm, holding him back purely out of instinct. He whispered, "You don't want to go in there," eyes still focused on the rosary.

You are getting very sleepy. . . .

Larry's face contorted, eyes rolling up into his head, lips twisting into a scowl. His throat swelled and undulated as if attempting to reject a large object. He then produced a loud, screeching cackle—a sound a hyena might make. Jyro flinched. So did the others. He heard someone say, "What the fuck?"

From behind Larry came a flash of light. It ignited the bathroom in intermittent bursts, throwing the eerie shadow of the praying virgin upon the wall again. Amid the bursts of light, Jyro could see tendrils of hot steam rising from the polluted matter on the floor, gathering about Larry like praying hands.

The flashlight, Jyro thought quickly, staring at the shadow. *It's working again.*

Larry's eyes, huge and white and shocking in their wickedness, filled with blood and spilled two red streams down his face. Someone prayed dully, "Jesus Christ . . . help us . . ."

The rosary kept swinging, back and forth. Jyro felt himself being pulled toward its promise of an answer to this whole eerie mystery.

Like a baby bird begging for a worm, Larry opened his mouth wide. From it, red vomit spouted, dousing his chin and his grimy shirt. A string of garbled words followed: "*One holds darkness; one holds light. Find the sinless one. . . .*"

A gust of cold wind whipped about the room, rippling their clothes. Waves of gooseflesh ran down Jyro's back. The wind grasped the bathroom door and slammed it shut, closing Larry inside. The icy gust moved across the hallway and the men clutched themselves for warmth.

Sickness nailed Jyro's stomach. A clear sense of panic rose in the room as the men cowered against the wall, crying out in fear . . . and then, as suddenly as it came, the cold air dissipated, leaving the men heaving for air in the rancid heat that once again dominated the hallway.

But not before delivering to them a message of hope amid the disaster threatening to kill them all.

Find the sinless one. . . .

Jyro could see the incredulous looks upon the men's faces as they gazed at one another.

Find the sinless one. . . .

They'd all heard it, the voice, like a call from a distant mountaintop echoing across a valley. It'd entered their heads along with the disturbing image now haunting them: an apocalypse in the form of an army of tattered men facing a great evil rising up before a wall of raging fire and blackened smoke.

"What the hell is going on here!" the thin man with the taped glasses cried, racing toward the landing. He teetered at the edge of the stairs and fell forward down the first few steps. Lunging, he grasped the banister, keeping himself from falling any farther. Tears sprung from his eyes. From the bedroom, Jyro could hear Rollo shouting a prayer like a minister delivering a sermon.

"Jyro!" Timothy called. Confusion suddenly spread over his face. He paused . . . then asked, voice trailing off, "How did I know your name?"

"Same way I knew yours," Jyro answered without delay, knowing that he'd never told the boy his name. Timothy just *knew*.

Timothy glanced down at his hands again, flexing them with a look of incredulity on his face.

The burns on his hands were gone. Healed.

Timothy gazed back toward Jyro, mouth agape.

Jyro narrowed his eyes. His bond with the boy was stronger now, giving them both a trace of comfort amid the gathering doom. If they could reach into each other's minds, the same thoughts would be there: *We were meant to be. It's a calling from God. We have no choice. We have to hear His word, receive His messages.*

In a voice barely above a whimper, Timothy said, "The rosary . . ."

There was a moment's hesitation, then Jyro replied, "Maybe the thief is the one," as the message from the rosary came into his mind: *One holds darkness; one holds light. Find the sinless one. . . .*

Find him. . . .

From the inside the bathroom came a quick succession of bangings on the door, as though Larry had finally slipped free of his trance. A long, fading gurgle emerged, like that of a man trying to yell with his mouth full. Then silence returned.

Jyro performed a quick head count. Everyone was out in the hallway now, gathered against the wall, looking to him for some sort of guidance. Marcus was trembling, staring at the floor as he sucked nervously on a Winston; Rollo had closed his eyes and was holding his tattered Bible to his chest, mumbling to himself; Wrath and Weston were looking toward the bathroom door, eyes narrowed, seemingly prepared should Larry come barreling out. There was the old tattooed man, the young dreadlocked man, and the lanky man with the broken glasses, who was still by the banister on the landing, clutching it like a squirrel on a tree branch. And then the silent albino, who remained trembling in the bedroom doorway, red eyes cast downward.

What a crew, Jyro thought. He realized suddenly that his experience in the bathroom had made him, by default, their leader, with Timothy second in command.

Little did the others know that it was he who may have brought all this havoc into their lives.

Jyro turned and looked toward Timothy. Despite being covered in sewage, the boy stood tall, seemingly prepared for whatever evils lay ahead. *He's one of us now,* Jyro thought, scanning the others in the room, his army—*an army of tattered men*—standing crookedly before him like forgotten mannequins. Jyro thought back to the message that had been delivered to him and Timothy.

One holds darkness.

The chalice filled with fire.

One holds light.

The rosary.

Find the sinless one.

The one. The rightful possessor would use the rosary's power to bring down evil.

Fragments of his dream slipped back to him, visions of the faceless men who had buried the crate beneath the church. As he'd slept he'd heard himself uttering over and over again: *The evil that promises man the end of days.* Now he remembered and saw its significance.

. . . promises man the end of days.

He focused on Timothy, the boy's eyes sharp beneath a mask of filth and fear. Without hesitation, Jyro said with authority, the shaky fear lessened: "We were brought here by God to fight a war. *All* of us. And we will. Why us? I don't know. But there is a reason. God never acts without a purpose. We'll uncover this purpose and use it to gain strength against the evil that promises man the end of days!"

He waited to see if any of the men would recognize the haunting phrase. They didn't. They all stood there unmoving, looking at him respectfully with a willingness to go along with him. Even Rollo.

Why?

Because, like me, they've been brought here for a reason.

He said, "Before we move on, before anyone else gets hurt, let's try to figure out why *we* were the ones called here. . . ."

CHAPTER TEN

He is walking amid a colorless landscape pitted with destruction. A city of death surrounding him, buildings and streets destroyed, their occupants long vanished. He is the last man standing, God's final living, breathing creature on an earth buried beneath the remnants of apocalypse. The skies shine red and black, the clouds thick and permanent, swollen with fatal acids. Black rain pours down on him, dousing his skin with disease. Should he live beyond this day, his flesh and blood will wither and rot.

But for now he remains whole and lucid, gazing out on the torn landscape. He is the one who made this happen. He is the cause of this destruction, simply because he did not find the strength within him to defeat the evil that had promised man the end of days.

A wind picks up. Wet debris flies in his face. For a moment, he shields his eyes, then takes a breath of searing pain and looks down at his hands. Here he sees blood, warm and wet against his skin. He gazes at his bare feet. The wounds are there too, bleeding. He struggles to say through split and bleeding lips, "Stigmata," but his voice is beaten back by the bitter vacuum and pouring rain that surrounds him. He holds his bleeding hands up to the dark pregnant sky, screaming, "Noooo!" Rivulets of blood wash up his forearms to his wasted biceps and shoulders. Bolts of lightning fill the sky like dead branches. "I am no savior . . ." he whimpers, utterly drained of strength, a sudden stench of ozone filling the dense air.

"But you are, Antonio," comes a familiar voice from behind. The Italian accent is thick.

"Mother . . ." He turns to face her. She stands before him only feet away, the black tattered robe shrouding her frail body billowing in the tainted wind. She is unaffected by the years of dementia. She looks entirely normal, perhaps as she might have been had she not been stricken with disease in her later years.

She places a gentle finger across her pink lips. Here he sees the ruby ring of scars she'd had for years around her finger. She speaks softly, eloquently, the wind tossing her gray hair across her face. "God has placed the blood on your hands because you have lived free of sin. He sends to you a message, Antonio, and you must heed it. If you choose to deny Him, then this will be your consequence." She waves a hand toward the ruined landscape.

"M-Mother," he stammers, dehydrated eyes unable to provide tears. "How . . . ?"

For a second time she silences him with a finger against her lips . . . just as she used to do when he was a child. The ring on her finger is darker now, the scars thick and wrinkled. "Antonio . . . long, long ago Christ came to me, and united with me, leaving with me this ring of flesh upon my finger. He made me His bride and delivered to me my son. Yet your purpose remained unknown to me in my time on earth. I kept His faith unsullied until the day I was called to sacrifice myself into the arms of His divine will. I went to Him in Heaven and celebrated the marriage that has no end—and it is why now, Antonio, you can see the ring I have worn for much of my life." She displays the finger with a ridge of flesh she professes to be the ring of Christ.

"Fear not, my son. It was Christ who gave you faith in my dying days. After I was gone, you maintained your faith steadfastly, which enabled Him to behold the strength in you. You are His son. And now, he needs you. Do as He says, Antonio."

He steps forward, thinking of the faceless man his mother had told him about only once when he was a teen—the man who had come into his mother's life, fathered him, and then left, never to return.

Was this 'man' Jesus Christ?

Suddenly, from within the tattered shell of a nearby building, a dog appears. It is large and black with eyes as red as fire. It begins to bark ferociously. Pilazzo looks back and forth, between the dog and his mother, who now bears lacerations upon her forehead that spell out the word CHRIST. Blood seeps down from the jagged letters into her eyes, which remain unblinking. "Mother," he calls, but she holds her hands forward and steps back, fading into the gray air and leaving him with an alarming parting message: "Your church awaits you. . . ."

Alone now, he looks back at the dog. His heart pounds with terror. The dog kicks up wet black ash with its hind legs and approaches him, foam-flecked jaws growling furiously.

Pilazzo shoves his bleeding hands toward the dog. Pain attacks his body at five distinct points: his hands, his feet, and at the right side of his torso. Where Jesus was speared. He cries out in the words of the Apostle Paul, "I bear in my body the marks of the Lord Jesus Christ!"

The dog releases a series of barks . . . and then leaps at him.

He holds his bleeding hands high and screams for his mother . . .

. . . but she didn't come. Instead he awoke from the feverish nightmare on the floor of his bedroom. He remained there for a long time. His breathing was slow and painful, his lungs rattling as if he had pneumonia. His mouth was parched, and so were his eyes. When he tried to open them, his lids stuck to them painfully. He reached out and touched the familiar knobby texture of the rug, then raised a finger to his face and gently peeled his eyes open, one at a time.

The first thing he saw was the Mother of God nightlight he had bought during his last trip to Rome, the small bulb painting the room a pale yellow. He looked up toward the mirror.

Your church awaits you. . . .

His hands—which in his dream, *and in my waking state*—had bled with the marks of Christ were now unblemished. Unmarked. He shook his head with both denial and confusion. Had he dreamed it all?

He struggled to his feet, groaning as the bones in his back popped. He was dimly aware of his head throbbing, feeling as it had when he'd drunk a bit too much red wine with dinner and awakened with a hangover. Silence ruled the world around him. He leaned against the dresser to rub his eyes. The room rocked and creaked back and forth. His legs and feet were numb.

Out of the blue, his mind began to pick up some images from his dream. They came back to him in glimpses, the horrific landscape and the warning from his mother. For a moment he tried to make sense of what he saw, but it was too overwhelming to think it through.

Still, his mind taunted him: *My mother, the bride of Christ. Me, the son of Christ?* She used to claim the scar on her finger was the ring of Christ, but he assumed her religious fanaticism was brought on by her dementia.

But now he wondered.

It was just a dream and nothing more. Or was it? His dream mother had alluded to a message he'd received while he was awake—*your church awaits you*—and warned that he had to heed it, lest he cause the apocalypse he saw in his dream. *The evil that promises man the end of days.* It was just as the homeless man in the confessional had said—and just as Monsignor Sanchez had mentioned.

He ran a trembling hand through his hair, feeling sweat. The clock on his nightstand was dark.

Was the power out?

Couldn't be. The night-light was on, jutting from the socket behind a frosted glass shell. He focused upon the Mother of God portrait hand painted on the shell's surface, her wide glossy eyes aimed remorsefully toward the wall above his bed.

Your church awaits you. . . .

He stepped to the doorway, felt for the light switch on the wall. With his eyes still fixed on the night-light, he flipped it up.

Then down. Then repeatedly, up and down.

Darkness.

He gripped the doorjamb and stuck his head out into the hallway, now a taunting, pitch-black hole.

The power *was* out.

Everything except the Mother of God night-light in his room.

He gazed back at it, intently now.

Mary's eyes were no longer aimed above the bed.

They were peering directly at *him*.

Gasping, he lurched from the room into the darkness of the hall. He was petrified. He fled unsteadily with his hands outstretched, bumping into the walls like a mechanical toy. He opened his mouth to shout, but only weak sobs escaped his bone-dry throat. He felt blindly along the right wall and came to an opening. He shoved his head into the unseen bedroom. *"Is anyone here?"* he cried out breathlessly, not seeing but somehow knowing that he was the only man left. *Like in my dream.*

No response.

Short of breath, he continued down the hall, fear sapping the strength from his body as if his blood were being drained. Tears left warm tracks against his cheeks.

He heard a noise.

Is that . . . music?

The next door he arrived at was closed. He leaned against the paneled surface, heart slamming so hard that it nearly drowned out the Bizet from behind the closed door.

Monsignor Sanchez's room.

He pressed an ear against the door, listening closely, and realized that something now sounded *off* about the usually familiar classical music. It could have been the fear that had him so confused . . . but in that surreal moment, he was almost certain of what he was hearing.

The music was *playing backwards.*

He silently ran a hand along the door and grasped the knob. Instantly he received a jolt of static electricity. In the darkness, he could see it: a flash of blue light, like a burst of sheet lightning through a rain-soaked window. It gloved his hand for a split second, then vanished, leaving blotches of imaginary light dancing in his sights. And it *hurt*, more than any static shock should, as though he'd just barehanded a few dozen volts from an exposed wire.

Despite the pain, he maintained his grip and turned the knob.

The door moved forward with a loud creak.

He stepped into Monsignor Sanchez's room.

Like his own room, there was a tiny bit of light in here: the same pallid splay from the bathroom he noticed during his earlier visit. The room was vacant now, eerie beneath the indistinct wash of light and sound of backwards Bizet. He eyed the turntable against the far wall and could see a small dark glow on the record's surface as it not only spun backwards, but seemed to skip over and over again: the same few seconds of music blaring from the tiny inset speakers. He stepped to the aged turntable, hearing now something else in the six or seven seconds of *Farandole* playing in reverse.

He shuddered. *My God.*

It was there. He could hear it. A voice. Barely a whisper, but still registering in his ears.

Rosary . . . rosary . . . rosary . . .

CHAPTER ELEVEN

All those present followed Jyro's lead downstairs to the lobby of the rectory. He felt, despite wanting to remain close to the rosary (none in their right mind was willing to try to get it from Larry), that it would be best to assemble everyone in a more open space so they could discuss their options.

Two emergency lights jutting from red fireboxes in the walls lit the lobby, each providing a hazy glow on each side of the room. In the center of the ceiling, a sole dome light shone dimly, the attached sprinkler dry and still, coated with dust. The vagrants milled about, feet shuffling heavily against the dusty carpet as they examined the bare room.

From somewhere outside the walls of St. Peter's, a woman screamed. The men fell silent and listened as it went on and on and on. . . .

"We're gonna die! We're gonna die!" the vagrant with the broken glasses yelled. His face was as red as a tomato. The tendons stood out in his neck, nearly as thick as bungee cords. He bolted across the room and launched himself at the closed door to the church. Timothy roared, "*No!*" But the warning fell on deaf ears.

The vagrant grabbed the doorknob and a sickly blue light hissed out. He howled in pain. A pungent stench saturated the room, of ozone and cooking flesh. He collapsed to his knees, wailing in a hysterical panic, holding his hands in front of his face and staring disbelievingly at the smoke spiraling from them.

The vagrants staggered back, pushing and shoving against each other. A few frantic discussions rose up. Wrath and Weston moved to within a few feet of him, but no closer, knowing they could do nothing to relieve his pain.

"It doesn't want us to leave!" Jyro shouted. He gazed incredulously at the burned man, promising himself to keep away from any doorknobs. "Whatever . . . whatever *it* is."

The vagrants looked back and forth between the injured man and Jyro, some nodding in defeat, the others too scared to do much more than tremble and hope the blue light didn't get them too. As Jyro looked at the men, he thought, *We're a bunch of hopeless saviors. Most of us have long hair and beards. Take away the bald guy, and it's darn safe to assume we all resemble Jesus Christ. . . .*

"Now what?" Weston blurted, looking at Jyro and Timothy, head moving back and forth. Despite his intimidating size, the big blond man looked apprehensive, the blue of his eyes seeming to have paled into an ill-looking gray. Jyro looked at Timothy. The boy was staring at his hands again, this time with fear on his face, as if he'd just awoken to find claws there instead.

"We wait," Jyro said.

"Wait for what?" Weston asked.

"I don't know." For a moment there was total silence in the rectory. Jyro tensed, thinking that their only logical course of action was to stay put and try to find out *why* they were all there. Perhaps then they could figure out what to do to get out. *It won't let us out,* Jyro thought with dismay, *until it's good and ready.*

The dreadlocked man said, "This really sucks, man. I ain't digging this one little bit."

Jyro nodded. "We have to remain calm. As long as we don't go near the doors, we'll be safe . . . at least for now." He twisted his head and looked at the injured vagrant with the taped glasses; he was sitting on the floor, crying like a child.

Jyro went to him and kneeled down. "What's your name, brother?"

The burned man gasped in pain, and managed to answer, "Seymour."

"Seymour. My name's Jyro. The boy is Timothy. The two big men are Weston and Wrath. The guy with the Bible, his name's Rollo. And his buddy with the smoking habit is Marcus." He peered over at the man with the dreadlocks. "If we're going to work together, we should at least know what to call each other."

The vagrant with the dreadlocks shook his head and spit on the floor. He muttered, "Wilson."

Jyro looked at the old man with the tattoos, sitting on a folding chair, elbows on his knees, bearded face rutted with sharp wrinkles. He was shaking terribly. "You with the tattoos . . . what's your name?"

The vagrant's eyes were wet and rheumy. "Dallas."

Jyro looked over at the albino. The pale man was leaning against the wall, staring at the ceiling. A long line of spit wavered from his trembling lips like a web in the wind. He seemed to have paled further, if that was even possible. Jyro decided not to drum up any conversation with him and let him be.

Wilson, tugging nervously on his dreadlocks, said, "Okay, now that we're all acquainted, why don't you tell us all how the fuck we're supposed to get out of here?"

"If there's a will; there's a way," Rollo replied, tapping the tattered Bible in his hands.

"Yeah, you can keep to your book of faith if you want," Wilson said, frowning with contempt and frustration. "The only way I see us getting out of here is through that door, and as far as I can tell, we can't even touch it."

"I think we need to figure out what the hell is going on first," Jyro said. "*Why* we're all here."

Wilson opened his mouth to protest, but remained silent. Everyone else stayed quiet as well. Perhaps there was no other course of action after all.

"Timothy, when you got here, your hands . . . they were burned like the others. But now they're not." Jyro's voice sounded oddly muted in his ears, as though something was trying to restrain him from making this observation.

Timothy looked grimly at Jyro, face still soiled with patches of waste, despite having tried to wipe it away with his hands. "The rosary . . . it must've healed—"

From the second floor came a scream, very long and razored with pain and terror. The men jerked their gazes toward the ceiling. It went on and on, seeming to vibrate the floor beneath their feet.

It was one-eared Larry, thief of tools (and now the rosary). He was still upstairs, trapped behind the closed door of the bathroom. The scream ended and a succession of banging noises followed: Larry's feet, perhaps, kicking against the door.

After endless seconds, the banging stopped, and there was nothing but silence in the room.

The albino staggered toward the lobby's only window. He bumped against the wall, gripped the sill, and looked out into the alley, mumbling incoherently to himself.

Jyro could see that it was dark outside now. *How . . . ?*

"How can it be night already?" Timothy blurted, echoing Jyro's thoughts. The boy's fists were clenched tightly at his sides.

"Christ, it can't be . . ." Jyro looked at Weston. "You said we were in that bathroom for three hours. . . ." He trailed off as a throb of pain settled into his head.

"That's right."

Timothy shook his head. He looked overwhelmed and weary. "It f-felt like we were in there for only fifteen minutes."

Jyro tugged nervously at his beard. He looked at the men, at the stairs, at the door leading out into the church. "Time is not on our side right now."

"And we are at its mercy," Rollo said.

"So what the hell do we do?" Wilson shouted, voice breaking. "How the hell are we supposed to get out of here?"

The albino raised a determined finger to the glass pane. "Through here . . ."

Timothy shouted, "No!" and with his right hand outstretched, lunged toward the window. The albino, buried in his own world, reached up and gripped the latch on top.

There was a sharp popping sound, as if someone had pulled a party noisemaker. At the same instant a flash of blue light, a *fire*, branched out from the window and covered the albino's hand. The sleeve of his tattered shirt went up in flames. He screamed piercingly. His legs buckled and he collapsed to his knees, waving his injured hand like he was trying to hail a cab.

Weston grabbed an old towel from the floor and smothered the fire before it could spread any further. Wrath shouted, "Oh God! Holy Jesus! What the fuck is going on?"

Still on the floor, Seymour skittered back against the wall in a panic, burned hands held high. He threw up on the floor between his legs, barely missing Marcus, who performed a lopsided jig in an effort to avoid getting splattered.

Feeling as though his army were dwindling, Jyro shouted, "Already too many injuries! Too . . . many! We need to gain control of the situation!"

Everyone in the room fell silent again. Except the albino. He was screaming hysterically. He was lying on his back, feet rapping the floor crazily, straggly hair falling into his bulging, red eyes. He looked up at Jyro, bottom lip quivering, saliva bubbling from his mouth.

Jyro paced, arms flailing, heart driving a heavy rhythm in his chest. "We need to stop making rash moves! We need to start thinking about why we're here and what we can do to get out!" His words carried volume but very little weight.

Wrath shouted, "You keep saying that, but you're doing nothing about it!"

"Okay . . . okay . . ." Jyro stopped pacing. Breathing heavily, he said, "We have to remain calm, all of us, myself included. We need to think this out. . . ."

Wrath looked at Jyro closely, dark eyes narrowed. "Man, how can you expect any of us to stay calm? Do you see what's going on in here?"

"Of course I do. . . ." He paused, composed himself, and said, "Look . . . I'm scared. We're all damn scared.

But it's here, and we're stuck in the middle of it." He considered Wrath's size. The big man had a glimmer in his eyes, the kind he'd seen too many times in the streets from those threatening to make off with his belongings. "As I said earlier, I really believe we're here for a reason. And the sooner we find out what that reason is, the sooner we can try to get the hell out of here."

Wrath's face was a mix of contempt and understanding. After a moment, he nodded, the harsh light in his eyes fading.

A moment of uncertainty followed where the men could only listen to the choking, sniveling sounds of the albino. He continued writhing on the floor like a soldier left for dead in a battlefield, his burned hand red and wet like a peeled tomato.

"Same thing happened to me," Timothy said, stepping into the loose circle that had formed. Weston and Wrath grimaced, as though reminded of having suffered their injuries. The others rubbed their palms, feeling their comrades' pain.

Seymour remained on the floor, seated against the wall amid his puddle of vomit. He was looking toward the group, body arched to one side. His glasses sat crookedly on his nose. They had specks of puke on them.

"What happened, kid?" Jyro asked.

Timothy said, "I've been here for three days." The emergency beacon above bathed him in colorless light, making him look like a ghost.

"Three *days*?" Jyro said.

"It seems that long, but I lost track of time. The days and nights have come and gone more quickly than usual."

When no one spoke, the boy continued quickly and anxiously, as if a gun were pointed at his head. "I woke up in my bed and remembered that I'd left a duffel bag full of clothes in my locker. It'd been more than three weeks since the church was locked up, but for some reason I felt like I needed to get my bag back. It was almost like something was calling me here, using my gym bag for a lure."

All of the men nodded, understanding on their grief-stricken faces, as if they too had been drawn in the same unearthly fashion.

Jyro realized that he himself might very well have been "called" here. Somehow he'd known the church would provide him with much more than a bed and a temporary roof over his head, as if there was a voice in his brain, calling all the shots.

Didn't you think it was odd that the air-duct grates leading from the subway to the church had come away so easily? And then you dreamed of the men and the crate . . . and then you found the crate. That's no coincidence. You're here for a reason. . . .

"On the way here, I remembered thinking not about my gym bag, but something else . . . something vague but so important—it was as though I *knew* I'd find something else here.

"It was midmorning when I got here. There was a foreman outside. At first I didn't think he would let me in, but when I told him that I'd left a few things behind, he just gave this creepy blank stare and showed me the door."

Jyro thought: *I saw this foreman. On the first day I arrived. And he saw me too, as I was rushing past the altar into the rectory. I thought for sure that he would chase me away. But he just stood there, staring at me with this weird look in his eyes, as though he were* frightened *of me.*

"So I came in the church and felt sick: dust and demolition everywhere. I mean, this place had been my sanctuary for months—to see it like this made me sick to my stomach." The boy shut his eyes, took a deep breath, and blew it out, long and slow. "There were a number of workers here who eyeballed me up and down as I stepped up to the altar. I remember feeling so scared I thought I was going to pass out.

"But I knew I *needed* to be here. So I ignored the men and went through the door that leads from here to the rectory. When I got here—" Timothy pointed toward the closed door in the lobby that gave way to the church hallway—"the door leading back out slammed shut. At first I thought one of the workers had closed it. So I ran back and tried to get out, but when I grabbed the knob, the . . . the blue flames shot out at me and burned my hands. I panicked and tried a couple times to get out, but got burned every time."

He displayed his hands. Unlike earlier, there were no tiny white blisters peppering the palm.

"You don't show no wounds," Wrath said.

"They were there," Jyro interjected. "I saw them. But . . . they're healed now." He gazed at Wrath's hands and saw the big man flexing them, grimacing as he did so. He thought: *If I had to guess, I'd say his hands are starting to heal too.*

Timothy added, "Even the doors leading into the rectory did the same thing: They shot fire at me. I was trapped in that hallway."

Timothy continued, "I waited. For hours it seemed. I screamed and yelled through the crack in the door, hoping that someone in the church would come and get me out. But nothing happened. The workers were out there—I could hear them drilling and hammering and sawing—but they didn't come for me. I even waited for the noise to stop before hollering, but it was no use.

"Eventually, their tools stopped altogether. Then the lights went out, and I was alone in there, in the dark."

"How did you get out?" Marcus asked, snuffing out a cigarette on the carpet.

Timothy cleared his throat. "During the night, the door to the rectory opened. A construction worker appeared. I was lying on the floor and acted like I was asleep. He must've not seen me in the dark. When I squinted I could see his outline. He walked right by me and went out into the church area. I waited a minute, then snuck out into the rectory. I heard some noise here, and when I looked down the hallway, I saw a light coming out from the rec room. I thought there was a fire."

And Jyro remembered: *The chalice, floating in the air, with its evil light and raging fire. It seems Timothy was set free after I opened the crate and went back upstairs with the rosary.*

"So I went down the hall, keeping my eyes on the flickering light, and looked into the rec room." Timothy paused, took another deep breath in an apparent attempt to gain composure, and said, "What I saw in here nearly killed me."

Wilson said, "C'mon man, 'fess up. What did you see?"

"An atrocity." Timothy took another deep breath, then gazed hard at Jyro, who nodded as if permitting Timothy to go on with his story. "At first I refused to believe what I was actually seeing. My mind . . . it wanted to reject it like a nightmare . . . but . . . but I knew it was real. It was just so hard to absorb! The place . . . it was barely lit from the emergency beacons on the walls, but it was enough for me to make out everything. There were a group of construction workers there. They were gathered around the hole. Some were tearing at the edges with shovels and crowbars; the others . . . they were . . ."

"They were what?" asked Wilson.

"Cutting up bodies."

The men stood motionless, staring at Timothy.

"Who were they cutting up?" Jyro asked, already knowing the answer.

Timothy's eyes darted back and forth, catching for a moment all the tortured eyes of the men in the room with him . . . and the burned albino, who had fallen unconscious.

"Homeless men."

"Christ, man, how were they doing it?" Wilson was clearly shaken, trembling, yanking nervously on his beard.

Timothy said, "With their tools. Saws, axes, knives. I . . . I saw it all."

Jyro peered at the carpet under his feet, noticing for the first time a smattering of thick, irregular stains. *Blood.* He stepped back a foot or so to an untainted section of the carpet. A dizziness beset him. The room seemed to grow very warm, and he nearly collapsed to his knees.

"And yet," Timothy said, "nothing could have prepared me for what happened next."

The men waited in silence.

Timothy opened his mouth to speak . . . then

stopped, frozen in unmistakable terror. He raised his hand and pointed to the wall.

Jyro spun around, along with the other men, who all began screaming as they staggered back toward the staircase.

The albino was crucified on the wall.

CHAPTER TWELVE

Rosary . . . rosary . . . rosary . . .

There was no mistaking it now. It was *there*, replaying in his head over and over again. The music remained as well: an eerie reverse-playing background to the whispering voice filling his head like a terrible headache.

And yet, despite its supernatural source and the fear it provoked in him, he knew that it was *good*, just as the stigmatic message from God had been. He saw no choice but to heed it and move on with his still unknown duty.

The rectory was empty, though he could not see so much as sense its barrenness. He'd been left to fend for himself by the others, all of whom were well on their way to setting their required tasks into action, whatever they might have been.

In Sanchez's room, the digital clock on the nightstand was dark. But the battery-operated clock (showing upon its face an image of Jesus herding sheep in a pasture) read exactly three AM. He assumed this was the correct time until he slowly felt his way through the darkness to the kitchen and saw the clock on the wall there, bathed in the pallid light from the overhead emergency beacon, also reading precisely three AM.

Struggling to see, he stumbled through the rectory passage (where he again received a sharp twang of static shock from the doorknob) and moved back into the dark and empty Church of Holy Innocents.

Utter silence prevailed in the church, save for the rush of air escaping his lungs and the blood pounding inside his head. Guided solely by the pulpit's faux candlelight, he crossed in front of the the altar and down the three marble steps into the nave. His footsteps creaked hollowly as he went. The eyes of the statues on the altar seemed to follow him down the center aisle. He shuddered. Never in his life had he felt so *unprotected* amid the consecrated walls that had always provided such security and comfort.

Halfway down the aisle he stopped. He thought he might not be alone after all. He twisted around and looked back at the altar. He saw the statues, gazing away from him as they should; the crucifix, hanging on the wall above the altar; and the confessionals, where hours earlier he'd seen those malignant images.

Visions of apocalypse. Of an army of tattered men standing before a wall of raging fire and billowing black smoke. Of its aftermath: death, destruction, and decay.

He heard a noise: a light tapping from above, as though a woodpecker were perched in the rafters, drumming out its boredom against a wide beam of wood.

He called out, "Anyone there? Monsignor Sanchez? Father Monteleone?"

No answer. The tapping ceased.

A wave of dizziness threw him off balance. He sought the firm stability of the closest pew.

The statues continued to look away from him, as though denying him their solace. The life-size Jesus hanging on the cross behind the altar maintained its pained gaze toward the heavens, seemingly in search of an answer Pilazzo could never provide. He thought of the night-light in his room and shuddered at the image of the painted Mary's eyes examining him, torn away from their usual point on the wall above his bed.

Your church awaits. . . .

The tapping in the rafters returned, a bit louder. He looked away from the statues and into the darkened heavens above. He could see nothing, as the flickering glow of the altar candles lacked the strength to reach such heights. Ignoring the senseless sound—*that tap, tap, tapping of some mindless bird*—he moved on, more slowly now, eyes tentatively exploring the pews. His blood raced hotly in his veins. He used a hand to wipe his perspiring brow.

Tap . . . tap . . . tap . . .

Louder now.

Directly above him.

Something warm and wet beaded down upon his hands; he flinched, clenching his hands in immediate, anxious prayer.

He looked down . . .

. . . and saw dark, wet drops pooling between his fingers.

Tap . . . tap . . . tap . . .

Dear Jesus . . .

Blood.

Gooseflesh sheeted his body. He could feel the skin around his mouth tighten with fear as he twisted his neck upward.

In the dark above the crossbeam, he glimpsed a pair of eyes peering down at him.

There was a man in the rafters.

A series of lightning-strike thoughts assaulted Pilazzo. Who was he? How did he get up there? Clearly he would need a ladder, as did the paint crews that had treated the beams a few weeks back. Now, as his vision adjusted to the gloom, Pilazzo could see that the man was dressed in a white jumpsuit, heavily spotted and streaked with paint.

"Hey . . ." the priest called out weakly. He stood still, listening to his voice echo away into nothing. And then, just barely audible, he heard the faint, wet drip of blood hitting the floor somewhere.

The man, eyes gleaming in the darkness, tapped something against the wood beam between his feet, *tap . . . tap . . . tap . . .*

Pilazzo saw what he held and felt the mounting fear in his body grow into unbridled terror.

The man shifted his knees closer to his chest, perhaps in an effort to maintain his balance. His face was an expressionless mask, but his eyes were feral, reflecting like an animal's gaze at night.

His hand flicked up and down as he pattered the flat edge of a priest's collar against the wooden beam, *tap . . . tap . . . tap.*

More blood dripped down, now onto Pilazzo's face.

Pilazzo staggered back. With the back of his hand, he wiped the blood from his cheeks and lips. Then he looked up again and saw the plummeting body of Monsignor Sanchez.

He had only a second to react. He leaped head first down the aisle, much like a baseball player trying to stretch a double into a triple. His ribs collided hard against the floor, sending a shock of pain through his body. His teeth came down stiffly on his tongue, bringing a sour tang of blood in his mouth.

Behind him, a hideous *crack* of bone against marble echoed through the church as the monsignor's body crashed to the floor.

Pilazzo snapped his head around and saw Sanchez's body lying motionless on the floor. The monsignor had fallen in a faceup position, arms and legs twisted at dreadful angles, eyes staring vacantly at Pilazzo. His head was arched back, gray hair like matted webs. A chisel or putting knife jutted from his exposed throat, the hilt drenched with blood. His purple robe glistened wetly from neck to crotch.

From above: *tap . . . tap . . . tap . . .*

Pilazzo skittered backward on all fours, gazing up at the rafters, at the man still perched there staring back at him with those horrible shimmering eyes. He continued tapping the plastic collar—*Sanchez's collar*—against the wood beam.

Pilazzo's shoes shuffled across the grainy marble in aimless fits. He cried out, expecting the man to leap down at any second and do to him what he'd done to Sanchez.

But the seconds grew, and suddenly Pilazzo found himself clawing at the front doors of the church, looking not at the man in the rafters but at the brass hand plate screwed into the door. He struggled to his knees and pushed against it. The left door swung into the vestibule with a dry screech. Pilazzo scrambled across the threshold, driven by his will to live—to carry out the still undefined task required of him by God.

Your church awaits you. . . .

The door closed behind him, shutting him in the foyer—in darkness. A cloud of dust rose up, tickling his nostrils and palate. Bitter silence washed over him. He crawled toward the front doors, his eyes wide in their sockets, his skin crawling.

He struggled to his feet and with sick terror plunged through the front doors of the Church of Holy Innocents into the darkness of the night.

CHAPTER THIRTEEN

The seconds felt like hours. The dim light in the lobby grew even dimmer as the emergency beacons struggled with their fading batteries. Jyro widened his eyes against the poor lighting.

The air grew suddenly cold and a slight breeze sprung up. Jyro felt his ears pop, and then a sharp pain clawed across his brain. He heard another noise—his breath running out of him in a sickly wheeze. The strength in his body, what little remained of it, seeped away too.

None of the men said a word—they just stood there, amazed and petrified, unable to tear their eyes away from the albino man hanging on the wall.

Like a wax statue, the albino's scrawny white body remained inexplicably suspended, arms extended, palms facing outward (his burned hand had smeared slimy blood on the wall behind it), each finger pinned to the chipped plaster. His legs were pressed together, bare ankles crossed as if knotted with hemp. A stink came off him like rotten garbage.

The man's eyes jerked open.

They stared at Jyro, red and ablaze with fire.

The man's mouth shot open, revealing bloody teeth

and gums. His body began to shudder and tremble, like that of a man caught on an electrified fence.

Jesus . . . oh my Jesus . . . help me . . . save me . . .

Jyro tried to turn away. He tried to move. He tried to scream. But only raspy breathing came out.

A hurting, helpless sound spilled from the crucified man's mouth, and a jolt of pain rose from the center of Jyro's brain. He saw the others in the room grimacing.

The albino's red eyes filled with blood. Thin red lines coursed down his parchment cheeks.

Jyro's mind screamed, *I can't take any more of this! Help . . . me . . .*

Lips barely moving, the albino spoke, voice weak and raspy: *"One holds darkness; one holds light. Find the sinless one. . . ."*

The man on the wall began to jerk and spasm, inhumanly quick, his face rippling as though caught in gale-force winds.

The words he spoke were broken but perceptible: *"Only the sinless one can bear that which holds light. . . ."*

To Jyro, its meaning was instantly clear: One of them would need to use the rosary to defeat the hideous evil taking control of the church.

But who?

Dark blood from the albino's palms ran down the wall. His eyes, still wide open, were completely white now, nearly as white as his skin. His lips drew back, revealing slick red gums. He made a hissing sound.

Bewilderment and revulsion crept through Jyro. He felt his sanity crumbling, unable to look away from the man whose body was caught in a struggle between Good and Evil. Here, Jyro realized, was a tug-of-war taking place with an albino vagrant as the rope.

Wind flooded the room, like it had upstairs. It blew over the men, whipping through their clothes, chilling their blood. The albino released a wretched scream—the agonized cry of a prisoner subjected to a thousand tortures. Brown vomit arced out of his mouth and landed in a splatter halfway across the room. Dallas gave a horrific yell and cupped a wrinkled hand over his mouth. Wrath was the closest to the line of fire and backpedaled away, catching a few bits in the leg. A second heave poured down the albino's chest. A horrible smell immediately saturated the room, like bad meat soaked in whiskey. Jyro's stomach leaped, and an acidic burp scorched his throat.

"Oh shit, oh Jesus!" Wilson shouted. He ripped across the room and staggered halfway up the steps. He spun and looked back.

Rollo blabbered a nearly inaudible prayer. Marcus cried out and coughed up a huge wad of phlegm on the floor. Weston slid an arm around Seymour and helped him away from the albino as everyone retreated toward the staircase. Timothy gripped his head, shouting, "Oh my God! It hurts, it hurts!"

The albino screamed, "*Castigo laudible, corpus meum!*" Then his trembling slowed. The force that held him up seemed to slip, and his hands fell away from the wall. His throat swelled like a balloon as he coughed, "*Destroy the evil . . . that promises man . . . the end . . . of days. . . .*"

Trying like mad to think past the crude image in front of him, Jyro tottered into the center of the room, away from the clutch of cowering men and toward what he felt was a solution to this horrific enigma, despite the cries of protest behind him. With each step he took, the answers in his head grew clearer. He could feel his bowels cramping furiously . . . but he could also feel his mind working overtime. Something inside him (damn, if it didn't feel like a little voice in his head) had helped him make sense of the man's words, which he knew now had not been said by the man, but were in fact a message from the undying will of Good lying beneath the shroud of Evil crucified upon the wall.

I can see . . . I understand. . . .

The twisting wind in the room hit Jyro hard. The tangle of hair on his head flew up like a wing, and he had to shut his eyes as grit flew into his face. Arms raised, he howled through the storm, praying his desperate words made sense to the Good inside the man: *"What is this evil?"*

The man uttered one word, *"Chalice,"* then slid off the wall and collapsed to the floor in a knotted heap of rags and flesh, leaving jagged smatters of blood behind. At the same instant, the icy wind dissipated, leaving everyone shivering in its wake.

Staring at the motionless man, Jyro muttered, "The chalice that belongs to the Darkest One . . ."

Dear God, help us. . . .

A few seconds of silence passed before the remaining men started milling about. Seymour leaped at the door again, this time with his coat wrapped around his hands. He screamed, "Get me the hell outta here!" As he came in contact with the door, a blue flame once again burst up and the coat immediately caught fire. He shouted in agony, the recipient of a smoking scald on his face. *"Shit! Shit!"* he screamed, tossing the coat to the floor. He collapsed on his rear, eyes wide behind the clouded lenses of his glasses, nose and cheeks red and blistered, oozing blood.

Jyro kept his eyes on the albino, twisted and lying in a puddle of blood and vomit. His pants were bunched up around his knees, exposing legs resembling snow-covered branches. He stared at the ceiling, drawn face coated in blood, mouth pulled into a rictus grin, baring slick red gums. He looked like someone who'd died after years of a debilitating illness.

Timothy hobbled over to Jyro and gripped his arm for support. "N-Now what?"

"We wait," Jyro replied automatically, eyes still fixed on the fallen man. *The dead man.*

"The chalice . . . the one he was talking about. I saw it."

Jyro nodded and after a few seconds replied, "So did I," realizing that he hadn't mentioned anything about seeing the chalice until this moment. He wanted to add, *I'm the one who released it from the crate,* but decided that would do no one any good.

He thought back to the rosary, still in the possession—he assumed—of one-eared Larry. He recalled holding the rosary in his hands, how it had offered him strength and resilience he hadn't felt for many years. *Protection.* And then, how it had healed Timothy's burns. How it seemed to be healing the wounds of the men burned in their attempts to flee. Clearly this rosary was a powerful talisman, a critical weapon in the hands of its rightful possessor.

"I saw it floating in the air," Timothy said, looking frantically at the others, all of whom listened as he spoke, except Seymour, who had repositioned himself against the wall, staring at his burns. "Right above the hole in the rec room. That's what I was saying be-fore . . . before . . ." Tears filled his eyes, and he shuddered.

"Tell us," Weston said, oddly composed and strong in contrast to Timothy's state of panic. He placed a hand on Timothy's shoulder. *A healed hand.* "What did you see?"

Timothy took a deep, labored breath, closed his eyes, and said, "It was swaying back and forth, like a pendulum. And it was big, maybe the size of a small barrel or something."

"Bigger than when I saw it." *Did it actually grow? Become stronger?* Suspicious of several accusatory stares, Jyro took a long, nervous breath, blew it out, and motioned for Timothy to continue.

"I watched while the workers dragged the body parts to the hole. They . . . they slit open the torsos and tilted them over the edge so that all the blood and guts dumped out into it. Jesus . . ." He moaned. "There was so much blood. . . ." He began to sob, shoulders hitching up and down.

"Go on, kid," Jyro said, tugging his beard. "It's important you tell us what you saw."

Timothy nodded. "After a few minutes, it . . . it started shooting up out of the hole."

"What did?" Weston asked

"The blood."

"Blood?"

"Yeah . . ." He nodded again. "It looked like there was some kind of pump down there. It just started squirting up in these thin streams and splashed against the floating chalice. The chalice must have been absorbing it, because I didn't see anything dripping back down into the hole. The whole time this was going on, the construction workers kept on with the bodies, dumping the blood into the hole. It seemed like with every body they gutted, another stream of blood would shoot up."

All on its own, Jyro thought. *Like the blood on the floor that gave life to the waste in the toilet. Did it give some sort of life to the chalice?*

Timothy breathed deeply through his nose in a struggle to gather some composure. "Some of the bodies . . . even though they were dismembered, I could *see them*. They were *still alive*. They were gutted! But I . . . I could hear them moaning. I could see their mouths moving. One of them, just a torso with nothing but the head attached . . . he was looking over at me. His eyes were bloody and . . . and *bulging* . . . and moving . . . and his mouth was opening and closing like he was trying to speak to me. . . ."

Timothy's voice trailed off. He started crying, hiding his face in his trembling hands.

"Jesus, kid, why didn't you say anything when you first came upstairs and found us?"

Timothy shook his head, confused, stammering through his tears, "I . . . I don't know. I was in shock at the time, and what I'd seen . . . I could only vaguely remember it. It was like it was being blocked, like something was trying to stop me from talking about it. Now . . . I mean, now I can remember everything. . . ." The boy ran his hands through his hair and shouted, "Jesus Christ, what's happening?"

"The shit's hitting the fan, that's what," Wilson said.

Jyro shook his head, looking sorrowfully at the men, all of them, eight strong plus one boy, gazing back at him pathetically, tattered before they arrived, now beaten down like roadkill, each looking worse than Jesus must've after rising from the dead.

"Lotta good my years as an altar boy did me," Jyro grumbled.

Weston shot Jyro a serious glance. "You were an altar boy?"

Jyro nodded. "Yeah. Why?"

"So was I."

"I . . . was . . . too," Wrath added, suspicion and shock narrowing his watery brown eyes. "And then after that, a minister."

The others followed suit, and in seconds the group of vagrants discovered that prior to falling from grace and turning to the streets of Manhattan, every one of them had once been either an altar boy, minister, or priest.

Holy men.

Wilson said, "It's obvious now why *we* were the ones called here."

Jyro nodded, smiled with no humor, and replied, "Well then, my brothers, let's figure out how we go about getting our hands on the chalice."

CHAPTER FOURTEEN

Darkness spread like a deadly virus. Not a single pin-point of light seeped from the windows around him. The streetlights on the block were out, standing like sentries at the gates of some dark palace. A boundless canopy lay gray and dismal across the sky like a woolen blanket, cloaking the moon, the stars, and the rooftops.

In the distance, however, Manhattan's power burned on, the faraway lights like dim beacons on a dark, billowing ocean. For this, Pilazzo was thankful. Head down, he raced from the church as quickly as his aching legs would take him. Not once did he look back, knowing that regardless of how this all played out, he'd never set foot inside the Church of Holy Innocents again. It was tainted now . . . tainted by a pure, nameless evil.

But what lies ahead in my church?

His footsteps echoed in the night. Guided solely by the dim and distant streetlights—*beacons*—he turned the corner and raced across the street, onto the sidewalk of Second Avenue. Here, thankfully, a few scattered streetlights burned on. He thought, *I'm having a breakdown, and I'm going to die soon,* feeling the heat of the night attacking him. He began to feel ill and thought it was from fear. Then he realized he hadn't eaten in more than twenty hours. He recalled stories of mystics who'd experienced stigmata and had apparently gone *weeks* without food, claiming to be guided solely by God. He wondered if that was happening to him now.

Guided by God . . .

The strength bled out of his legs, and he had to slow down to a walk. He could feel his lungs burning, wheezing for precious air. Light-headed, he nearly collapsed to the pavement.

In a sudden blare of light he beheld an image, that of the crumbling Church of St. Peter. *My home—my sanctuary.* The image appeared as a defined silhouette, beckoning him forward just as the words scrawled in ash upon his bedroom wall had. He again came to realize that he was being guided by some greater power, and the clues being provided to him would point the way.

Your church awaits. . . .

So he forced himself to press on, seeking the parking meters for precious support. He reached the corner and leaned against a mailbox, a flyer slapped on it advertising a techno nightclub called Atmosphere. He swallowed past the lump in his throat and looked across the street to the opposite corner. It seemed unreachable, caught in shadows.

His thoughts whipped about his mind like a sandstorm, demanding that he move on . . . into the impending war of Good vs. Evil. *I can't!* his fatigued body screamed. But he knew some higher authority— *God!*—needed him in a specific place, and the time to go there was now, without delay. He only hoped his mission would in some way be explained upon his arrival at St. Peter's.

He looked around and saw that the city lay in terrible silence, with no cars or cabs racing up on Second Avenue. Typically, even in the early morning hours, life existed everywhere in the city. Here and now, looking both ways, he could see that nothing existed.

Nothing . . . except the man standing in the middle of the street.

The man remained at a distance . . . a *safe* distance. Pilazzo immediately gathered by his intense, troubled stare and downcast scowl that in some inconceivable way, this strange man—the only other living being in sight—appeared afraid of *him*.

Pilazzo straightened and stepped backward, across the sidewalk. He kept his eyes trained on the man, who wore jeans, a dirty white T-shirt, and a leather utility belt wrapped around his waist.

A construction worker.

Standing with his muscled arms at his sides, the worker opened his mouth and released a screeching howl on par with the sound a dog might make upon having its leg chopped off.

Pilazzo backpedaled into the storefront behind him. There was a loud crash as the store's gate wavered back and forth.

He thought back to the construction workers he encountered on the subway platform the previous day. *They were scared of me,* he remembered. With an odd mixture of sick dread and relief, he saw that this man remained unmoving, like the other workers had, stiff and wide-eyed in the center of the street. Despite the warmth of the night, his breath was visible.

Pilazzo staggered along the length of the gate, then

darted across the street. Heart pounding furiously, lungs pulling hopelessly for air, he continued racing away from the man, down the street toward Third Avenue.

Just ahead another figure emerged from an apartment doorway.

Pilazzo gasped. He put his hands to his heart, but felt nothing.

Nothing but fear and the clear image of horror before him.

In the semidarkness, Pilazzo could see the figure—a man—was dragging a body. Holding it by the arms, he dragged it down the sidewalk toward the priest.

Pilazzo skidded to a stop against a parked sedan, now aware of sirens blaring in the distance, of acrid smoke saturating the air.

Fire.

The man looked at Pilazzo and grunted. The flickering light of the street lamp reflected off his sweaty, hairless dome.

Dear God, what's happening . . . ?

This man too was a construction worker, clothed in jeans and an orange safety vest. Tattoos ran the length of his flexing arms. His clothes were painted with patchy, black stains. The body in his grasp appeared to have been a homeless vagrant, judging by his tattered clothes and straggly beard. He was dead, having met his fate beneath the thrust of two orange-handled screwdrivers jutting from his eyes like road flares. Blood had poured from his sockets down his face.

The worker stopped, then grabbed the body by its matted hair and arched the head back, placing the vagrant's face beneath the street lamp's flickering light. The screwdrivers wavered up and down like batons in the hands of a guide.

The worker laughed, deeply, gutturally.

Pilazzo was momentarily paralyzed. In his mind, a voice whispered, *Your church awaits*. . . . The simple line provided him with the fortitude to carry on with his task, whatever it might be.

He heard a shuffling noise behind him and spun around.

The worker who had stood in the middle of the street was now leaning against the corner street sign. His eyes were rolled up into his skull, baring only stark whites. His teeth were bared, white and glimmering.

From around the corner, another man joined him, a yellow hard hat on his head . . . and a circular saw in his hands, its electrical cord dangling like a tail. He jabbed the saw forward, grunting with each movement, "*Uhrr . . . uhrr . . . uhrr . . .*," childishly imitating the saw's rev.

Pilazzo slid between a pair of parked cars and staggered across the street. Only now did he scream out loud in the deadly silence of the night.

He lurched drunkenly down the sidewalk, seeing peripherally more workers gathering, not coming after him but keeping a watch on him from a distance with their poisoned, white eyes. They were murderers, Pilazzo thought. Every one of them wanted only to kill. Something dark and evil was driving them, just as something *good* attempted to guide him and protect him from the workers who wanted to kill him.

He glanced over his shoulder and saw with horror six or seven men now—all construction workers— milling about on the sidewalk with utter disregard for the dead man at their feet, eyes pointed unwaveringly in his direction as he fled down the street.

Reaching Third Avenue, he saw smoke billowing from a distant building, sirens blaring nearby.

He instantly remembered his vision: *an army of tattered men facing a great evil rising up before a wall of raging fire and blackened smoke* . . .

People shouted in the distance . . . and now a number of confused individuals, who'd apparently caught news of the anarchy going down in the city, ran aimlessly across the shadowy street.

Soon, Pilazzo assumed, there would be many more people crawling from their beds to witness the hellfire in the streets of New York City.

He turned and saw the construction workers slowly, tentatively approaching, stalking him like a gang of prowling jackals.

A girl ran by them, her face sickly white.

They paid her no interest.

They kept their gazes on *him*—the priest they inexplicably *feared. How can this be?* he wondered. *What would happen,* he thought for a crazy moment, *if I spun around and charged after them? Would they run?*

Or would they grab him, kill him?

He didn't want to find out. He turned and ran away from the men, toward Lexington. He stopped at the corner and gripped the steel post next to the entrance to the subway for support. Somewhere close by, a woman screamed. Even closer, a dog started barking ferociously.

Pilazzo took a hurried breath, then, seeing no other option, stumbled down the steps, deep into the bowels of Manhattan.

CHAPTER FIFTEEN

In the battered rectory of St. Peter's Church, the home-less men drew together in a loose circle, all of them unable to come up with any answers.

Marcus lit another cigarette from his seemingly never-ending pack and blew a cloud of smoke out toward the downed albino. Seymour had fallen into a pained stupor and was sitting on the floor with his head drooping between his raised knees. His hands had turned an angry shade of purple with cut skin hanging from them. Rollo wore out a path between the men and the steps, mumbling some unheard prayer. Weston and Wrath were whispering to each other, each man giving Timothy a guarded look.

The room had grown very cold. A light steam rose from the blood and vomit beneath the motionless albino.

Wilson was the first to speak. "So what we need to do is get our mitts on this chalice you're talking about."

"And how are we supposed to do that?" Dallas asked, hugging his frail body for warmth. He'd been running his hands through his grizzled hair, setting it into an Einstein style.

Both Jyro and Timothy had claimed to see the chalice

floating over a deep hole. From the chalice, Jyro had said, fire rose six feet in the air with a gush of foul-smelling wind that had knocked him down. Again Timothy described the streams of blood that spewed out of the hole like a fountain.

Wrath said, "Even without all that, trying to get a trophy too far out of reach is dangerous."

"We should see if it's still there first," Jyro said. "And then decide what to do."

"And if it isn't there?" Wrath asked.

"Then we look somewhere else."

Wilson yanked nervously on his dreadlocks, eyes glued fearfully to the twisted heap that used to be the albino. "I sure hope it ain't there."

Jyro peered down the dark hall. He remembered seeing the light from the chalice's fires flickering against the hallway wall. Now the hall lay in darkness, the twin doorway on the right nearly buried in shadows.

"We need flashlights," Wrath said, moving beside Jyro. His bald head glistened in the pallid light.

Jyro looked toward the ceiling. "Larry's stockpile of tools. I lifted one from there earlier. Timothy found a penlight there, too. There might be more."

Wrath looked up the winding steps with the trepidation of a child checking under the bed for monsters. "I'll go," he said quietly. "Where are they?"

"There's a sliding closet in the bedroom. The tools are inside under a blanket." Jyro said.

Marcus, voice clogged with phlegm, said, "Maybe the tools could be used as weapons. Something to protect us." He coughed, then pulled another Winston from the tattered pack in his pocket and lit it with the one he'd just finished.

Jyro tried to see how a few screwdrivers or awls might prove useful against the inexplicable evil possessing the church. He considered the painful absurdity of the idea . . . then realized that, if anything, the tools might at least make the eight desperate men feel less helpless.

Wrath said, "I'll gather what I can."

With silent determination, the big black man climbed the dark staircase, those downstairs watching with a mixture of fear and caution. As soon as Wrath disappeared around the turn, Weston climbed a few steps and waited, while Marcus and Wilson gathered at the bottom step, listening.

"Shout if you see anything," Weston called, and Jyro wondered whether any of them would dare race up those steps if the biggest and strongest one of their bunch started screaming bloody murder. Certainly not the elderly Dallas, whose pale tattoos looked older than Jyro himself.

The men waited in silence. Jyro felt an odd disconnection from himself, as though his mind were floating away from his body. He shivered and a despondent voice inside his head screamed, *Help me!* not a second before Wrath shouted, "Holy shit!"

Jyro shuddered back into reality. He staggered as Weston leaped down the steps, not in fear of what had Wrath so startled, but simply to get out of Wrath's way. Weston lunged past Wilson and Marcus, then spun into a defensive posture and watched along with the others as Wrath bounded down the steps like a pissed-off bull.

The big man lurched into the center of the group, screaming, perhaps on the verge of losing all control, then turned around and peered up the steps fearfully.

"What is it?" Jyro demanded. *What could be more*

frightening than a possessed man crucified on the wall?

Wrath pointed a trembling hand toward the stairs, lips drawn back to reveal huge white teeth, saliva running from them in loose smatters. His barrel-like chest heaved.

From upstairs came a series of plodding footsteps that were soon muffled as they met the runner covering the upper landing. The men waited, watching as they listened to the footsteps slowly descend the steps, one at a time, *thump . . . thump . . . thump . . .*

From around the turn, six steps up, they saw.

First the booted feet, doused in blood, leaving wet footprints behind as thick as mud tracks. Another step, legs up to the calves, the trousers as saturated with blood as the boots. Another step, the thighs now in view, the blood there substantial but in streaks, winding up to the tattered shirt. As the hands came into view, Jyro realized they were looking at one-eared Larry, thief of tools.

Wilson yelled, "Oh man, oh my God, oh man . . ."

Rollo blurted, "Dear Jesus!"

The world swam around Jyro. He could see the rosary dangling from Larry's filthy leathery fingers, the carved cross swinging back and forth in his outstretched hand, beckoning him once again. Jyro squeezed his eyes shut, denying himself the charm's lure. He clasped his hands together and shook his head vigorously.

When he opened his eyes, he could see the whole horror of the man before him, two steps up and standing there in all his filthy glory, staring at the men through a mask of shit and gore: the nose pulverized, lips split, cheeks battered and bloodied, smeared with black waste. And his eyes . . . still very much alive, aglow with fearlessness.

Jyro thought, *There's no way this man could be alive.* Then he added, *or human.*

The thing that Larry had become stood, one arm at his side, the other extended, twisted fingers clutching the rosary. His arms—mere bones covered in scant flesh—were fixed and motionless. His teeth glistened wetly.

And the rosary swayed back and forth and back and . . .

It was a standstill, Larry on the second step, the rest of the men, all eight of them, a dozen feet away, unwilling to make a move.

Except for Timothy.

He took a step forward.

Jyro whispered, "Kid! Get back here now!"

Weston reached out to grab him, but the boy took another step, out of his reach. Now perhaps three feet away from Larry (whose freakish eyes continued to remain the only part of him moving), the boy reached out with a shaky hand, to grab the rosary.

Larry didn't move. He didn't look at Timothy. He just stood there, arm extended, dead skin flaking off in tiny peels, dusting the floor.

The rosary swung slowly from side to side.

Timothy took another step closer, and Jyro could see that no one, himself included, was willing to move between them.

The boy's outstretched hand was only eighteen inches from the rosary now. Jyro closed his eyes and winced, fearing the next moment. He heard a shuffling commotion.

He opened his eyes and saw Larry lunging forward, his fist flying toward Timothy's face.

In the split second before contact, Jyro could see the panic on Timothy's face as his arms went up, too late to block the punch. Larry's fist connected with Timothy's right eye socket with a sharp thud.

The boy made an *"Oomph!"* sound and thumped down on his rear, both hands pressed to his face. Weston and Wrath immediately grabbed him under the arms and dragged him away from Larry.

Larry darted past the men toward the exit. Jyro (and perhaps a few of the others) thought about charging him. But the beaten vagrant, clearly under unnatural influence—*like the shit-beast,* Jyro thought—was too great a threat to confront.

Larry grabbed the doorknob with both hands.

Cobalt fire lanced out. The bright flash shot up Larry's arms like lightning. Jyro shielded his eyes, expecting the man to go up in flames. But the fire fizzled out and didn't seem to affect the mad vagrant, as though his clothes were fire retardant. Larry fled through the door, leaving it slightly ajar behind him.

A few seconds passed. There was no sound except the door leading out into the church slamming shut and Seymour sobbing from his spot on the floor against the wall. His hands had exchanged their purple hue for a freshly healed pink sheen.

Wilson stepped to the door and peered through the slight gap. "I can't see anything. It's dark."

"Let him go," Jyro said, the room rolling in and out of focus. It was a struggle for him to speak, but still he mustered the strength to add, "The rosary . . . it'll be delivered to its rightful owner. We . . . we need to find the chalice now."

"How can you be so sure?" Weston looked at Jyro, face pale except the dark circles under his eyes.

"Listen to the man," Wrath said, voice deep and booming. He put a hand on Weston's shoulder, gentle but firm. "Our message has been delivered, our mission laid out for us. Let's do it as a group. There's strength in numbers."

Jyro nodded vigorously, thankful for the support.

"The chalice . . ." Timothy rasped painfully, looking as if he were going to puke. "We . . ." He trailed off, seemingly drained of the strength to continue.

The men needed to hear no more. They knew. There would be no chance for escape without it.

Jyro stared at Timothy for a moment, then, working against his fear, motioned down the dark hallway toward the rec room. "Let's go see if it's still there."

CHAPTER SIXTEEN

The subway station lay silent and desolate. Like the street outside the Church of Holy Innocents, not a soul could be seen. The main overhead lights were out, but all the emergency beacons still glowed.

Pilazzo passed the attendant booth and saw with dismay that someone had smashed the Plexiglas casement and looted what cash they could find inside. A sunburst of blood was painted over the subway system map inside. Pilazzo guessed that on the floor below, amid the shards of inch-thick Plexiglas he'd always presumed to be shatterproof, the body of the attendant lay in a dead heap.

He stooped beneath the turnstile and walked briskly down the steps to the platform.

A subway train sat on the tracks, its doors open, interior lights flickering; he could hear them buzzing, a stench of ozone and urine saturating the air.

Seeing no place to sit, he leaned against the closest support column and began to cry. It was just a few sobs at first, but soon the floodgates opened. The wails spilled from him ungoverned, and warm tears streaked down his face. After a while, he stopped and gazed up the stairs that led to the outside world . . . and then to the train sitting motionless amid a thin wisp of acrid smoke and sputtering lights.

The open door beckoned him.

He was afraid . . . but wasn't *terrified* as he felt he should be and couldn't fathom why. There were murders being committed on the streets, chaos erupting . . . and yet he maintained his composure—his *will* to press forward and move on with his mission.

Your church awaits. . . .

He took a step toward the open train door.

From behind him came a voice, a mocking call: *"Uh-boo-hoo-hooooo,"* the type of feigned blubber a schoolyard bully might make after shoving a nerdy kid into a mud puddle.

Pilazzo froze. He looked over his shoulder and saw four men standing perhaps twenty feet away. They were huddled together, staring at him, eyes feral beneath the dim lighting.

The tallest called out with derision, "Time to play, priest. Time to plaaaayyyy!" His head jerked back and forth, shoulder-length hair brushing in and out of his face.

The men moved forward as a group, their gait hideous and unnatural, as if manipulated by intermittent surges of power. Pilazzo could see none of them boasted any kind of construction gear, but he knew they were workers. They had muscles. They were tan with soiled jeans and T-shirts emblazoned with graphic logos.

Despite it all, he sensed they were *afraid* of him.

Like the others. Here I stand, utterly defenseless. They could murder me like they did Thomas and that homeless man. But they can't. I don't know how I know it, but it's perfectly clear in my head.

It is the Goodness that protects you, Antonio.

Through the splay of watery light, he could see a large wrench clutched in the hand of one worker. The worker grinned and gnashed his teeth, slamming the tool into his palm in an intimidating I'm-going-to-club-you gesture.

Pilazzo took a step back, icy breath suddenly misting.

The tall worker's laughs persisted. Pilazzo could see his eyes rolling up into their sockets, showing slick whites.

In Pilazzo's head, a whispering voice: *rosary . . . rosary . . . rosary . . .*

The worker mocked, "Come plaaayyyy with us, priest!" His wicked laughs continued.

A brutal welling of emotions beset Pilazzo, intense fear coupled with pure disgust and anger. Part of him wanted to shout out and defy the evil that was toying with him, attempting to lure him into its bizarre trap, but he followed his heart and the will of the message sent to him and staggered into the train.

As soon as he stepped inside, the doors closed. The lights continued flickering, leaving him in intervals of light and darkness. He grasped the closest pole, palm slick against the silvery surface. Dizziness rolled over him. He closed his eyes tightly, praying.

With a sudden *smack*, the hands of the workers struck the dirty windows. He started, watching as blood smeared the clear plastic. They peered into the train, only the whites of their eyes clearly visible, fingernails scratching harshly against the hard surface.

The worker with the wrench drove it right through the window, and suddenly Pilazzo understood how the token booth had been smashed. The worker bucked and thrashed outside the train, trying to batter his way through, shoving his face forward and cackling.

"No!" Pilazzo screamed. He backed up against the opposite door . . . but couldn't pull his eyes away from the men with their bloodied hands bludgeoning through the shattered window. The lights continued to buzz and flicker, and then the train started moving forward. Pilazzo knew that if he raced to the front of the train he wouldn't find a motorman.

The four workers kept pace with the train as it moved, whipping their heads back and forth like Dobermans gnawing at a steel cage. The worker with the wrench reached farther inside, and the flesh of his forearm tore open on an exposed shard of plastic. Blood gushed, painting the seat below.

Pilazzo's mind ran like mad: *If they're afraid of me, then why come after me? Do they simply want to scare me?*

The train picked up speed, too quickly for the workers to keep up now, and they abruptly fell away. All of them except the worker with the wrench. His arm was still snagged on the shard of plastic. Sprinting, the worker roared like an injured animal as he tried desperately to yank his arm free. More blood burst from his wound.

He lost his footing and fell. The speeding train was dragging him.

Crunch!

Pilazzo flinched as the worker disappeared, and the darkness of the subway tunnel swallowed the train. The lights buzzed out at that instant, and in a quick flash of blue volts from inside the tunnel, Pilazzo could see the worker's severed arm thump onto the bloody seat across from him, the hand open, the wrench it held clanging to the floor. An abrupt spatter of warmth hit his face, and he knew as the lights flickered back on that he'd been sprayed with the worker's blood. He wiped his eyes in a panic and watched with sick horror as the fingers shriveled into the severed hand like the legs of a dying spider.

The train moved at a rapid clip, passing the next station without a hint of slowing down. The station he regularly got off at was four stops away. He wondered if the train would stop there at all.

Somehow he felt it would.

He quickly recalled Monsignor Thomas Sanchez's final words: *We are being summoned. Follow the message that God delivers to you. Heed His word and do your part to bring down the evil that promises man the end of days. . . .*

And in his mind: *Your church awaits. . . .*

"Priest . . ." This voice, low and gravelly.

He shot a startled glance down the length of the car.

Seated at the opposite end was a vagrant, the same homeless man that had touched his shoulder upon returning to Holy Innocents yesterday afternoon.

In his mind, the vision returned, as clear as a television transmission: *blackened skies and an army of tattered men facing a great evil rising up before a wall of raging fire and billowing smoke . . .*

His breath escaped him. He felt his lungs gasping for air. Dizziness shrouded his ability to see, and he had to close his eyes.

He heard the vagrant speak: "*Your church awaits, priest. . . .*"

Grasping the seat's handrail, he opened his eyes.

The vagrant now stood only ten feet away, staring at him, eyes mournful, wet with tears. He extended a callused hand, displaying a thick crimson scar around his ring finger.

Pilazzo gasped. The lights in the train blinked out, and in the darkness he saw his mother standing there, just as she had in his dream, garbed in a black billowing robe, a single finger pressed against her lips. He heard her utter one word: *Antonio . . .*

Oh my God . . .

The lights flashed back on.

His mother was gone.

So was the vagrant.

The train pulled into a station. The brakes squealed, sending up an odor of burning metal. He wobbled as the train slowed, grabbed hold of the support pole, and looked out the blood-smeared window. The signs indicated he was at the Seventy-seventh Street station.

I'm here. My church awaits . . .

The train stopped. The doors opened.

He hesitated, tried to swallow but couldn't. He heard nothing. Saw no movement.

The train planned to travel no further.

Mumbling a prayer, he exited onto the platform, staggered away from the train and leaned up against the closest support column.

He gazed up the steps leading to the street.

One block away from the Church of St. Peter.

CHAPTER SEVENTEEN

The men moved as a loose group, Jyro leading the way. He held a lighter out before him, the faint hiss audible in the tense silence. Jyro could see the pile of debris at the end of the hall, flickering like a restless ghost. But that was all. The wall beyond lay entirely in darkness.

Weston moved beside Jyro, holding a small plank of wood with both hands, ready to swing it should the need arise. Following close behind were Seymour and Dallas, then Wilson, Timothy, Marcus and Rollo, with Wrath anchoring the procession. They passed the lunchroom and the lockers, all of them peering ahead to the doors leading into the rec room. Just inside the entrance, a white light blared, much brighter than the emergency beacons in the lobby, enabling them to see the hole in the floor as they went inside.

Aside from the big hole, nothing seemed out of the ordinary in the room. There was no floating chalice. No fires or wind. And no fountain of blood.

From the back of the line, Wrath called out, "What do you see?"

Jyro stepped forward. His feet crunched on bits of debris, some of it wet, but most of it not. Weston and the others shuffled in close behind him.

"Nothin' but a big hole," he said. A cold chill traced its way up his back.

"Plenty of light here," Dallas said. He raised a tattooed arm and pointed to the lightbulbs. "They replaced the hazards with a pair of halogens. See? They're aimed down into the hole." He grinned thinly, adding, "Used to be an electrician in my former life."

The group stopped and stared, and Jyro realized that seeing this hole had confirmed to the others the incredible story they'd heard from him and Timothy—a story they did not want to believe.

Jyro separated himself from the group and stepped to the edge of the hole. He looked down into it and gasped at what he saw—at what he *felt:* a sudden dislocation from reality, forcing him to sense much more than the hole's depth and exposed skeletons (many now shattered by the workers' boots) lining its dark bottom.

A rush of nearly painful tingles enveloped Jyro's body—this was how he had felt upon first investigating the hole. There'd been an unmistakable presence looking down on him, *touching* him, making certain that he moved and acted exactly as it wanted him to. He shuddered. The presence was still here. He could feel it. And it wanted him to peer into the hole.

A faint acrid smell drifted up from the hole. Twisted pipes jutted angrily from the walls of the pit, hunks of brown rock and earth surrounding them. At the bottom of the hole he could see the wooden crate, a tiny island drowning in a sea of shattered bones, four feet long and three feet wide, odd writing burned into its rough surface, its depth partially buried in shadows.

It was open, just as he had left it.

He could not see the interior of the crate, but the men from his dreams, the forefathers of the church . . .

. . . and they are wrapping the chalice in burlap and placing it inside next to the shrouded rosary. Beside the crate are a line of lifeless bodies—men, women, and children—lying faceup, eyes gouged from their decapitated heads, crucifixes piercing their hearts. There are perhaps two dozen dead packed in the bottom of the pit, sacrifices made to the evil that threatened to bring down mankind. . . .

He could see it all in his mind's eye, like a recent memory still fresh.

He struggled to step back from the hole's edge. He wiped his forehead, feeling weak and ill, scared. A jolt of pain grasped his heart, and he shied away from this vision, seeing in his mind now the evil entity that had tormented these people. And it terrified him. He could feel his body trembling. He wanted to scream, but his mind had become a prisoner in his own head. This evil . . . he could *see* it, a dark and formless thing able to take any menacing form it chose. Somehow . . . somehow, Jyro understood this, as plainly as the excavated hole before him—it had composed itself of waste, it had entered the albino and one-eared Larry. All representations of the beast released from its bonds, now in possession of the church.

Oh dear God, help us all. . . .

And yet something buried deep inside his mind made him see that there was some good present in all these terrible representations . . . that within each of the beast's forms, a certain level of goodness was there struggling to keep it at bay: the rosary in Timothy's hand, enabling him to down the possession of the waste; the messages from the crucified man and from Larry.

Jyro jolted, and the piece of his mind making him

see and understand everything happening *today* lapsed back into the past he so desperately wanted to escape . . .

. . . and he can see the men, who appear as real as the men standing behind him, the crate and the dead bodies now buried deep in the darkness of the soil— sacrifices made to the beast that threatens the existence of every man, woman, and child on earth. And along- side them he can see a boy, and in the boy's bleeding hands are the rosary and the chalice. . . .

He fought away the image for a second time, seeing now that the good of the rosary had been used by the boy to keep the evil of the chalice at bay. It was as if the pieces of some mysterious puzzle had magically come together in his mind. A voice uttered in his head: *One holds darkness; one holds light. Find the sinless one.* And he knew: The rosary was the only weapon against the evil that promised man the end of days. And that evil was flourishing because the chalice and the rosary had been separated. He heard this in his head as if it had been spoken aloud. And it made him painfully aware that all those in the custodies of the chalice and rosary would become part of their amass- ing armies; the workers, retrievers of the chalice from its lofty point above the pit, now incarnations of Evil; and Jyro's finding of the rosary made those like himself—the city's homeless—to form Good's army.

The city's homeless vs. the city's workers. Good vs. Evil. The only means of beating back the beast was to bring the chalice and the rosary back together and lock them inside the crate, again and forever. Just as the church's original ancestors had done more than a hundred years ago.

A task easier said than done.

The images faded from his mind. Faintly, dimly, he sensed himself being pulled away from the hole. He tried to resist the pull, but a wave of dizziness consumed him and the real world rolled back into his sights. His feet tangled together, and he collapsed . . . into the waiting hands of his brothers.

He could hear them shouting at him from every direction, hands slapping his cheeks as he came to. He looked up, saw Timothy and Weston staring down at him, their outlines bobbing crookedly in the light as they dragged him out of the rec room.

"Are you okay?" Timothy asked hurriedly, helping him sit down against the lockers in the hallway.

Jyro saw the scene before him coming into focus: seven men and one teenaged boy, pathetic and filthy but brimming with spirit and strength.

"What happened?" he asked.

"You almost toppled into the pit," Timothy replied quietly.

"It looked like you were in some sort of trance." Weston kneeled down before Jyro; the big man's face was so red it was almost purple. "You started mumbling, and when we looked at you we could see your eyes had rolled up in your head."

Timothy said, "We left you alone at first, but . . . but then you started trembling, and that was when you leaned forward, and we had to pull you back before you fell into the hole."

There was a long pause as Jyro marshaled his thoughts. He rubbed his eyes and shook his head, then climbed to his feet and leaned against the lockers. With the events of a hundred years ago still gnawing at his mind, he figured there was only one course of action: to do as they had done, all those years ago. If he could put this hellstorm off for another hundred years, then so be it. He told the men: "We need to find the chalice. The sinless one, whoever he is, will bring us the rosary. We need to put them both into the crate at the bottom of the hole and bury it someplace where no one will ever find it again."

Just like the founding fathers of the church did all those years ago.

The group of men nodded weakly. Timothy, right eye nearly swollen shut, asked, "So where do we look for the chalice, then?"

Jyro looked through the open doors of the rec room. "As far as I can tell, it ain't in there." He took a deep breath and motioned toward the partially open door in the rectory lobby.

"We have to get into the church, don't we?" Weston said, looking edgy.

Jyro nodded, and the men spread out as he trudged through them and moved down the hall.

"How, man? How are we supposed to do that without getting burned?" Wilson asked.

Jyro said, "You used to be an altar boy. Didn't they teach you that where there's a will, there's a way?"

Wilson stared back at Jyro, utterly silent.

"C'mon. Let's go find a way into the church."

CHAPTER EIGHTEEN

"My . . . dear . . . Jesus . . ."

Pilazzo stood at the top of the subway entrance, aghast at the scene playing out before him. It was still early in the morning, the sun's rays a faint glimmer over the horizon. The streetlights were out, but he could see flame and black smoke spewing from a building's windows not two blocks away. Distant sirens blared. A few taxis and cars zoomed past, alarm on the drivers' faces.

A girl of perhaps eighteen wearing running gear rushed up to Pilazzo in a panic.

"Help me!" she cried, eyes red and swollen with tears. Smears of ash and soot marked her sweaty cheeks and forehead like war paint. Her thin brown hair was plastered to the sides of her face.

Pilazzo startled and shoved her away. She raced blindly into the street . . .

"Oh God, *No!*"

. . . right in front of a speeding cab. With a hideous *crack!*, the cab slammed into her and sent her flying into the windshield of a parked vehicle, driving portions of skull and brain across the webbed glass. Pilazzo watched with horror as the center of the windshield caved in and her body slid down onto the front seat, bloody legs sticking out.

Somewhere nearby people screamed. A few feet away, a shirtless man sprinted across the sidewalk, clutching a wound on his chest. Blood seeped out from between his fingers. He collided into a mailbox on the corner, and quickly disappeared down Seventy-seventh Street.

Short of breath, Pilazzo shambled down Lexington Avenue. Terrors filled his senses at every angle. Cars screeching, people shouting, sirens calling out to one another in the distance.

The world around him fell into a blur, making it difficult to make out any details. Nearby he heard the wail of what he thought was a circular saw combined with bloodcurdling screams.

A cold wind blew across the avenue. He shivered, holding his arms close, blinking as dust invaded his eyes. He moved across the littered sidewalk. In the gutter he saw a dead dog, its injuries still wet. Its tongue was bloated and black. Beside its mouth were two human fingers, bitten off below the knuckles.

Grimacing, Pilazzo jogged across the street, listening to the sounds of destruction, relentless in the distance. Ahead a homeless man lay next to a crashed vehicle, one leg pinned beneath the car's front tire. Pilazzo hurried to him and kneeled at his side. The man was unconscious. Blood oozed from his nose and lips.

Pilazzo grabbed the man's wrist, felt for a pulse.

The vagrant's eyes snapped open. He pulled his arm away and grabbed the priest's wrist. A quick jolt of pain ripped through Pilazzo's arm. He cried out, tried to pull away but couldn't.

Through split and bleeding lips, the vagrant said,

"Your church awaits. . . ." He then let go of the priest and fell motionless, empty eyes staring blankly toward the gray skies.

Pilazzo stood and ran into a grocery storefront. The front door was shattered, bits of glass crunching beneath his shoes. Inside he saw a man standing in the center of the store, eating an orange, babbling as he chewed, juicy bits slathering down his chin. A young man blanketed in tattoos sat at the foot of the register, jabbing his arm with a hypodermic needle. Neither of them looked at the priest.

Pilazzo fled the storefront and moved farther up the avenue. He saw a car speeding across the empty street toward him. He hurriedly slipped into an alcove of a building under construction. The car zigzagged, side-swiping a parked delivery truck before speeding on. Somewhere nearby, a girl screamed.

Pilazzo emerged from the alcove and gazed up at the unfinished structure looming over him.

From within, he could hear them: shouts and laughs and the harsh clanging of tools.

The workers.

He ran as fast as he could, which wasn't very fast at all. A cold breeze lanced his face. His cassock billowed behind him. He turned the corner onto Seventy-eighth Street.

Halfway up the block, he saw the Church of St. Peter and staggered toward it. All the trees on the block— planted in cement cutouts every ten feet—were gray and leafless now, dead. Beneath each tree lay dead birds, wings withered and jutting like the branches surrounding them.

What in God's name . . . ?

As he approached the church, he saw something in

his peripheral vision. He skidded to a stop, looked to his right, and stared.

In the center of the street was a mob of construction workers.

They were looking at him.

They were covered in blood.

The men—seven or eight in all—began staggering toward the priest in the same monstrous way the workers in the subway had: arms punching forward, eyes turned up into their heads.

Pilazzo slid between two cars, then lunged across the sidewalk and grasped the rusty handrail on the steps to St. Peter's.

The men, blood streaking down their stubbled chins, continued moving forward. Pilazzo saw in their hands a variety of blood-drenched tools: screwdrivers, wrenches, box cutters. They were swiping the air with them, like explorers in the jungle digging through dense foliage.

They can't hurt me because they're scared of me. Pilazzo tried desperately to convince himself, but fear kept him from standing his ground. He struggled up the church steps, tripping over his own feet, all the while watching the workers.

Instead of going around a car at the curb, the workers began climbing over it, leaving bloody smears in their wake. The tools in their hands gouged jagged lines into the shiny finish. As they climbed, they maintained their hideous grins, snickering between their clenched teeth.

Pilazzo groped blindly for the handle to the church door . . . the same handle he had grasped every day for the last seventeen years. He managed to get a hold of it.

It felt warm, *different*.

He pulled it.

With a loud screech, the door opened. A gust of bitter air rolled out, sending whorls of dust and grit up into his face.

The workers stopped, frozen in their tracks. One of them, a middle-aged man with a dark sunburn, slid off a BMW's roof and landed face-first on the sidewalk. In no noticeable pain, he leaped up on all fours like a cat righting itself and glared at the priest, white eyes glistening.

Pilazzo stared wordlessly at the man. His nose had been crushed to a pulp. His tongue flitted in and out of his mouth, making a horrible gargling sound. He held a bloody box cutter in his hand and jabbed the air with it.

The other workers were also staring at the priest, sniggering, showing bloodstained teeth. They began clanging their hand tools against the car, creating a wicked tolling sound that echoed up and down the street. In the distance, Pilazzo could hear a chorus of loud shouts—other workers answering the call of the men eyeing the priest.

Pilazzo's eyes burned from the dust. He performed a hasty sign of the cross and slipped inside the church.

In the vestibule he turned back to the staring workers. They kept their distance, heads weaving back and forth, trying to keep their sights on the priest. Their clanging went on and on. . . .

The church door ripped free of Pilazzo's hand and slammed shut, closing him inside. For a tense moment he stood there with his back to the church, pulling on the now immovable door, listening to the echo of the slam fading away. Outside he could hear the workers laughing and clanging, some of them now only inches away on the other side of the door.

He let go of the door's handle and stepped back.

Then, with his heart beating furiously and his nerves screaming bloody terror, he turned around and faced the gloomy interior of the Church of St. Peter.

CHAPTER NINETEEN

Jyro was standing five feet from the door, eyes glued to the darkness beyond the ten-inch opening. Timothy stood directly beside him, arms crossed tightly in front of his chest. Weston was close behind, nervously wielding the wood plank like a baseball bat. The rest of the men were poised at various points in the lobby.

"I sure as hell ain't gonna try it," Wilson said uneasily.

With a show of determination, Weston stepped around Jyro and Timothy and examined the slight gap. He held the plank inches away from it. Jyro could see his eyes shining in the dim glow of the emergency lights. "Well . . . what do you guys think?"

A pause followed where everyone contemplated what might happen if he touched the door with the plank. Jyro frowned and shrugged. This was a crapshoot he didn't want to bet on.

"I don't think that's a good idea," Marcus said firmly. He coughed into his hand, and this was the first time Jyro had seen him without a Winston tucked between his lips. Perhaps he was finally out.

"I think you should go for it," Dallas said, tugging his beard. "What's there to lose?"

Marcus answered, "He could end up with french fries for fingers."

Wilson tucked a dreadlock into his mouth and chewed on it nervously. "Hell, man, he used to have 'em, but not anymore."

That much was true. Weston's hands—and Wrath's, for that matter—were free of burns. Something was healing them, perhaps even making them *stronger*. It was all they had to rely on at the moment. "He's got a point, fellas. Your hands are cleaner than they were before you hit the streets for a living."

Rollo held up his Bible and shouted, "It's a miracle of the Lord! He protects us all from evil. We are His children, and He will guide us to safety!"

For once, Jyro thought, the chubby preacher had it right.

"So let's try it, then," Weston said indulgently. Ever so slowly, he arced the plank down into the gap between the door and the jamb.

Nothing happened.

There was a great sigh of relief in the room . . . but, no sense of accomplishment. He still had to push the door open a bit farther, enough so they could slip through.

Don't do it, Jyro thought, but he said nothing.

"This is crazy, man," Wilson said. "Just fuckin' nuts."

"May the Lord be with you, brother Weston!" Rollo went on. "Let Him shine down upon you the gift of everlasting life!"

"Enough, Rollo, that ain't helping any," Jyro said anxiously.

Sweat ran down the sides of Weston's face. He looked back at Jyro, plainly scared, like a man whose sense of normalcy had flown the coop. A moment passed where it looked as if Weston were going to pass the torch to someone else ... but then slowly ... slowly ... slowly, he moved the plank to his left until it came in contact with the door ...

   ... Whoosh!

A blue flame burst out of nowhere. It swallowed the wood and then Weston's arm. He tried to drop the plank, but the flame instantly fused his hand to the wood. A horrible stench of burning flesh permeated the room. He collapsed back into the group of men, who scattered like fish in a pond. Then he tore around in a circle before tripping over the albino's legs. He landed on his side with a dull thud. The plank splintered into blackened pieces as it hit the carpeted floor ... except for the square section that still burned freely in Weston's hand.

Weston's scream gave way to a sickening wail. He shrieked, "Put it out! Put it out!" His eyes bulged horrifically. He held up his cooked arm and ogled it stupidly. White blisters coated his red skin like a froth of boiled milk. Flames burned on it in scattered patches.

A man's scream came from inside the church, seemingly answering Weston's. The men turned toward the door, terror painted on their faces. *Larry,* Jyro thought quickly. *What the hell's happening?*

Outside St. Peter's, something exploded. The walls shook, and Jyro and Timothy rocked on their heels and covered their heads with their arms. Dust rained down on them. Wrath fell to his knees and attempted to snuff out Weston's arm with the same dirty towel he'd used on the crucified man.

Weston begged loudly, "Help me, please help me!"

A blue flame lanced out from Weston's arm. Wrath yelled, let go of the towel, and lurched back from the burning man, eyes wide, hands shaking. He fell to his knees, grimacing. Tendrils of smoke rose from his fingers. He'd been burned again.

The fire, Jyro thought. *It's as if it's . . . alive.*

Jyro got a firm grip on Timothy's arm. He looked at the boy protectively and then at Weston. For a moment he considered trying to help the injured man, but ultimately stayed back like everyone else, to protect himself and Timothy. Wrath had given it a good try, anyway. There wasn't much more he or anyone else could do.

Timothy looked at Jyro with a dark and vacant gaze. He shook his head in confusion. Jyro thought he looked utterly lost.

Weston emitted a croaky *"arck!"* His eyes rolled up into his head, and another gagging sound exploded from his throat, startling everyone in the room. His fingers, white and oozing, clawed against the floor as he struggled to his knees . . . but no further. Here he remained wavering like a scarecrow in the wind, smoldering hands floating loosely at his sides.

"What the hell . . . ?" Wilson screamed.

Weston's posture changed. He stiffened up. His face turned a sickly shade of blue, upturned eyes wide. His arms pumped up and down like pistons. His throat swelled profusely, like a frog's.

"I think he's swallowed his tongue!" Dallas shouted. Still no one moved to help.

But then Wrath, in a brave yet hopeless move, lunged forward again and positioned himself behind Weston. He wrapped his arms under the convulsing man's rib cage, hands fisted into Weston's gut. He managed to perform one or two Heimlich maneuvers on him, but that was all. He couldn't hold on. Weston was bucking and thrashing too much; plus his arm was still on fire. Wrath surrendered his grip and stumbled back. Weston collapsed beside the albino, arms and legs drumming the floor crazily.

He choked one last time, a final effort to push his tongue out of his throat, and then he fell silent. At that moment, the flames on his arm subsided, giving way to winding curls of smoke. It was as if someone had cut off their source.

The men stared at Weston's body. It was stuck in a mannequin-like pose, head arched back, limbs at odd angles. His burned arm was as black as charcoal.

One by one, the men backed away, eyes wide, mouths agape.

"Is he dead? *Is he?*" Timothy asked.

No one responded. The answer was all too obvious. Weston had met his maker. Jyro leaned back against the wall, holding his head in his hands, listening to the blood roaring in his ears.

Rollo broke the silence with a sudden, boisterous prayer. "May the good Lord look down upon our brother—"

"Will you shut the fuck up!" Wilson shouted. "We don't need that shit right now."

Jyro looked up.

Timothy was standing just inches from the church door.

"Hey, kid . . ."

Timothy turned. "The gap . . . it's wider," he said quietly. He shifted sideways, eyes moving between the door and the jamb. "I can do it," he said.

Jyro shook his head vehemently. "No, you don't."

Wrath said, "You're gonna end up like Wes if you try." The big man leaned against the wall, dazed and unbelieving. His skin glimmered, coated in sweat.

"But he caught fire when he *touched* the door. Just look at the gap . . . I can fit through. I'm the thinnest one here by far, and the door's open a few inches more."

Seymour warned, "You'll get burned, kid. Just like I did. Just like he did." Jyro looked over at the frail vagrant. His hands, although healing, still looked painfully pink and shiny. His eyes were dead blanks behind the dirty lenses of his glasses.

"I won't get burned if I'm careful."

Jyro nodded. "And then what? What will you do after you go through?"

Timothy peered through the opening into the dark hallway. He tilted his head sideways. "I can see the door leading out into the church. It's wide open. I'll go in there and look for the chalice."

"Larry's in there," Jyro cautioned. "Or what used to be Larry." He looked through the gap but couldn't see much in the darkness. "Evil's got him. You don't need me to tell you to be careful."

Timothy nodded, and before anyone could protest— to Jyro, it didn't seem anyone planned to—the boy slipped an arm between the door and the jamb.

All the men flinched . . . but nothing happened.

Timothy pulled his arm back and blew out a long, nervous breath.

Then, sizing up the space one more time, he twisted his body sideways and stealthily slipped through the gap into the dark hallway.

Silence followed. Jyro stepped to within inches of the door, peered through the gap, but saw nothing.

"Kid? You in there?"

Timothy appeared, standing about a foot away from the door. His face was bathed in shadows. "I'm here."

He looked different to Jyro in the darkness of the hallway. Older. Wiser.

"You made it!" Jyro said in an excited whisper.

"Just stand close by," Timothy said. "I know that if anything happens, you won't be able to help me, but . . . I'll feel better knowing you're there."

For the first time since this all began, Jyro smiled, and the bond between them grew stronger, more definitive. If there had been any doubt that the two of them were supposed to be here, it was now gone; just as Jyro knew Timothy's name earlier, he now knew the boy would risk his life to make certain every task set upon him was accomplished. *And so will I.*

"Just go see what's in the church," Jyro said. "And . . . and while you're at it . . ."

"What?"

He looked Timothy right in the eye and said, "Find the sinless one, and tell him to get us the hell out of here."

Timothy smiled grimly, then disappeared into the darkness of the hallway.

CHAPTER TWENTY

Pilazzo flinched at the explosion, perhaps only a block away. He could feel the church vibrating in its aftermath, the faint din of screams and shouts outside seeping in through the closed doors.

He took a deep breath and scanned the vestibule. It made him sick to his stomach. This used to be his *home*, the place for years he slept and ate, prayed and worked. Now it was the victim of a great evil trying to tear it down.

He saw the antechamber bulletin board hanging askew by one rusty nail, the glass shattered, pointed shards tearing two-month-old activity announcements. The threadbare carpet beneath his feet was ripped by the weight of construction equipment. Splinters of pine lay about like tiny carcasses.

The only thing that remained untouched was Henry Miller's fold-out table of yellow hard hats and orange vests. *There's some protective gear on the table to the right, as soon as you walk in. There's also a yellow envelope. Inside are the documents for you to sign.*

Pilazzo didn't see an envelope.

He leaned down and looked under the table. A wave of dizziness hit him. He closed his eyes and gripped his head, taking slow, even breaths through his nose. When the dizziness faded, he opened his eyes and waited until his vision readjusted to the gloom.

He placed his hand against the doorjamb and gazed at the miserable scene inside the church.

A wicked sin has been committed. May those guilty of this travesty burn in the fires of . . .

He thought of his mother, presumably the bride of Christ—*does this make me the son of Christ?*—of how she'd maintained her devout convictions all her life, even more so during the later stages of her mental illness. He recalled her image from the dream, how she'd stood in the ruined landscape and told him: *After I was gone, you maintained your faith steadfastly, which enabled Him to behold the strength in you. You are His son. And now, He needs you. Do as He says, Antonio.*

I am the sinless one . . .

Indeed, he'd remained true to his faith, even in his mother's dying days. And now he had no choice but to do the same.

He beat back an impulse to flee.

Your church awaits. . . .

Then he whispered a silent prayer to his mother and left the vestibule, entering the Church of St. Peter.

What used to be the Church of St. Peter.

The interior of the century-old building had little natural light, except for what filtered through the stained-glass windows at either end; with the church sandwiched between two buildings, the windows on both sides that depicted the events leading to the birth of Jesus had never seen any daylight.

Lights gleamed from the altar. He fixed his gaze on the two industrial spots at the front of the church. For a fleeting second he wondered why the crews had left these on, but then nothing came as a surprise to him anymore.

He noticed the marble holy-water basin at the entrance to the nave, coated in sawdust and plaster chips. He walked to it, slid his fingers through the grit, and crossed himself. He frowned. There wasn't the usual bountiful feeling, no impassioned touch of God.

Dear Lord, I pray for Your strength.

He pinched his dry lips and advanced into the church.

The Gothic architecture was not as he remembered it. Without the yellow glow of the dome-shaped fixtures above, the columnar supports and vaulted ceilings that had always suggested a heavenly presence lay shrouded in darkness. Half the pews were gone, the only evidence of their existence the rectangular marks of wood and glue on the marble floor where they'd once stood.

Strangely, the altar remained untouched. He admired the power it demonstrated, even now despite the destruction, its marble solidity somehow balanced by the delicacy of what surrounded it: a half dozen blessed statues draped in drop cloths and shadows, waiting to be delivered to the various parishes who'd requested them.

The statues made him think of the conversation he'd had with the foreman, Henry Miller. . . .

Our crews aren't insured for moving valuables, Father. I strongly suggest you hire a moving company to handle them. We won't be able to move them out unless you sign a damage waiver . . . but I advise against that. Our men aren't trained to be delicate, ya know what I mean?

Gracing the wall behind the altar was the great

crucifix, twelve feet high, intricately carved in wood, its extraordinary detail still visible despite the film of dust and dark shadows enveloping it. Pilazzo could almost feel the pain carved in the face of the crucified Jesus: the thorned head; the tortured eyes searching the heavens for an answer to this disgrace of God; the mouth contorted so passionately that Pilazzo could almost hear echoes of its pained suffering.

It looks different. . . .

He cleared his throat and walked farther down the aisle, footfalls gritty in the sediment, crunching hollowly. He ran his hands along an untouched pew as he kept his sights upon the wooden Jesus. *The blood . . . it looks more real.*

He heard a noise ahead. Footsteps shuffling across the dusty floor.

From the shadows at the left of the altar emerged a dark figure.

It moved in a stooped position up the three steps to the altar and disappeared behind the statues.

A gust of wind rose up from out of nowhere and sent a whirl of dust about Pilazzo. He squeezed his eyes shut, hiding his face beneath his hands. The wind, howling amid the exposed beams and stained-glass windows, seized the inner doors of the church and slammed them shut with a forceful *bang*.

Heart pounding furiously, Pilazzo pulled his hands away from his face and cowered alongside the side rail until the wind died down and the echo of the slamming doors faded.

He looked back toward the closed doors. There was nothing there.

He faced the altar again.

He could see the shadowy figure standing before a

shrouded statue, face pointed away. It bobbed up and down for a few moments, as if praying, then limped to the great crucifix, where it gazed up toward Jesus's face and began bobbing again.

Pilazzo took a step forward, then another.

"Hey . . ." he called weakly, thinking, *This is no construction worker.*

He took another step, now a foot away from the altar steps.

Without warning, the inner doors to the church slammed back open. Pilazzo whipped around and watched as the doors slammed shut again with the same tempestuous ferocity. A cloud of dust billowed up and out over the pews.

He reminded himself that with all he'd seen and heard today, all he'd dreamed and experienced, nothing should come as a surprise.

It didn't.

It scared him to death.

He faced the altar again.

The shadowy figure was still there, standing beneath the crucifix.

A little more loudly, Pilazzo called out: "Hello? Can you hear me?"

No answer. No movement.

The hunched figure stepped to the left and stood before another covered statue, this one at the very front of the altar.

Pilazzo went to the foot of the altar steps. He could see the figure's hands now. They were moving fervently over what appeared to be a rosary.

Follow the message that God delivers to you. Heed His word and do your part to bring down the evil that promises man the end of days. . . .

"What are you doing here?" Pilazzo called out, voice cracking. A tingle ran along his spine, causing the hair on his neck to stand.

The figure ignored Pilazzo ... or was wholly ignorant of his presence.

He could see the figure's fingers moving. He stepped to the left, finally escaping the glow of the construction spots.

Now he could see that the figure was a man, and that he was not a worker but a vagrant. Pilazzo sighed in relief. The man's clothes were covered with filth and dark stains.

Pilazzo stepped closer. He could hear fervent but unintelligible whispers coming from the man's mouth, and also noticed a twisted mass of scar tissue where one ear should have been. "What are you doing?"

The homeless man kept to his prayers.

Pilazzo stepped up to the altar ... and heard something oddly familiar in the vagrant's mumbling.

Pilazzo could see the man's hands clearly now. In them was a large rosary, made up of what appeared to be unpolished wood. He was grappling at the marble-sized beads, the cross.

Rosary ... rosary ... rosary ...

As the vagrant increased the energy of his prayer, Pilazzo was able to distinguish a word or two amidst his mumblings.

And it struck him. *How can this be? This man's speaking Latin.*

"Are you okay?" Pilazzo asked.

Turn away! his mind shouted.

Pilazzo came within inches of the praying man ... and that was when he saw the blood, a dark splotch of it on the white drop cloth covering the statue. Pilazzo stepped back, gazing fearfully at the stain. It was *seeping* across the pallid whiteness of the drop cloth, bleeding out from all sides, a circular shape with jagged edges halfway up the height of the statue.

Pilazzo tried to shout, but fear knotted his tongue. He planted a trembling right hand on the praying man's grimy shoulder.

"Are . . . you . . . okay?" he asked again.

The homeless man stopped his prayers. In the damning silence that followed, Pilazzo could hear the wet blood as it continued to saturate the drop cloth, as thin rivulets branched out and trickled down.

Still facing the statue, the vagrant replied, "This is the end of days . . . *priest.*"

CHAPTER TWENTY-ONE

Jyro stood at the door, waiting. He heard nothing, but he could see Timothy's shadow hovering about ten feet away in the hallway.

"What are ya doin', kid?"

"It's too dark . . . I can't see anything."

"Did you go to the end of the hall? Did you look in the church?"

A brief pause. Then, "No."

"You need to go there and see what's happening."

Jyro felt a hand on his shoulder. He turned.

Wrath looked down at him. "In the bedroom . . . I'll look for a flashlight for the boy. It's safe there now."

Jyro nodded. Indeed, it did seem safer without Larry up there. He turned back toward Timothy. "Wait right there, kid. We're gonna find you a flashlight."

Wrath told the men what he was doing, and Wilson offered to go with him. Like a dark shadow, the hippie followed the big man up the stairs. Both of them disappeared around the bend.

The seconds felt like minutes as the small group waited in the center of the room. They all looked up at the ceiling and listened as the pair's footsteps made their way into the bedroom. Jyro could then hear them rummaging through the closet: feet shuffling and the errant clanging of tools. Moments later, their footsteps traveled the length of the upstairs hallway and the carpeted stair coming back down.

They appeared around the turn like angels in the mist, Wrath in the lead holding a flashlight and a hacksaw. Wilson was right behind him with an awl, a screwdriver, and a claw hammer in his hands. Jyro thought, *We were pretty useless before, just waiting for our tickets to heaven to be punched. Now we're warriors. We're being healed. . . .*

"There's a level and a ruler up there too, but that's it." Wrath handed the flashlight to Jyro, who turned it on and returned to the hallway door.

"Here ya go, kid. Keep it aimed at the floor so no one will see you coming."

Timothy reached through the gap and took the flashlight. Jyro could feel a slight charge of electricity as the exchange was made.

"Thanks." Timothy aimed the flashlight's beam toward his feet, then walked off into the shadows. Jyro and Wrath watched as the light wavered across the dark floor.

From behind them came a loud tearing noise, like the sound Velcro makes when it's pulled apart, only bigger. It came again. Jyro spun around and caught Marcus's eye. There was a delayed chorus of groans from the men as they all saw what the thin, raspy-voiced vagrant was up to.

Marcus had a broom in his hand. He was using it to roll Weston's corpse against the wall alongside the crucified man's body. As his body rolled over, Weston's burnt arm—quite stuck to the carpet—tore off at the elbow, making that noise. Black stuff oozed out from it onto the carpet.

Marcus shrugged stupidly. "Just gettin' 'em out of the way."

Jyro shook his head, unsure what to say. He decided it wasn't worth the energy and turned his attention back to the hallway, where he saw only darkness beyond the slight gap.

The flashlight was out.

"Timothy," he whispered. "You still there?"

No answer.

A moment later, someone screamed.

CHAPTER TWENTY-TWO

The praying vagrant twisted around to face Pilazzo.

The priest screamed, looking not just at the vagrant's bloody eyes but at the rest of his face: cheeks, stripped of their skin, wet and glistening beneath the shadows. Nose, a running channel of gore joining bleeding lips.

The vagrant uttered one word. "*Priest . . .*" Then he grabbed the bottom of the bloody drop cloth and yanked it off the statue.

It flew away like a ghost in a haunted house, landing on the altar near the pulpit. Pilazzo shrank back as dust assaulted his face. He coughed, rubbing his eyes.

Again, low and guttural: "*Priest . . .*"

He looked back at the vagrant, who was still staring at him with those bloody eyes . . .

. . . and then Pilazzo saw the exposed statue.

Sickness struck him like a sudden charge. His mind refused to accept what he was seeing—it wasn't logical. And yet here it was, the statue of the Virgin Mary, cradling a porcelain baby Jesus in her arms.

She was *bleeding . . .*

. . . and in his mind, he sees a shadow on a wall, and it is in the shape of this statue, and at the same

place where the blood taints the statue, there is a stain on the wall, just like this horrific desecration. . . .

The blood ran from the statue's groin, down across its base and onto the floor. Pilazzo could see a hole in the floor.

Oh my God . . .

Within the hole existed a . . . a *thing* like nothing he'd ever known before . . . a patch of gnarled flesh that . . . that . . . *oh dear Jesus* . . . looked exactly like the vagrant's knotted ear.

It was moving.

The fleshy thing was fused to the hole's jagged edges: splinters of wood merging with tangled lumps of soft tissue. It pulsated like a slow-moving heart, sickly rhythmic. The canal at its center opened and closed hungrily.

A jet of blood shot out of it, spattering the statue.

Pilazzo attempted another scream but could not so much as wheeze.

Is this, dear God, truly the end of days?

The vagrant started sobbing. Pilazzo noticed the wooden rosary in the man's hands. It was glowing slightly, a reddish illumination spreading over the vagrant's crusty fingers. Tiny flames fluttered across his exposed arms like hummingbirds. His neck swelled like a balloon and erupted with yellow pustules that oozed down his chest in rivulets.

And his ear, that knotted hunk of flesh . . .

While Pilazzo stared in disbelief at the vagrant, the thing in the hole *bulged*. He could see that it was undeniably *alive*, sentient in its own right, expanding to show dark jagged teeth inside its orifice. They were wet with blood, grinding up and down to create the wickedest of sounds.

Pilazzo broke away and backpedaled down the steps away from the altar. With a muffled thump, he fell and landed on his rear. Sawdust rose around him in a cloud. He shot his hands up and made the sign of the cross over the hellish scene before him.

A deep, strident chortle surfaced from the ear creature. Blood erupted from it in intermittent spouts, covering both the statue and the vagrant. It opened wide and from within its depths swelled a bulbous membrane—a great blister bursting with pus—swelling nearly three feet up and out.

Pilazzo could see something writhing beneath the membrane's pinkish surface.

With a slick, wet burst, the membrane popped. Pilazzo flinched, seeing something hideous birthing from it: two reptilian claws covered in greasy scales, swaying and writhing back and forth like entranced cobras. They reached a height of two feet and unfurled three curved talons..

The vagrant fell helplessly forward, face and arms burning as they came in contact with the carpet. Dark puffs of smoke rose around him.

Pilazzo struggled to his feet, watching as the vagrant's heavy, trembling hand extended toward him. In it was the rosary. The vagrant twisted his sightless eyes toward Pilazzo, eye sockets gushing thick, oily fluid. Tiny flames swarmed on his face as he attempted to speak. The words were broken, but intelligible:

"Take it. . . ."

The wooden rosary fell from his grasp onto the steps, a few feet from Pilazzo.

Rosary . . . rosary . . . rosary . . .

In a response that was little more than instinct, Pilazzo dove forward and grabbed the rosary.

He cried out; it was extremely hot in his hands. He nearly dropped it, but managed to hold on despite the searing pain. He crossed himself, then held the beads up and began reciting a Hail Mary. Thin tendrils of smoke rose from the rosary like incense.

The vagrant made a vain attempt to crawl away, hands clawing at the bloody carpet. With a horrible gushing sound, the reptile arms lunged from their fleshy womb and seized his head.

"Kill it!" the vagrant cried, his words nearly unintelligible. He began to shriek with amazing force.

Pilazzo looked on, terrified and aghast.

Hail Mary, full of grace, the Lord is with thee . . .

The claws squeezed the homeless man's head. The vagrant jerked and writhed, arms pistoning frantically. Blood gushed from between the constricting talons. The vagrant's face took on a reddish-purple color from the horrible pressure. He let out a long, shrill wail that was cut off with a terrible bone-crushing sound. His legs swept weakly across the dusty floor in spasms and then fell deadly still.

Blood poured from his eyes and ears. The talons remained hideously still as they continued squeezing, like a vise with unimaginable force. There was a *pop* like a firecracker. Pilazzo flinched and shut his eyes, feeling warm pieces of the vagrant's head pepper him. When he opened his eyes he saw a shocking spray of blood geysering upward from the vagrant's neck stump. The body fell to the altar. The claws still clutched and clasped.

Clutching the rosary tightly, Pilazzo screamed hoarsely and shambled back down the aisle to the closed doors at the rear of the church. His footsteps were wet and tacky, and he imagined a long line of blood trailing behind him.

He grabbed the door handles but didn't have a chance to pull on them before a blue flame came out of nowhere and buried his hands in agony. He howled and fell to his knees, and gazed at the white blisters rising on his skin. The rosary, still wrapped around his fingers, glowed faintly red, appearing undamaged by the otherworldly attack.

"Help me!" he screamed, eyes searching the heavens. "Help me! Is there anybody here?" A tremendous pain shot from his burnt hands to his spine. He could hear his labored breaths inside his head.

And then came a string of bone-crushing sounds from the front of the church.

Wide-eyed, Pilazzo turned and faced the wicked scene. The beast in the floor was devouring the vagrant, claws operating like the pincers on a crab, grabbing the headless body, puncturing the waist as it pulled the torso down to feed itself. The body was gone to the hips, legs in the air. The arms were twisted back, still out of the hole. But as the thing surged, chewing and eating, the vagrant's legs jerked, waving through the air like batons.

Pilazzo tried to look away. He tried to not hear the wet, crunching sounds, to concentrate only on the painful burns on his hands. But a new set of cracking sounds came, like tree branches splintering. The thing had swallowed the body to the knees, claws grabbing thighs, guiding it in. Thick, viscous grunts emerged from somewhere deep inside the thing. The vagrant's legs were at last sucked in like strings of spaghetti.

He was gone.

Pilazzo could hear the man's bones crunching, like hard candy. The thing swelled as it chewed. It turned purple, with dark, winding tendrils expanding beyond its splintered edges. Blood gushed everywhere. Dime-size drops of gore spattered the altar as far as twenty feet away.

Pilazzo whispered a desperate prayer before crawling into the rearmost pew. He sat on the floor, trembling, listening to the beast's croaky breaths.

Over the top of the pew, he looked to the crucified Jesus and shuddered.

Its heavenward eyes were crying tears of sorrow.

CHAPTER TWENTY-THREE

Jyro stood a few feet from the open door, straining to see into the hallway. They'd all heard Larry's screams and were stricken with terror. Jyro tried desperately not to imagine what was happening.

Looking into the dark hallway, he called, "Kid? You all right?"

"Yeah." Timothy's voice emerged from the darkness a notch above a whisper and not too far away. Jyro felt a great wave of relief. "Did you hear that?"

"We all heard it," Jyro answered despondently. The low rumbling growl of the beast still resonated in his ears.

"It's the beast. I think it got Larry."

"You hear anything else?"

"A man. He was screaming, but . . . but not anymore."

"Can you tell if he's still out there?"

"I don't hear him."

This unseen man might very well be the sinless one they were supposed to find.

"Kid . . . listen to me. You have to go out there. You have to draw attention to this guy. If he's the sinless one we're supposed to find, then . . . then he's our only hope." He paused. "But be careful. If he's *not* . . ."

Silence followed.

Then, in a weak but determined voice, the boy answered, "Okay."

CHAPTER TWENTY-FOUR

Endless seconds passed. Many thoughts came and went, but to Pilazzo all that really mattered were his only clear choices: remain in place and pray that everything would return to normal, or confront the thing in a do-or-die attempt to . . . to *what*? Kill it? Exorcise it?

Is this what I'm supposed to do? Exorcise the demon?

Then it hit him suddenly.

Rosary . . . rosary . . . rosary . . .

He squeezed the beads tightly, praying for an answer. *Dear God, please! I implore you!*

Nothing.

After a minute, he stood in the pew. Unable to face the monstrosity on the altar, he turned to the rear doors of the church. For a moment he expected them to open and slam shut again as they had earlier, but they remained unmoving and silent.

He wondered whether the possessed workers were out there right now, waiting for him.

An ancient war has begun anew, a war between Good and Evil. I've been chosen to play a role. I am the sinless one. . . .

With no other choice, he turned back despondently to the altar. Tears formed in his eyes, and he wiped them away with his dirty hands.

He shuddered. *My God . . . how can I face such a monster?*

He looked at the rosary in his hands. . . .

How is this possible?

The burns on his hands were gone. Healed. The pain of his injuries had been so intense, but now it was as if they had never been there. And the rosary was no longer glowing. It looked as unremarkable as the healed skin on his hands.

He told himself: *This rosary is a work of God. He's watching over me now, giving me the strength to carry on with what's expected of me.*

He took a deep breath and slowly walked back up the aisle, clutching the rosary tightly. The unnamable beast continued to writhe and pulse before the statue, and he wondered again how in God's name he might confront such a monster.

Rosary . . . rosary . . . rosary . . .

As he neared the altar, he held up the rosary and said a prayer. He was speaking English, but the words coming from his mouth were Latin: *"Castigo laudible, corpus meum . . ."*

At once he could see tiny lumps rising on the beast's bloody surface. The flesh shrunk into itself. It changed color, from deep purple to black. All of a sudden it no longer resembled a gruesome ear, but rather a rotten plum fallen from a dying tree.

Pilazzo swallowed and felt his legs tremble as he moved closer. The rosary swayed back and forth in his hand.

A tearing sound cut into the silence.

Pilazzo watched as the thing severed itself from the floor. Black oil oozed from it as it slid away from the splintered hole. It jerked flaccidly, like a landed fish, until it plunked down onto the steps. Here it remained utterly motionless amid a fresh puddle of blood, devoid of life. A ghostly hiss emerged from the hole, then tapered down into a sickly wheeze before completely fizzling out.

Pilazzo shuffled forward in the sawdust and blood, terrified. He stared disbelievingly at the lifeless hunk of flesh on the steps . . . then at the dark hole it had come from.

Still holding out the rosary, he uttered another prayer, gazing at the slaughterhouse the altar had become.

In my hands, with my prayer, this rosary is a powerful weapon against evil.

The rosary moved slightly in his hands. Gooseflesh pricked his arms. He held the rosary close.

And at once he felt *something* . . . a trigger inside him that blocked out the scene before him, leaving only the rosary.

Of their own accord, his fingers began working the marble-sized beads that dangled from his eager hands. He was mesmerized, with no option but to analyze the beads—to seek an answer in their intricate structure. Soon, he lost the sense of all time passing. His fingers grew hot as they picked and prodded at the beads. Tunnel vision had set in. He was deaf and blind to everything else, completely focused on the beaded heart of the rosary. He became convinced that the rosary would provide answers to the evil if only he could unravel it.

I see something in them, he thought. *And . . . it . . . is . . . good.*

"Father . . ."

A light shined into his eyes.

Pilazzo pulled out of his reverie, distressed as the rosary returned to something utterly ordinary. The priest looked away from the invading light and once again beheld the butchery on the altar—the same altar he'd performed Mass on for seventeen years.

The light cut away from his face. He turned back and saw a young man behind the flashlight. Only now did Pilazzo realize that the construction spots had gone out.

As surreptitiously as possible, he shoved the rosary into his pocket.

"This is your house," the boy said, his voice echoing hollowly.

Pilazzo took a step forward.

He pointed the light back into Pilazzo's face. "Stay where you are."

Pilazzo, shielding his eyes from the light, nodded.

After a moment, the boy pulled the flashlight's beam away again. He moved into a golden shaft of light, enabling Pilazzo to see him more clearly. He was perhaps six feet tall, but no more than sixteen years of age. He'd seen some abuse recently, right eye nearly swelled shut, a dark purple bruise encircling it like a damaged halo. A fresh wound festered on his cheek, lips cracked and bleeding. His face was coated in dirt. He wore jeans and a filthy yellow shirt that hung slackly on a thin, angular frame.

He looked familiar.

Pilazzo nodded, slowly, tentatively.

"I recognize you," the boy slurred. "Father Pilazzo."

The priest remained silent at first, observing the

boy's injuries with both concern and distrust. "You're hurt," he remarked, keeping his place against the first pew. He looped his fingers through the rosary in his pocket. It felt warm and appeared to have taken away his pain—suddenly he felt stronger, more alert.

It's a miracle.

"I'll live, for now." Pilazzo could see a spot of fresh blood oozing from the boy's earlobe. "You don't remember me, do you?"

Despite the boy seeming slightly familiar, Pilazzo prepared to fight back if he attacked or went for the beads.

My God, am I losing my mind?

"Timothy Stafford. I am . . . *was* a member of the parish. An altar boy under Father D'Auria for Saturday evening Mass. We met once when you filled in for him."

He looks as frightened as I am. But . . . can he be trusted? Timothy's tortured eyes seemed to read his thoughts. "You feel the pain that's here, don't you?" Pilazzo asked.

"I've seen a lot the last three days."

"Three days?"

Timothy glanced down at his grimy hands, then motioned to the altar with the flashlight, his voice a monotone: "I had it in my hands and used it against the beast . . . but . . . but it wasn't meant for me. Then L-Larry took it . . . he was different from the rest of us. We thought he might be the *one*, but we were wrong. Something had him . . ." Timothy paused, as if trying to see the logic of what he just said. "The beast was in him, using his sins to gather strength . . . but there was some goodness inside him too . . . and it was fighting the beast to deliver the rosary." He lifted his heavy gaze back to Pilazzo.

Pilazzo wasn't quite able to make sense of the boy's rambling. Still, his mind latched on to something the boy had said: *There was some goodness inside him fighting the beast to deliver the rosary.*

To me? The sinless one?

"What rosary are you talking about?" Pilazzo asked slowly, fingers secretively massaging the beads in his pocket.

"It's powerful. Without it, the beast can't be defeated. But in the hands of the sinless one . . . then maybe it *can* be brought down." The way Timothy was speaking led Pilazzo to believe the boy didn't fully comprehend what was happening, but . . . he did seem to *believe* what he was saying.

Sinless one . . .

Pilazzo remained silent and held the rosary. *I can feel its goodness. It's protecting me. Healing me . . .*

"That thing I saw on the altar . . . was that the beast?"

Timothy nodded, eyes downcast. "It can take on different forms. I've seen it. Fought it."

Pilazzo's mistrust faded. The rosary told him to trust the boy, and he followed its guidance. "I have no choice but to believe you."

"It's clear to me now that *you* are the sinless one, Father." He looked at the priest with admiration. A thin smile appeared on his filthy face.

Pilazzo shuddered at the words. *Sinless one.*

"Come with me," Timothy said, looking back toward the open door. "We have a lot to tell you."

"Who's with you?"

"Please . . . come with me now."

"And if I don't?"

"It won't let you out."

Pilazzo remembered the fires that shot out of the front doors and burned his hands.

His hands that were now healed.

There was an uncomfortable hesitation between them. The boy's eyebrows arched curiously. "I *saw* Larry hand them to you."

"Hand *what* to me?"

"The rosary."

Pilazzo nodded. The rosary moved about his index finger, providing reassurance, comfort, and strength. "The workers . . . they're outside. Are they planning to enter the church?"

For a moment the boy didn't answer. His battered face paled, eyes wet with tears. Then he spoke in a different voice, deeper, more alert, as though some unseen force was speaking through him. *Like the workers . . . only different.* "Good is battling Evil right now. We can only assume that it's keeping them away while we search for the chalice."

"The chalice?"

"Things outside are not the same anymore, now that you're here. The beast has what he wants. You, Father, are God's chosen one, an adversary to the beast and his minions." He paused, then added, "The end of days has begun, and it is our mission to stop it."

At those words, the bloodstained statue of Mary slid forward through the gore, cutting into the saturated carpet. Pilazzo yelled, "Look out!" and he and the boy dashed out of the way just as the statue toppled over the first step and smashed onto the marble floor. It shattered into a thousand marble shards. A sea of gore exploded from within, flooding the floor in a horrific display.

Pilazzo yelled, "My God, what is going on here?"

His voice back to normal, Timothy said, "I've seen more in the last three days than any man has in his lifetime. Come with me, please, we need to tell you what we know."

Pilazzo studied the boy's injured eyes long enough to realize the boy did indeed know something. Despite the evil thriving in St. Peter's, there still might be a chance for life, for goodness. It existed within the altar boy and within the rosary of the Mother of God he held in his pocket.

And me.

I am the sinless one.

Father Anthony Pilazzo nodded, then followed the boy into the shadows, seeking reassurance from the wooden rosary that wrapped itself gently around his caressing fingers.

CHAPTER TWENTY-FIVE

"The flashlight. I can see it."

Jyro stood beside Wrath, peering into the gap in the door.

"He's got someone with him," Wrath whispered tentatively.

From behind, Dallas chimed in: "Is it the sinless one?"

"I don't know . . ." Jyro was worried. What if this *wasn't* the person they'd been waiting for? What if this was another one of the beast's workers?

He stepped back from the door, pulling Wrath with him. The big man wiped the sweat from his forehead and stared down at Jyro with dazed eyes. "What do you think?" Jyro asked.

Wrath looked at the others. They were grouped together by the stairs, each holding a tool or a piece of wood as a makeshift weapon. "Be very cautious."

Jyro agreed. Despite the possibility of something finally going their way, he agreed that their guard needed to remain up. "Let's assume the worst until we know for certain we're safe."

Wrath nodded.

Jyro reached into his pocket, removed the awl Wrath had given him earlier, and moved to the door.

CHAPTER TWENTY-SIX

The boy led Pilazzo through the door to the left of the altar, into the rectory hallway. They followed the flashlight's beam down the dark, hot passage, footsteps crunching over debris. Pilazzo had traveled this hallway countless times, but he had never felt so lost in his life.

A sudden headache attacked him. He stopped and leaned against the wall, closed his eyes, and wiped the sweat from his forehead. His thoughts turned to the construction foreman and the conversation they'd had before he arrived at the church:

"Father Pilazzo? This is Henry Miller of Pale Horse Construction. I need you to come down here right away and sign off on the list of statuary donors."

"Today?"

"Please, Father, we can't continue with the work until you approve the requests. And . . . I recommend that you hire outside movers for the statues. We can't move them . . ."

We can't move them, he'd said.

Can't . . .

My God.

It all made sense now: just as Pilazzo had become a

chosen representative of God, the foreman had been used as a pawn by the beast. His task was to convince Pilazzo to remove the statues from the church. The Old Testament said that for Evil to gain rule over man, it would need to abolish all that was good. It seemed logical that the presence of the statues and crucifix proved too much 'goodness' in the face of Evil, and that Miller and his workers were unable to proceed with their dark task. They needed them gone. And they needed someone else to get rid of them.

"Father . . . are you okay?"

Pilazzo nodded and gestured for Timothy to walk on. Still, his mind remained on his—the sinless one's—entry into the church. If the beast had appeared upon the altar in an attempt to harm or weaken him, then perhaps the presence of the statues and the crucifix had been what prevented it from succeeding. It certainly hadn't seemed that way at first—the beast had appeared strong when it slaughtered the battered vagrant. But once the rosary had found its way to the sinless one . . . a simple prayer had forced the beast to abandon the altar.

There is hope. . . .

Timothy stood a foot or so from the partially open door. He studied the gap, which seemed just wide enough for him to squeeze through. Not Pilazzo, though.

The boy told the priest, "When I got here three days ago, the construction workers had just started removing the pews. When I came through the church, I thought it was weird that the workers ignored me." He then went on to tell Pilazzo of his days and nights trapped in the dark hallway, unable to escape because of the blue fire.

Awe filled Pilazzo as he listened to Timothy's story. Apparently he *wasn't* the only one trapped in this web of Good vs. Evil, and he wondered how many more there were. "I was burned by the fires as well," he revealed. "But the rosary'. . ." He looked down at his hands. *"It healed me."*

"It healed me too."

The priest shot an uneasy glance at Timothy's swollen face. "But . . . you still have wounds."

Gently, Timothy touched the bruise near his eye. Outside a sudden wind howled, rattling the stained-glass windows. "These came later. . . ."

Feeling the rosary winding about his fingers, Pilazzo removed it from his pocket. Something warned him against displaying it, but the goodness of his heart compelled him to help the boy.

The boy's good eye widened. He turned his head away.

"Let me heal your wounds," Pilazzo said, his headache suddenly gone.

Timothy shook his head vigorously. "No . . . put it away. It's too powerful . . . you should only use it for its *true* purpose. Please . . ."

Pilazzo gazed down at it in awe. The beads shifted slightly in his open palm but remained devoid of the mysterious red light. He placed it back into his pocket, keeping his fingers close to it.

"Thank you, Father."

Pilazzo nodded. "How did you get the injuries?"

"I told you, I've seen a lot here in the last three days."

Timothy looked over his shoulder into the lobby. "We need to get you through."

Pilazzo's fingers deftly sought the comfort and strength the rosary provided. He was eager to hear more about Timothy's experiences, despite the impending threat.

Timothy remained silent, however, focused on the door. He slowly placed his left hand through the gap . . . and nothing happened. He pulled it out.

"You can fit through there," Pilazzo said.

Timothy's face was filled with shadows. "It's how I got out. But . . . I don't want to chance it again. This time . . . I . . . I don't trust it."

Pilazzo understood. Timothy had told how the doors had burned him before and how the others had been hurt too. Yet he said Larry had been left unharmed, probably because he was holding the rosary. Pilazzo too had been spared injury with the rosary in his hand. It stood to reason that Pilazzo—and, he hoped, Timothy—would be all right as long as they sought the rosary's protection going through the door.

Pilazzo pulled the rosary from his pocket.

"Maybe now would be a good time to use it," Timothy said.

Pilazzo knew what needed to be done. He stepped forward, chest heavy and tight with panic. Timothy edged up behind him and wrapped an arm around his waist, face against the priest's back.

He said, "Open the door."

Nervously, Pilazzo held the rosary out before him. The cross swung back and forth like a butterfly in the wind. He inched forward—Timothy keeping right behind him—and pushed the door with his protected hand.

A small flame shot up, but only a fraction of what had burned him at the front doors. Still, Pilazzo could feel the raw heat on his hand, a wicked shock of pain that cruised through his body and sent his brain floating.

The door swung away, and he felt a parade of blisters march up his arm. He screamed as a wave of undamaged skin trailed the blisters from his fingertips to his biceps, healing him. With it came an immediate end of pain.

Timothy released his grip on the priest and stepped in front of him. "Are you hurt?"

Pilazzo shook his head, staring at his arm with gross fascination. "Not really." He looked at Timothy. The boy's one visible eye was dilated. Pilazzo motioned toward the dim room, feeling dizzy, hot, and fevered.

The boy took a deep breath and crossed the threshold.

Pilazzo looked into the dim lobby but saw nothing. "Timothy?" he called. He could feel his heart beating.

He returned the rosary to his pocket and followed the boy into the hall.

CHAPTER TWENTY-SEVEN

With no warning, a wide-eyed vagrant rushed out and seized Pilazzo by the shoulders. The filthy, bearded man shoved him against the wall beside the door and held a pointed awl against his neck. A pinpoint of pain shot through him, cold and icy.

"Is he tne one?" the vagrant asked the boy, breath hot and stinking in Pilazzo's face. *"Is he?"*

Timothy nodded and backed away, his open eye registering confusion. "Jyro . . . what are you doing?"

"What's this about?" Pilazzo cried. Two additional vagrants appeared from the shadowy reception area, one a large black man holding a hacksaw; the other a thin, dreadlocked hippie with a screwdriver in his hand. Both men looked and smelled as if they'd been on the streets for years.

"What's your name?" the lead vagrant demanded. The man, despite his condition, had a sharp, authoritative manner. And given the fresh wounds on his face, had apparently encountered some of the same misfortunes as Timothy.

He grabbed Pilazzo by the collar and shook him hard, the awl jabbing into the priest's neck. "I said what's . . . your . . . name?" He punctuated each word by slamming the priest back against the wall.

"Jyro!" Timothy yelled. "Don't! He's a *priest*, for Christ sakes!"

The man Timothy had called Jyro pulled Pilazzo forward until their noses were almost touching. "Name," he said in a low, gravelly whisper.

"Father Anthony Pilazzo. Please . . . please don't hurt me." For a quick moment he wondered how he could survive a throng of possessed construction workers and an otherworldly beast, only to be taken down by some raving bum with hideous breath.

"Have you sinned in your lifetime, Father?"

"Huh? What? What's this about?" He didn't think he'd get any sort of logical answer.

"Answer me!" Jyro spat, pushing the priest against the wall again.

Timothy shouted, "Jyro! Stop!"

"No," Pilazzo sobbed. "I haven't sinned. I only forgave the sins of others." *And allowed my mother—the bride of Christ!—to die alone because of my faith.*

Jyro examined Pilazzo suspiciously. He leaned close to the priest so that his beard brushed Pilazzo's cheek, then pointed toward two corpses on the floor beneath a bloodstained wall at the opposite end of the room. "You see those men? You see what's left of them? That's what'll happen to you—to us—if there's any sin in your priestly blood. So tell me again, Father, *have you sinned?*"

Pilazzo shook his head vigorously, staring at the dead men.

Jyro grinned, lines cracking his dirty face like asphalt.

An elderly vagrant covered in tattoos asked, "Does he have the rosary?"

Jyro approached Pilazzo, a fresh gleam in his eyes. "If he does, then for sure we have our man." With no warning, Jyro started sifting through the priest's clothing.

Pilazzo didn't think twice—he had to protect the rosary. *God's telling me to.* He shoved Jyro back. The bum backpedaled, arms pinwheeling. The awl dropped to the littered carpet with a quiet *thump.*

"Yes, I'm the sinless one!" Pilazzo shouted, looking back and forth among the small group of men.

Jyro caught his balance and turned toward the priest with perhaps a bit of fear.

Pilazzo swallowed hard. "I am the sinless one," he repeated quietly, his mind adding, *and the son of the bride of Christ.*

"Leave him alone, Jyro. We have our man. Now it's time to let him do his job. He isn't going anywhere."

Jyro glared at Timothy. Pilazzo slumped and blew out a long, nervous sigh. Timothy grabbed the priest by the sleeve and led him away to the reception area.

"Water . . . please . . ." Pilazzo said as he collapsed into a chair, bewildered. His headache returned, sharp and pounding. He felt weak.

Timothy looked at him curiously. "We don't have any."

"Look in the closet." Pilazzo motioned with his chin.

Timothy opened the door. Sitting on a shelf inside, like an oasis in the desert, were three dust-coated cases of water bottles, next to a few bundles of paper towels and a small box of plastic cutlery. The boy tore open the plastic coating on a case of water and handed a bottle to the priest. Then he handed bottles to the other men and gulped from one himself.

Wiping his lips, Timothy said, "Jyro and I have something to show you."

"Jyro," Pilazzo repeated. He looked over at the aggressive drifter.

"That's me, Father. . . ." Jyro walked over to the priest, eyeing him guardedly. "I used to be an altar boy, you know," he said, his demeanor changing from defensive to respectful.

Pilazzo nodded. In his pocket, he could feel the rosary moving slightly.

Jyro pointed to the eldest of the homeless men. "And so was Dallas." He then pointed to the two dead men tucked against the wall. "Weston over there was a minister for more than ten years. Didn't do him much good."

He leaned down close to Pilazzo. "So tell me, Father, sinless one, what do we do next?"

Your church awaits you. . . .

Pilazzo shrugged. He let his empty water bottle fall to the floor. Tears were welling in his eyes. He looked up at Jyro and felt a strange empathy for him, as if they'd known each other for years, or would become very close in time. He glanced around the room and asked, "Who are you people, and what in God's name is happening here?"

Timothy quickly introduced all the men to Pilazzo, then filled him in on everything that had happened.

Wrath stepped forward, bald head glistening with sweat beneath the dim emergency beacon overhead. His shirt was torn, and his pants were burned away to the knees. He spoke with authority, voice deep and focused. "We assume that wherever there's evil, goodness is with us struggling to keep it from winning."

Yes, this is true. . . . Pilazzo thought.

"We can only guess that's what's kept us alive so far,"

Wrath went on. "But time's passing and the beast is getting more powerful. I can feel it. *We* can feel it. This goodness . . . it can't continue to give us strength." He spread his hands in a pleading gesture and said, "We have to find the chalice. It's the only way."

"Or?"

"Or we'll witness firsthand the end of days."

The end of days.

Pilazzo looked around his former home. It had seen quite a battle already. But it still stood strong, providing a shelter from the horrific developments in the outside world. How long would this protection last? The men claimed to have been here for two weeks, sleeping despite the clamor of the construction crews as they'd worked to tear it down. Battling the beast in its many forms. Pilazzo felt a wave of exhaustion wash over him. He wanted to simply stay put and allow events to unfold. Maybe everything would go back to the way it had been.

Monsignor Sanchez's voice broke through his thoughts like a hot needle through warm flesh: *We are being summoned. Follow the message that God delivers to you. Heed His word and do your part to bring down the evil that promises man the end of days. . . .*

Pilazzo could feel the rosary writhing in his pocket, a constant reminder that he had work to do. He said, "Tell me more about this chalice. . . ."

CHAPTER TWENTY-EIGHT

"Jyro! Jyro!" From the hallway leading to the recreation room, the bum with the beard and dreadlocks whom Timothy had introduced as Wilson shambled into the room. He was holding an old transistor radio with an analog dial. "I found it in one of the lockers. It still works. . . ." Holding the radio by its handle, he adjusted the dial until the signal came in clearly. All the men—Pilazzo counted eight, including Timothy—crowded around Wilson and listened to the fairly panicked voice of a male newscaster describing what was happening outside the walls of St. Peter's.

Having witnessed the very beginnings of it all, Pilazzo listened to the sobering report:

"Right now there are multiple incidences of violence in the streets of the city. We have reports, and I know this all sounds difficult to believe . . . but it is reported that an entire construction crew working on an Upper East Side building project has seized a homeless shelter two blocks from their work site."

"That's just a few blocks from here," Pilazzo said. It was the shelter the priests used to call to take in the homeless from St. Peter's on cold winter nights.

Jyro held up a hand, and the men listened in silence as the announcer went on:

"Witnesses are vague, but from what we can gather so far, at least thirty men entered the shelter armed with power drills and nail guns. Reports state that soon after the workers went inside the shelter, screams erupted and—this is as disturbing to report as it is to believe—but the construction workers are purported to have murdered a number of the people inside the shelter. Police are at the scene now, and although not much else is clear, we do know that gunshots have been fired. A news crew has also just arrived, and they've informed us that a man is on the roof of the shelter right now hurling body parts out onto the street. And this is not the only occurrence of violence being reported in the city. According to the reports coming in, there are random acts of extreme violence being committed all over the city by what appear to be city construction crews. I . . . uh . . . excuse me, a breaking story has just come in. Parishoners of St. Michael's Church on Fifty-ninth Street are reporting multiple murders taking place inside the church during this afternoon's Mass. The attackers, numbering in the dozens, have also set the church on fire. Numerous witnesses claim that those committing the crimes are males, and that they are armed with box cutters, screwdrivers, knives, and other hand tools. Others are purported to be committing murders with gas-powered tools. Police have requested that if you are inside, stay inside. Do not leave your home or your workplace, as there is panic in the streets at this time. . . ."

There was a pause, and they could hear the reporter shuffling papers. The men continued looking at the radio, as if it would give them answers. All it gave them was more hell:

"There are now reports of looting at another midtown site where six men working on a water-main break near the United Homeless Organization's main offices have set the building on fire. Witnesses report that the men, armed with blowtorches, entered the building and began attacking the people inside. Numerous deaths are being reported."

"Enough!" Pilazzo reached out and abruptly turned off the radio. "We don't need any more proof! I saw the beginnings of all this before I got here." *And I saw the end in my dream.* "We have to find a way to end this chaos now. Before it's too late!"

Marcus shouted, "Jesus Christ! How the hell are we supposed to do that?"

"The chalice," Jyro said. "We have to find the chalice!"

"Yeah, and where should we look?" Seymour shouted. "Huh? Where?"

Jyro shrugged, then pointed toward the hallway door. "There's a way into the church now. . . ."

"I don't think it's in there," Timothy replied.

Rollo looked to the ceiling and declared, "We will beseech the good Lord for His guidance! He will tell us where to look."

Wrath said, "No . . ." He walked over to Pilazzo and said, "The sinless one will tell us."

All the men turned and looked at Pilazzo.

Pilazzo's mind whirled. He still didn't know what to make of all this horror or this talk of a chalice. And now they were thinking he was some kind of savior, the one to go to for answers. *I need answers myself!* He surveyed the homeless men, God's supposed army. *Are we at war? Are we the army of tattered men I saw in my vision?*

"Timothy . . . Wrath . . ." Jyro said. "I think we should bring the priest to the hole."

Panic ripped through Pilazzo at the mention of being taken to a hole. He bolted from the group and made it to the foot of the stairs, where Marcus and Wilson grabbed him forcefully and held him back.

"Don't go up there, man," Wilson said.

"Father! Please!" Timothy shouted, approaching the priest. "You have to trust us. We've received messages."

As have I, Pilazzo thought, pulling away from the men. *And they're not telling me what to do now. Dear God, tell me what's next. I've arrived at my church. Should I wait for another message? Or . . . should I follow this mangy bunch of derelicts?*

"Where's the rosary?" Jyro asked Pilazzo. "You say you have it. Show it to us."

"Look in his pockets," Seymour said. Wrath, Marcus, Wilson, and Jyro formed a loose circle around the priest. A few feet behind them, Pilazzo saw Rollo looking back at him, tapping the tattered Bible he held against his heart.

Pilazzo shoved his right hand into his pocket and grasped the rosary. It coiled protectively around his fingers like a snake on a tree branch. Jyro grabbed the priest's elbow, and Pilazzo pulled away, shouting, "I have it! I have it!" He broke through the circle of men and entered the rec room hallway.

Ever so slowly, he pulled the rosary from his pocket and displayed it to the men.

The small crowd gasped.

Pilazzo leaned against the lockers, thoughts raging like wildfire. The rosary offered not only strength, but an intimidating power as well. The evidence was unmistakable. He himself had used it to drive the beast from its place on the altar. Timothy had used it to defend himself and Jyro against another of the beast's incarnations. Indeed, it had power—power that controlled men and monsters alike. He could *feel* it.

Still, his mind burned with questions: Where did it come from, and why was it here at St. Peter's? He squeezed the beads tightly, quickly concluding that there would be no time for logical answers; as a priest, he'd learned to acknowledge a world full of achievable miracles, and thus he accepted the rosary as an object with divine intentions.

He looked at the gathering of homeless men. They stared back, their droopy eyes filled with awe. Even Jyro now seemed to accept Pilazzo as the sinless one they'd been waiting for.

A loud explosion outside shook the church walls. Dust rained down on the men. Pilazzo jolted and stood upright, feeling the reassuring power in the beads as it seeped through the skin of his hand, into his blood, his heart.

Jyro screamed at one of the other men, something about "gathering the troops." His tone rattled Pilazzo, and by the looks of it, everyone else too.

Pilazzo shoved the rosary back into his pocket and asked, "What do you need me to do?"

Timothy separated from the small crowd. "Come to the hole."

CHAPTER TWENTY-NINE

Following Timothy, Jyro, and Wrath, Pilazzo walked unsteadily down the hall. He took a series of deep breaths in an attempt to calm himself as he watched their moving shadows against the wall. A mess of splintered wood jutted across his path as they approached the entrance to the rec room.

"I'm gonna warn you, Father," Timothy said. "It ain't pretty."

Pilazzo nodded, fearful of what additional horrors might lay in his path. He stood before the open doors to the rec room, seeing no choice but to allow fate to carry him forward under the watchful guidance of God. He told himself that as long as he kept the rosary with him, he'd remain safe.

He hoped.

"Let's go."

They entered the rec room. Pilazzo placed a supporting hand on Timothy's shoulder. A chill of dismay invaded his body as he took in the scene before him.

Illuminated by a pair of halogen lights over the entrance, the small gymnasium was practically gone. A few months ago the place had been alive with parish members gathering with their children to organize fund-raisers, play Ping-Pong and pool and socialize amongst themselves with prayer and song, coffee and cupcakes. Now a hole in the center of the room swallowed up nearly half the wooden floor space. The edges were jagged and splintered upward, as if something huge had burst out from below. Deep brown irregular stains ringed the floor around the hole like a grisly aura.

Pilazzo slowly stepped to the edge of the pit. At once the hot, pissy stench of the city's subway tunnels filled his nostrils. He looked down into the hole and gasped.

A wasteland of bones: femurs, ribs, and skulls, the remains of what might have been a dozen or more people partially exposed in the dark surface.

Along the exposed walls of the pit twisted pipes and severed cables jutted from hunks of soil and cement. Then his eyes were drawn to what appeared to be a wooden crate at the bottom. He estimated it to be about four feet long and three feet wide, with odd writing burned into its rutted surface.

The crate was open. He peered into its dark depths . . .

. . . *and in his mind he can see the builders of the church dismembering and gutting bodies of innocents in a sacrifice to the beast. His mind screams and the scene fades into another where Pilazzo sees the beast. It rises from the depths of the pit, a dark shapeless form with huge red eyes like exposed organs in a freshly eviscerated gut, glaring at its offerings. Lambs to the slaughter, Pilazzo thinks as the beast thrusts itself upon the quartered and decapitated corpses. The scene blurs into an image of a boy wrapping the rosary and a glossy black chalice in burlap and placing them both into the crate— Good working to keep Evil from emerging unfettered*

*into the world. The boy closes the lid of the crate . . . and
then turns and looks directly at Pilazzo. They lock gazes
through the barrier of time. The boy's lips part and he
whispers one word: "Brother . . ."*

Pilazzo looked up from the hole, trembling. The
rosary was performing a mad dance about his trembling fingers, and he had to ball his fist up good and
tight to keep it from leaping out of his pocket.

Timothy walked up beside him, his one good eye
swollen with tears.

Still looking into the pit, Pilazzo asked, "What is
that?" He twisted around and saw Jyro and the other
half dozen wide-eyed vagrants standing behind him.

"It's something that maybe the Bible never told us
about," Jyro replied, his demeanor now calm and co-
operative. In an unexpected display, the vagrant performed the sign of the cross, then folded his hands
together and looked to the heavens.

Beyond the walls of the rectory, they heard another
explosion. The floor beneath Pilazzo's feet shook. The
men looked around, as if expecting the ceiling to
come crashing down upon them, but it didn't.

A nervous cramp hit Pilazzo's stomach. Making an effort to ignore the disaster taking place in the outside
world, he said, "What happened here?" He scanned the
bones, trying desperately to find some righteousness in
their presence.

Timothy did his best to explain what he'd seen the
night before: how the workers had been disembowel-
ing and dismembering a group of homeless men beneath the floating chalice, how the chalice seemed to
draw their blood, *drinking* it.

I just saw this, Pilazzo thought.

"Are these the bodies?" Pilazzo asked, pointing down to the bones in the hole.

Timothy replied, "No, the beast took them."

Pilazzo recalled the news report of the worker hurling body parts off the roof of a building, and his mind replayed the scene he had witnessed on the altar, of the beast devouring the homeless man. Suddenly he had a startling revelation: If the bones before him were not those of the bodies Timothy described, then what were they? No, these bones had been here for years, since the church was erected. *These are the bones of those I just saw sacrificed.*

And it was at this moment he realized with unequivocal certainty that the horror he was dealing with was far beyond anything merely supernatural; it was something all-knowing and all-powerful, an immortal presence that could never be fully brought down.

It could only be contained. That was their only option.

Timothy went on, pulling Pilazzo away from his fearful reverie. "There were growls coming from the hole. Father . . ." He began to sob, then blurted, "There was blood everywhere! The chalice . . . it was expanding, getting bigger and redder. I-I couldn't take my eyes off it. I remember wanting to touch it. I couldn't control the urge to just leap out over the hole and grab it!"

He cried, tried to wipe his eye but only smeared dirt around on his face. "I stepped forward and was at the very edge of the hole when I heard a whisper inside my head. Over and over it called: *rosary, rosary, rosary,* and it distracted me enough to make me realize where I was, what I was going to do. I panicked, seeing how close I was to the workers, who were ignoring me as if

I wasn't there at all. I ran out of the room and back down the hall. I was going to leave though the church, but I remembered that there were workers out there, and if they were anything like the ones I'd just seen, then I couldn't take a chance having them see me. So I decided to go upstairs, and that's when I saw Jyro holding the rosary."

Rosary . . . rosary . . . rosary . . .

"The second I laid my eyes on it, nothing else seemed to matter. The workers, the chalice, the bodies, they were all like a dream to me. The word . . . it kept whispering around in my head, over and over, *rosary, rosary, rosary*. It somehow gave me the strength to explore the rooms. I'd found the homeless men sleeping in the bedroom, and for some reason, I knew their being in the rectory was somehow *right*." He halted here as if gathering his memories, then said, "Eventually I got my hands on the rosary, and it ended up saving my life—and Jyro's life—from the beast."

Pilazzo nodded and looked over Timothy's shoulder toward Jyro. The vagrant's scraggly beard was littered with filth, face scarred and pimpled, eyes sagging from the weight of their experiences. He looked like a living dead man.

And Pilazzo thought, *This is your doing, isn't it?*

Jyro looked the priest in the eyes, and as if reading his mind, confessed, "Forgive me, Father, for I have sinned."

CHAPTER THIRTY

Pilazzo led the group back into the hallway, the rosary giving him a sense of authority.

"I opened the crate," Jyro said, leaning against the wall. His voice was clear and articulate, despite the pained look on his face. "At first I thought the workers were just tearing down the church. But then I realized they were also in the rec room, jackhammering the floor."

"Did you see them?" Pilazzo asked, wondering if they were possessed like those he'd confronted in the streets and subway.

Jyro shook his head. "No."

"Then how did you know where they were and what they were doing?"

Jyro grinned thinly. "Father . . . when you're living out in the street, you learn very quickly how to survive. It heightens your senses, makes you hear things and see things the average man might miss."

Pilazzo nodded. "What made you come *here?*"

"I knew the church was going to be shut down. For months it had been posted on the bulletin board outside. After it closed, I'd kept my eye on the place, on the comings and goings of the workers. About a month ago, I snuck in through an air duct and hid upstairs in one of the rectory bedrooms—imagine my surprise when I discovered there were still beds here. Of course, no good secret lasts forever. Word got around, and soon enough there were more than a dozen of us living here."

He rubbed his eyes. "Of course we immediately thought it was strange that the workers never came up. They were making a helluva racket below, a week's worth that eventually got the best of some of the men. One night, after the crews left, I came down here to check it all out. And that's when I found the hole."

Pilazzo struggled to find a response but failed. The real world had been extinguished permanently.

Jyro continued, "I went to the edge. It was dark, and I lost my footing. I fell in. I wasn't hurt badly, but something real hard hit against my hip and it's still hurting me something fierce. I had a flashlight and dropped it, but it was pointed toward the edge of the crate sticking out of the ground. In a few minutes, after digging around it with my fingers and hands, I uncovered the crate."

Pilazzo, feeling the rosary beads slowing down against his fingers, said, "And you opened it."

Jyro nodded grimly. "And released all Hell on earth." He looked around the room. Pale, frightened faces stared back at him. "But . . . I didn't mean to . . . and if it hadn't been me, then the workers would have done it— I'm sure of it. The evil in the crate was calling them . . . just like something good had been calling me."

Something is calling me, and I must follow. . . .

He paused, then added more quietly, "Something *good* has us under its control." He motioned toward the others in the room. "It has a purpose for all of us. I believe mine was to retrieve the rosary from the crate and find its rightful carrier. Father, it's no coincidence that all of us at one point in our lives have been altar boys or ministers."

Pilazzo asked in a low, hoarse voice, "What happened when you opened the crate?"

"It took me a while. I dug around it until it eventually came free from the dirt. When I opened it, I found two crumbling burlap cloths. I unwrapped the first one and found the rosary. I put it in my pocket and reached for the second cloth. Inside was the chalice."

Pilazzo noticed the reactions of the homeless men listening to Jyro's account. Apparently this was the first time they'd heard all this too.

"The chalice was hot. I let go of it, but it didn't fall to the floor. It floated up to a spot just above the center of the hole, and stayed there. I was stunned. There was no way I could get to it."

"What about the rosary?" Pilazzo asked. As soon as he mentioned it, it became warm against his clenching hand.

"It started moving around in my pocket . . . I could feel it. I climbed out of the hole. The chalice . . . it started spinning and a bright light came out of it and filled the room. I felt dizzy and heard what sounded like a raging fire. I remember the sound filling my ears with a pressure that hurt like hell. A hot wind sprung up that stunk of something awful, and all I could do was stagger out into the hallway, afraid for my life. Eventually I found my way back upstairs with the rosary. The next thing I remember is waking up in the hallway, the rosary clutched in my hands. I went into the bathroom to examine it, and when I came out, Timothy was there."

Pilazzo glanced back at the unmoving crowd. All eyes were upon him. He grinned uncomfortably.

Michael Laimo

Suddenly he felt the need to examine the rosary alone. It called to him, just as it had earlier in the church. A strange feeling of excitement filled him. Could victory really be found in the beads?

"How much time do you think we have?" he asked Jyro.

The vagrant shrugged, stepped closer to the priest and said quietly, "Father . . . the workers are getting stronger; the beast has them in his command. You heard the radio reports. It's using them to spread chaos throughout the city. Who knows what they're truly capable of?"

Another explosion outside rocked the building. The exposed lamps in the ceiling swayed in the blast's wake. Wrath and Dallas leaned against the wall to avoid falling, chests heaving.

"What's going to happen to *us*?" Wilson shouted. "I don't want to fuckin' die, man."

"We'll wait for the priest's command," Timothy answered.

A series of grunts and protests emerged from the frail group.

Timothy spread his arms out. "If anyone has another suggestion, I'm all ears."

Pilazzo gripped the rosary, feeling another surge of power, of strength. *Of command . . .*

Timothy said to him, "You're the sinless one, and we're here to support and defend you. God called upon you to lead His army against Evil. Come on . . . we have to prepare for battle."

CHAPTER THIRTY-ONE

They went upstairs to the bedroom, where they milled about in a loose group; Rollo and Marcus at the door, Dallas and Seymour near the wall. Wilson and Wrath stood out in the hallway, respectively armed with a hacksaw and a screwdriver. Jyro and Timothy led Pilazzo to one of the beds and told him to sit and rest. "Spend some time in prayer," Timothy said. "Try to find out what we should do next."

"Tell us where to find the chalice," Jyro said.

Pilazzo shuddered as he sat down on what used to be his own bed. He placed a hand on the soiled mattress in dismay. At one time the room had smelled of soap; now it reeked of body odor, urine, spoiled food.

He performed the sign of the cross and searched the room for an unblemished feature of his past. The only thing he recognized was the silver crucifix that hung crookedly on the wall like a wounded soldier.

Jyro said, "Pray, Father. You have to be clean of mind and soul in order to confront the beast."

Pilazzo stared up at the vagrant, stricken with panic. "Confront the beast?"

"Yeah."

"How do you know that's what I'm—?"

"The rosary," he said. "The rosary."

Pilazzo felt the warmth of the talisman in his pocket and knew. Both Jyro and Timothy had had it in their possession at one point, and they'd been given a piece of the answer to the dilemma at hand. With it he saw things and felt things too powerful to be ignored. *Will it give me the wisdom to defeat this beast?*

Timothy said, "The rosary contains the power of God. You only have to seek one answer in it: the way to stop the beast again. I know this because . . . because God told me."

Pilazzo gazed at Timothy with awe. "You spoke with God?" The once senseless question seemed all too valid now.

Fixing the priest's gaze, Timothy replied, "God delivered to me a message, and I've followed it."

Pilazzo's trembling hands folded insecurely in his lap. "If I hadn't seen His message with my very own eyes . . ."

Timothy nodded fervently. "Evil's running rampant outside . . . God knows what atrocities the beast has in store for mankind. Father . . . it's your game now. Find an answer in the rosary. When you're prepared to confront the beast, call us, and we'll support you."

Pilazzo understood despite the flood of denial consuming him. *How can I prepare for this?*

Again Monsignor Sanchez's voice answered: *Follow the message that God delivers to you. Heed His word and do your part to bring down the evil that promises man the end of days. . . .*

Jyro limped from the room; Timothy and the others followed in silence.

"Where are you going?" Pilazzo asked anxiously.

Timothy said, "We will be right here in the hallway, waiting for you."

They shut the door behind them, leaving Father Anthony Pilazzo alone, sitting on the edge of his moldy bed.

CHAPTER THIRTY-TWO

Pilazzo stood and stretched. His bones popped loudly, and his muscles ached painfully. He reached into his pocket, carefully removed the rosary, then held it in front of his face and studied it curiously. It *was* spectacular, much larger than your average dime-store beads, hand carved of wood that should have deteriorated years ago. There were five charms dangling from it, small wooden stars and a single meticulously carved cross. He toyed with it slightly, just as he had at the altar when he first examined it.

Immediately he felt its magnetism, its significance. Its purpose, Pilazzo suddenly knew, would be revealed now that it was in his hands, the hands of the sinless one.

He let the rosary slip through his fingers. The beads danced of their own accord, as though seeking a comfortable position. It grew warm, glowing faintly crimson. His hands became translucent, their inner workings visible to his disbelieving eyes. He could see the flow of blood rushing through his veins; the flexing muscles and tendons as his fingers massaged the beads. His vision blurred . . . but his instincts heightened to new levels. The beads slithered quickly in his grasp now.

Pilazzo felt encouraged by this immediate progress, and he worked harder against the smooth grain of wood, feelings of imminent triumph lifting his eager soul.

He began to recognize the rosary as something sentient, and in doing so he was able to acknowledge and obey its direct command to sit back down on the bed. Tiny sparks of electricity danced along the surface of the glowing beads, growing more distinct, more colorful. Pinpoint lights emerged from the grain of the wood onto his fingers like drops of rain, guiding them with determined precision. The redness enveloped his translucent hands, all the way to his wrists, where he could see the tiny bones there executing their precise movements.

He could hear the pounding rush of blood in his body as it escaped his heart and bulleted into his brain. *Yes*, he sensed. *I am the sinless one, and I am mastering God's all-powerful weapon. He has chosen me to lead His army. I shall carry the world away from Judgment Day.* He gazed hard at the rosary. It pressed and pulled at his willing fingers, the charms caressing his skin. The red light spread to his elbows, his hands now completely consumed by the glow. He peered deeply into it . . . and saw something that wasn't his hands.

Fires . . . I see fires rising.

His heart beat an anxious rhythm in his chest. He prayed aloud but could not hear himself, the pounding now making its way into his head, deafening him. A sudden wind sprang from his clasped hands and whipped harshly against his ears. The air felt dense, thick, like stifling smoke.

In the surge of agony consuming him, the ruined landscape reappears around him, and his mother stands before the open entrance to the Church of St. Peter. She is naked and charred amid the flames rising about her, her skin sloughing off in blistering slabs, her blood pooling out onto the ashes, winding about the charcoal ground, flowing toward him, twisting up his legs like tentacles and settling into pools in his open palms.

He watches his mother as she pleads with him, her eyes melting from their sockets over her skinless face. "Antonio, He needs you. Do as He says. . . ."

From out of the ashes, a rabid Doberman appears, muzzle spraying thick white foam as it barks furiously. Behind the dog, the Manhattan skyline looms in the distance, buried in red flames and billows of black smoke.

And the dog keeps barking, growing stronger, fiercer, and more confident. . . .

Vicious pain rips through his hands and feet, as though heavy iron spikes are being driven through them. His mother's body is no more than a pile of ash and bones on the ground.

In agony, he raises his face to the blackened skies and screams toward the fires rising high over the ruined buildings of New York City. . . .

The door slammed open, the wood splintering on impact.

Everything disappeared: the landscape, the wind, the pain. His sight was still blurred, but the real world returned slowly and clumsily. Jyro and Timothy appeared in the doorway, Wrath immediately behind them.

"Father? Are you okay?"

Heart racing, Pilazzo looked down at his hands and saw blood pooled in the center of each palm, dripping through his fingers onto the floor, the rosary squirming eerily in his bloody grasp like a worm in a rain puddle.

"He's coming," he said, his mind nearly paralyzed from the vision he'd just glimpsed. "And he's bringing his army."

CHAPTER THIRTY-THREE

Pilazzo gripped the rosary tightly. The others in the room cowered at the mere sight of it—now drenched in the priest's blood. Timothy kneeled before the priest, hands clasped in prayer. "What can you tell us? How do we prepare ourselves?" The boy's good eye flicked back and forth between the bloody rosary and the priest's face.

Pilazzo took a deep breath. "I'm not certain there *is* a way to prepare for the horrors I just saw."

"What did you see?" Timothy looked over at Jyro as if the two had discussed this coming to pass.

"Fires . . . tremendous flames rising high above the city."

"You saw the future," Wrath said, holding the transistor radio in a swollen, scabby hand. "A future you have to stop."

"Father," Timothy said, "we knew we had to find you—the sinless one. It's just as important that we find the chalice."

Pilazzo shook his head, a cold bullet of pain shooting into his brain. "I don't know where it is. All I know is that the beast is coming." He gazed suspiciously around the room, images of the dog from his nightmare haunting him. It had grown stronger since his first vision, more vicious, more powerful. He ran a hand through his sweaty hair. "I need some water, please."

In seconds Seymour appeared with a bottle, which he handed to the priest.

"What happened, Father?" Timothy asked. "Did you sleep?"

"Sleep? No. But I dreamed. And I saw."

There was a pause of uncomfortable silence. Then Jyro said, "It's getting dark outside. The city is in bedlam."

Pilazzo glared at the vagrant. "Dark? Is it night?"

Jyro's eyes narrowed. "It's getting close. . . ."

"How long was I in here?"

"About two hours. We stood outside the door the whole time, listening to you praying. We left you alone until you started screaming."

"Screaming?"

"Yes."

Pilazzo looked at the rosary, still in his bloody grasp. The images from his dream lingered.

Fires . . . huge flames rising over the city.

"God's power is in you," Timothy said. "He works in mysterious ways."

Pilazzo nodded. *And he works quietly and suddenly too.* He took a deep breath, listening to his heart and the rush of blood pumping through his veins. "I do feel . . . something in me. But I can't explain it."

He remembered that he'd seen some buildings on fire as he was returning to St. Peter's. Everything around them seemed to warn of chaos. "How bad are the fires?"

"Let him hear, Wrath," Jyro said.

The large black man flipped the switch on the radio.

The announcer from earlier, who once sounded merely concerned, now spoke over constant static in a frightened tone, pausing ominously between sentences:

"Authorities are insisting that you stay in your homes. Make certain that all doors and windows are locked. It is also recommended that you arm yourself. As reported earlier, rampant violence has made its way almost as far north as the Bronx. At this time, there seems to not be any violence reported outside the borough of Manhattan. . . . Again, it appears that most of the violence is being committed by employees of the city's construction crews. Those individuals appear to have no goal other than to destroy anyone they see as a threat to them, namely the city's homeless and the clergy. The city has brought in its entire police force, resulting in gunfire and bloodshed. Hundreds are dead, some officers and many more civilians. The president has declared a state of emergency, calling upon the National Guard to intervene. Troops have been dispatched to the city and are now poised at the entrances and exits of all the city's tunnels and bridges, while shelters have been set up to care for the wounded. The attackers, seemingly numbering in the thousands, are purportedly fighting back by starting random fires throughout the metropolitan area. Recent reports claim at least twenty fires burning out of control at this time in the city. Hundreds of additional firefighters have been brought in from seven counties, but so far they are unable to keep the fires under control. This sudden wave of violence is being watched by the world, and although other cities are showing scattered reports of copycat activity, nowhere is there evidence of a similar situation. As the fires in the city rage out of control . . ."

"I've heard enough," Pilazzo said despondently.

Jyro said, "Turn it off," and Wrath complied.

The priest motioned toward the radio in Wrath's hands and said, "I've seen the results of this. The city *will* burn to the ground. Millions will die."

Pilazzo stood, the rosary gripped tightly in his bloody hands.

As if in response, an explosion rocked the building. Everyone in the room yelled. Rollo shouted a prayer. Wrath and Seymour raced away to investigate. Jyro and Timothy looked hard at the priest, seeking a desperate answer.

Pilazzo said simply, "It's time."

CHAPTER THIRTY-FOUR

Pilazzo went downstairs to the lobby of the rectory, flanked by Jyro and Wrath, with Timothy leading the short procession. The other men remained in the lobby, struggling to make sense of what had just occurred. Dallas appeared out of a cloud of dust from the hall leading to the rec room. His shirt was gone, and Pilazzo could see a landscape of tattoos on his scrawny chest and stomach.

"Something happened at the hole!" he cried, baring a row of brown teeth. "I didn't go in the room, but there's a lot of smoke coming out."

"Anyone hurt?" Pilazzo asked.

Timothy looked around the room, counting the men. "Marcus is missing. Where is he?"

Dallas said, "He was with me. I told him not to go in there, but he went anyway, and then . . . and then something in the hole exploded. I shouted for him, but the smoke got too thick, and I had to get out."

"Is there anyone else in there?" Pilazzo asked.

Dallas shook his head. "I don't think so."

Pilazzo walked to the door. "I'm going in," he announced. Timothy joined him, but Pilazzo quickly put a hand up.

The rosary dangled from it.

Timothy stopped dead in his tracks and stared at the priest's bloody hand . . . and the swaying rosary.

"I'm protected. Let me go," Pilazzo said.

There was no further debate, save for one weak protest from Timothy, which Pilazzo ignored. He went down the hallway, the thirty-second walk feeling much longer as he worked his way through the settling dust. He squinted against the invading grit, the reassuring rosary in his hands.

About halfway down the hall he beheld an odd red glow emerging from the rec room. He quickened his pace and upon reaching the open doorway witnessed a bizarre spectacle.

The chalice—*Evil's* chalice—was there, floating above the hole just as Timothy and Jyro had described it. It was spinning. Blood oozed over the rim. A spectacular array of dark red beams emanated from it, bounding and flickering about the room like lasers on a concert stage. Pilazzo stepped into the room, entranced by the horrifying sight, the rosary in his pocket suddenly writhing. He stopped and gripped the beads, seeking direction.

Behind him, concerned voices called out: *Father! Be careful!* They sounded like distant whispers in a crowded room, barely making their way to him. He felt mesmerized, hovering somewhere between wakefulness and sleep, dreams of *happiness* suddenly tempting him. Despite these strange feelings of impending bliss, he sensed the approach of something else . . . something dark emerging from the hole. A gush of pungent subway air invaded his nose. The distant moans of pained voices filtered into his ears.

He chose to ignore the warning signs. *Somewhere in*

here is pure happiness. Heaven and peace on earth. He stepped forward, arms outstretched.

From behind: *Father! Come back!*

Ahead in the storm of light and dust he could hear the scuffle of eager feet against grainy cement, of tools punching into hard soil.

In his mind the swift promise of comfort came to him, and he saw himself as a young boy again, smelling the sweet aromas of his mother's cooking as he settled down to do homework in his kitchen.

No . . . she's gone. Dead and gone.

The rosary shifted in his hands, and although his chest was not in contact with it, he could feel the pressure of its message in his heart. He shook away the reverie. Suddenly he was no longer feeling comfort. Fear gripped him as he saw the construction workers climbing from the hole, emerging from the red light and smoke like apparitions. Their faces were coated with grime and blood, crazed eyes upturned, teeth clenched.

The chalice was spinning faster now, the blood beginning to spill on the men as they used grappling hooks to pull themselves up onto the wooden floor.

Pilazzo squeezed the rosary. Fear engrossed him, and he tried painfully to pull away from the threat only a few yards away. He looked down at his feet, buried beneath a pile of twisted rubble.

As the smoke cleared, he could see the tail end of a subway car sticking out of the bottom of the hole, construction workers covered in blood and dust and tattered clothing, crawling out from the door at the end, onto the splintered floor of the rec room.

Pilazzo's lungs heaved, taking in dirt and dust with every painful gasp. A moment passed in which no additional workers emerged from the pit. Then, with the subway car jostling slightly, two very large men climbed out.

They were carrying the crate between them.

With a crooked lunge they heaved it up to three other workers kneeling by the edge of the hole. It hit the floor with a weighty thud, attracting the other workers like jackals to a carcass.

The men lumbered from the hole on all fours, some of them using hooks to gain purchase on the hard soil, others simply using their bloody hands. The filthy men were all over the hole's edge, and Pilazzo imagined more of them down there, making their way up.

Pilazzo instinctively held out the rosary before him and cried, "Be gone, foul spirit, and take thy demons with you! Return to the depths of Hell! God of heaven, God of earth, God of all creation, I implore You. The power of the Lord, Jesus Christ commands you! Lord, hear my prayer!"

The room went silent. The workers stopped moving, eyes wide and white, peering up at him. The priest held the rosary forward challenging the minions of the beast.

Suddenly, a deafening roar tore through the silence. It struck Pilazzo's ears like daggers. And with that, his lucidity seeped back to him. He saw his arm extended, the rosary dangling listlessly from his trembling fingers, the smoky air parting to reveal the true terror of the scene before him.

He shoved the rosary into his pocket . . . and at the same moment the minions echoed the evil roar with high-pitched screeches of their own. Eyes rolling, they began staggering again toward the priest. Two of the men dragged a dead body with them.

Marcus.

Oh God, no . . .

Without warning, strong hands grasped his ankles. Pilazzo startled and screamed. Thin arms dragged him away from the unholy threat that was seconds away from him.

He tripped backward and landed on his rear. He flailed only slightly, focusing on protecting the rosary writhing in his pocket.

The hellish screams filling the room were deafening. The workers came at him with arms outstretched and red mouths gaping, their tattered jeans and construction vests spattered in blood.

He felt himself moving backward, not of his own doing, but pulled by the homeless men trying to protect him. He was dragged out of the rec room, and the doors were slammed closed.

He gazed up at the doors, terror ripping through his body. He shoved a hand into his pocket and yanked out the rosary; it dangled in his hand, the tiny cross and two of its stars glowing red. He prayed for assistance. The charm grew warm, then hot. He heard a loud popping sound and could see the golden glimmer of the deadbolt's bar locking the minions inside the rec room.

From behind the doors a wicked chorus of howls ensued. Heavy pounding exploded against the polished wood, raining dust down from the ceiling. *They'll break through in a second,* Pilazzo thought. He shoved the rosary back into his pocket and yanked his hand away from the burning beads. He smelled the stench of cooking flesh. His strength seeped out of him like water in a sieve. In the gloom he saw Timothy staring at him.

God's power is in you, Timothy had said. *He works in mysterious ways.*

Heart pounding, Pilazzo closed his eyes and listened to the incessant banging of the workers against the twin doors of the rec room.

Indeed, He does . . .

CHAPTER THIRTY-FIVE

Like a drill sergeant, Jyro shouted for everyone to arm themselves. Pilazzo struggled to his feet, watching the six vagrants taking up arms with their meager arsenal of screwdrivers, hammers, and awls. Wrath, Seymour, and Dallas stood by the twin doors, while Jyro, Rollo, and Wilson moved alongside the priest.

Brothers in arms.

"Come on, Father," Timothy shouted, pulling him by the arm. With a flashlight in his left hand, the boy led Pilazzo to the lobby, where they paused to gather their wits.

Pilazzo looked at Timothy. The boy's face seemed even more battered and bruised, pale white in the beam of the flashlight.

"You're badly hurt."

"The world outside is badly hurt—*that's* what you have to protect." There was something eerily detached about his voice.

Pilazzo nodded slightly with a sickly resignation, squeezing his eyes shut like a child struggling to block out a particularly scary scene in a movie. "Dear God . . . how can I defeat such a thing?"

"The beast . . . it must have a weakness," Timothy replied.

"Perhaps, yes." The rosary moved in Pilazzo's pocket as if confirming Timothy's observation. "An Achilles' heel . . ."

The boy stood unmoving. Unanswering. His eyes seemed to stare *through* the priest.

"But how do we find out what it is?"

"Ask God," Timothy replied. "He'll tell you."

In that instant, shadows shifted, as did the rosary in his pocket . . . and the men closest to them began to scream. Pilazzo saw Jyro leap sideways and grab Timothy. Then Jyro tried to latch on to the priest . . . but with no success.

Something else had him: the same cold, dead grasp that now seized Rollo and Wilson and had them screaming for their lives. Wilson's mangy dreadlocks flew up like flags, and then he went down, the unforgiving grasp of Weston's lone dead-fish hand burrowing deep into his neck.

As Pilazzo came to the horrible realization that the larger of the two dead men lying against the wall had somehow come back to life, something else lunged out of the gloom, the once-crucified albino, also back from the dead.

Pilazzo screamed and grabbed at the first thing he saw: the flexing wrist of the albino. The pale, dead man latched his raw-boned fingers on to the priest's cassock and wrenched it violently. In the jerking beam of Timothy's flashlight, Pilazzo could see Weston's hulking body falling down on top of Wilson, his remaining hand (the severed one, burnt to a charcoal crisp, was still stuck to the floor) tearing into Wilson's throat.

Blood spurted from the gaping wound. A terrible wheeze emerged.

The albino met Pilazzo face-on, eyes reddish-purple but oozing yellow. His hold on Pilazzo was weak, and the priest was able to break away with a single powerful jerk. Having lost his first pick, the albino settled for second best and honed in on Rollo, who was flailing his fat arms and shouting verses from the Old Testament.

"Get back!" Jyro yelled, a hand on Timothy's biceps. Pilazzo backpedaled into Jyro's waiting grasp, the rosary painfully hot in his pocket. They pressed themselves against the wall. Dallas, Seymour, and Wrath, amid the earsplitting assault of hammers on the rec room doors—leaped into the fray with their tools raised high.

Wrath was the first to strike. Apparently realizing he couldn't save Wilson (the bottom half of his dreadlocks and beard were saturated with blood), he calmly raised his hammer and buried the claw deep into the back of the albino's skull, producing a sharp crack like a bat on a baseball.

The albino released Rollo, bellowed a great scream, then fell sideways to the floor into a twisted, motionless knot.

The Weston-ghoul, having finished with Wilson, lurched up and made a move for the now unarmed Wrath. The big man, dripping with sweat, screamed something unintelligible and threw up his arms to defend himself. The Weston-ghoul made a play for Wrath's throat. They tussled harshly and crashed into the bloodstained wall where the albino had been crucified. Wrath leaned a beefy shoulder against the ghoul and heaved it back. Weston tripped over his own legs and tumbled into the puddle of thick blood oozing from the albino's punctured skull.

This gave the vagrants a window of opportunity. Both Dallas and Seymour, armed respectively with an awl and chisel, bounded forward and impaled the Weston-ghoul. Seymour punched the chisel through its sternum, and Dallas drove the awl into its forehead. There was a striking one-two-*pop*, and then black blood burst from the wounds. The ghoul let out a terrible roar so loud and deep it could be felt more than heard. It thrashed about frantically in a convulsing dance of death, filmy eyes finding the priest in its final seconds.

Pilazzo remained against the wall, held there by Jyro. He quivered with terror and the truth of the situation: with Wilson now dead, there were only four vagrants left, plus Timothy. And himself.

Wrath leaned against the wall, huge chest heaving. His shirt was glued to his muscles, drenched with sweat. Seymour stood panting, glasses gone and crushed on the floor, while Dallas—who may have just committed his very first murder—paced in a circle, the spattered blood on his face glistening wetly.

Rollo, trembling madly, located his tattered Bible and whispered a quiet prayer. It was then that Pilazzo realized the workers had stopped slamming into the rec room doors.

Pilazzo pulled away from Jyro and peered down the dark hallway.

"What happened to them?" Dallas whispered hoarsely.

From behind came a low, metallic screech. The men startled and spun, tools drawn.

The door to the hallway leading into the church was now wide open.

Tentatively and quietly, Pilazzo crept toward it. He could see the dim outline of the exit at the other end of the hall, but that was all.

The church beyond lay in darkness.

He whispered, "I don't see any—"

An explosion ripped through the rectory. The twin doors of the rec room burst into the hallway, adding to the piles of debris already there. Screams erupted, from both the homeless men and the marauding workers who'd apparently set off the explosion. Smoke filled the hallway and rectory.

"How . . ." Pilazzo cried. He saw the quick flash of an orange vest spattered with wet blood. Gray shadows moved in the white smoke. Horrible thumping noises spilled out. Slashing noises. Tearing noises.

In one terrifying moment, the smoke parted, and Jyro appeared, his face strangely calm. He stretched his arm toward Pilazzo and Timothy, fist opening slightly to reveal something . . . but then a dark shadow in all the gray smoke moved behind him. Jyro grimaced and closed his fist tightly as a pair of bloody hands grabbed him by the shoulders and jerked him back into the billowing smoke.

Pilazzo remained frozen. *He had something to show me. Something . . . good.*

"God's showing you the way!" Timothy shouted, jerking on Pilazzo's arm. The boy pointed the flashlight toward the dark church. "Let's go!"

CHAPTER THIRTY-SIX

They entered the church, the priest pitching forward as though guided by some unseen force. With no warning, the hallway door slammed shut, closing them in darkness. Timothy aimed the flashlight back toward the door, fixing the beam on the doorknob. Behind the door, shrieks of murder and death ensued.

Pilazzo grabbed the boy's trembling wrist and motioned toward the pitch-black church.

Slowly they turned to face the sea of darkness. The air was frigid; frozen plumes fled their lungs. Pilazzo shivered, from both cold and fear.

He took a step and the smell hit him: wet, organic, reeking of blood, feces, and burnt flesh. Pilazzo continued forward, slowly, feeling Larry's fluid remains beneath his feet.

Here in the darkness of the Church of St. Peter, death lived.

As the screams and wails and horrid thumps of weapons meeting flesh rang from the rectory, he realized that the stench was too horrible to have been caused by only one dead body.

No, there had been a multitude. But where?

"It's so dark," Pilazzo whispered. "I can't see anything."

The rosary began to twitch in his pocket.

Timothy pointed the flashlight toward the altar. There was blood everywhere, on the carpet, drop cloths, and the great statue of Jesus. A desecration. *In my home . . .*

Timothy pulled the flashlight away from the altar and shined it across the dark church.

"Oh . . . my . . . God . . ."

Pilazzo jerked around, half expecting to see a worker hiding in the rafters like he had at Holy Innocents.

What he saw instead was far, far worse.

Bodies. Perhaps two dozen of them, slaughtered like pigs. Homeless men, religious men, all sitting upright in the remaining pews, heads bowed on gashed necks. One by one, the flashlight spotlighted their lifeless faces, frozen in terror.

Pilazzo fought back his gorge and tried to find an answer to this travesty.

None came. The rosary remained cool and motionless.

To the left were more bodies, eight or nine of them charred black, the whites of their teeth shimmering in the flashlight's beam. Farther along the gruesome procession sat two additional bodies, wholly flayed of skin.

"Take it away," Pilazzo ordered Timothy, and when the boy didn't comply he shouted louder, "I said take it away!" Trembling, Timothy pointed the beam to the floor, away from the butchery.

Pilazzo could only muster enough willpower to beseech the rosary, to seek its guidance. But it remained cold. Unresponsive.

"What happened here?" he asked God.

Timothy, beside him, answered, "The end of days."

Their senses turned again to the burgeoning threat inside the rectory. The shouts and screams there had quieted, replaced with weak groans of agony. Both Pilazzo and Timothy stood motionless, listening.

Timothy ran his free hand through his hair. "They're coming for us. Are you prepared for battle, Father?"

The priest looked at the boy, whose swollen eye twitched nervously. "No. But I'll try—"

There was an explosion just outside the church. Two of the stained-glass windows shattered and colorful shards sliced through the air. The windows' lead frames buckled and collapsed inward. Pilazzo pitched forward, reached out both arms to keep himself from falling, and grabbed on to a . . . a *body . . . a warm, slimy, wet, naked, corpse . . .*

Neither he nor Timothy had seen it in the gloom. In the beam of Timothy's flashlight Pilazzo saw that the body was hanging from a noose leading up to a beam in the dark ceiling.

With dreadful silence, the flashlight abruptly went out.

The beams creaked, and the body swayed. Still fighting to remain standing, Pilazzo latched on to it with both hands. His fingers sunk into the pliant flesh. His feet slipped in the puddle of blood beneath him. In a panic he squeezed the body even tighter. His cheek pressed against a wet patch of flesh. A flurry of dust rained down on him from the ceiling.

Lungs heaving, he called for Timothy—but the boy remained dishearteningly silent.

"Timothy?" he repeated, his voice faint.

No answer.

His hands flew away from the hanging corpse. The body swayed.

"Timothy?" he cried out, a bit more loudly now.

No answer.

His heart sank into a black hole, a tiny voice in the back of his head yammering, *The boy's dead! The boy's dead!* And then he thought, *And what about all the others? The rectory's quiet. There isn't even the cries of the workers. Dear God, WHAT IS HAPPENING?*

The rosary began to move.

He managed to reach into his pocket and grasp it. It calmed as soon as he touched it. And so, for the moment, did his anxiety.

From behind, near the rear of the church, Pilazzo heard footsteps—they crunched debris, echoing in the strange silence like drops of water in a cave.

Pilazzo was able to gather his thoughts. He mustered a bit of strength, took a deep breath, and turned away from the hanging corpse. He desperately searched the all-encompassing darkness as he staggered into a pew. A jolt of pain ripped through his hip as he collided against the hard wooden seat.

With a deafening crack the beam supporting the hanging corpse snapped. The body plummeted to the floor with a sickening thud, and a loud rain of wood followed it to the floor.

He shouted, "Timothy?" He lunged from the pew toward the altar, preparing to confront the evils awaiting him in the bitter darkness. He skidded to a stop somewhere near the steps, suddenly aware of the sticky blood on his hands and face. He clawed at himself as if trying to brush away a swarm of insects.

The footsteps he'd heard earlier grew louder, seeming to approach from every direction. He jerked his head around, but could not make out their source in the dark. Quickly, he removed the beads from his pocket.

He held them out and spun around like a vampire hunter brandishing a crucifix.

He heard a loud creak.

He turned.

The door to the rectory was opening.

CHAPTER THIRTY-SEVEN

Amid the gleam of yellow light, the workers emerged into the church. The first two held the ancient crate between them. Those behind carried the severed heads of their vagrant victims: Seymour, Dallas, Rollo, Wrath, Wilson, Marcus, Weston, and the albino.

But where's Jyro? he thought, recalling how the vagrant in his final moments had tried to show the priest something in his hand. *Is he still alive? If so, how? And where is he now?*

So many questions and no time to find the answers.

The workers shambled through the doorway. Their injuries were painfully clear. Many of them were bleeding—or drenched in the blood of their victims. Some were missing an eye or limb. They didn't seem to feel the agony that must have been tearing through their bodies.

They filled the transept at the left of the altar like a chorus of parishioners. There were at least twenty-five of them in all, those holding the heads standing in front, flanking the pair with the crate on both sides. *There's so many of them,* Pilazzo thought, realizing with dismay that there were even more wreaking havoc in the outside world. *A whole damn city's worth.*

He trembled uncontrollably as he held out the rosary, instinct forcing him to shout, "Be gone, foul demons!"

The workers laughed.

Pilazzo swallowed hard. He clutched the rosary so tightly his nails dug half-moons into his palm.

Amid their laughter, deep livid voices shouted, *"Bow to the beast, priest! Bestow upon him the rosary! The vagrants have lied to you! The rosary is a sham! A useless piece of junk!"* On and on their hideous lies went.

A cold wind blew into his back, sending ghostly chills up and down his spine. He jerked around as if someone had shouted, but saw only the dark church, its shuttered doors dim shadows in the light spilling from the rectory door. He turned back toward the bloody mass of construction workers packing the transept . . . but . . .

. . . *but they're staying away from the altar,* Pilazzo realized with a shock of revelation. *And I understand.* . . . His mind again went back to his meeting with Henry Miller and how during their conversation outside the church the foreman had said: *Our crews aren't insured for moving valuables, Father. I strongly suggest you hire a moving company to handle them.* . . .

The Achilles' heel of the beast became utterly clear.

The porcelain statues and the great wooden Jesus. The workers couldn't move them because they *couldn't touch them.* Miller had tried to convince Pilazzo to get someone else to move them—someone not under the influence of the beast—because his workers could not do it.

He remembered then his confrontation with the beast, how it had manifested itself upon the altar amid the circle of statues—and before the great crucifix.

Pilazzo wondered, *If the workers—the minions of the beast—aren't able to approach the altar, then how did the beast itself manage to do it?*

Pilazzo squeezed the rosary—now warm—and as if by magic an answer bloomed in his mind.

The doomed vagrant Larry had tried to use the rosary for its true, benign purpose. He had not been pure of heart, however—*a sinless one*—and had therefore failed to invoke God's power. Instead it had backfired, and he opened a door for the beast to emerge and gain strength.

But goodness had *used Larry* to intervene at the exact moment Pilazzo arrived at the church. So Larry could deliver the rosary to the priest while the beast was exposed, and vulnerable to attack.

Yes, Pilazzo thought. *It was divine intervention. Larry taking the rosary and being there when I entered the church. Timothy being there for me soon after that. It's Good combating Evil, every step of the way.*

The entire truth had finally been revealed, spread out before him: a gift to him from the rosary. *From God.*

He had no choice but to use it to his advantage. *Follow the message that God delivers to you. Heed His word and do your part to bring down the evil that promises man the end of days. . . .*

"Father!"

Timothy. Pilazzo spun around and saw the boy.

Trapped in the arms of Henry Miller.

CHAPTER THIRTY-EIGHT

The foreman had one great arm wrapped forcefully around Timothy's neck, his free hand clutching a fistful of the boy's hair. The boy's good eye bulged—even his swollen eyelid had managed to open a bit—as he pulled furiously at Miller's beefy forearm in a bid for escape.

Pilazzo rubbed the rosary frantically, seeking assistance. He felt the heat of the wood, but failed to gain any help in his moment of need.

"Timothy . . . I'll get you out of this," the priest promised emptily. *Please, God, I implore You, help me. . . .*

Miller grinned, mouth filled with thick brown teeth. As though reading Pilazzo's mind, he barked, "God can't help you now, priest." His voice was feral, barely recognizable as human.

And yet, the foreman wasn't all that threatening in his appearance. He might've been just another balding, overweight man in his fifties, face red and pudgy, puffy bags sagging under deep-set eyes. He looked more unhealthy than evil.

Still, Pilazzo knew the evil dwelling inside this man could move worlds.

To save all mankind (it all sounded so B-movie, but

damn if it wasn't the fact of the matter), Pilazzo needed to kill this man at once, end his command of the workers.

He shuddered at the thought. How could he possibly do this? He was a priest, a holy man, truly incapable of murder. He reminded himself that he wouldn't be killing a man so much as eliminating an evil entity, but he still couldn't find it within himself.

"Father!" Timothy shouted, squirming in Miller's tightening grasp. The tendons on his neck stuck out like cords. His feet slipped in the carpet of blood, drawing streaks into it.

The foreman grinned. "Come and get him, Father. The boy for the rosary."

"What good is it to you?" Pilazzo felt his face go hot with anger.

"It's everything . . . so long as its rightful possessor surrenders it to me."

"The boy is doomed either way," Pilazzo replied. "We all are." He contemplated Miller's words. *"So long as its rightful possessor surrenders it to me." Which is why the beast needed me to come here, why it couldn't have simply taken the rosary for itself. It needed Good to surrender it . . . to bow to the beast. Just as the Bible says: For Evil to gain rule over man, it would need to abolish all that was good. The sinless one.*

Miller laughed at the priest's logic. "So true." And then the foreman *changed,* exposing the evil lying below his human surface. His face turned repulsively gray in the dim light, bloating slightly. His head jerked up and down, and he barked, gagging up clots of thick white foam. When he looked back at Pilazzo, his nostrils widened and green fluid leaked out.

Pilazzo couldn't believe what he was seeing. He

clutched his stomach as a wave of nausea gripped him.

"Give me the boy, Miller," he said, trying desperately to ignore the transformation he'd just seen. He turned away from the foreman and looked at the rosary in his hand.

He raised it in battle. *Or am I preparing to trade it for Timothy?*

One life for millions?

"No, Father!" the boy shouted, squirming in the foreman's—*the beast's*—grasp.

Pilazzo jerked the rosary back.

The foreman grinned. Then, with a similar flick of the wrist, he grabbed Timothy by the chin . . .

"No!"

. . . and with cruel and inhuman strength wrenched the boy's head sideways and snapped his neck, producing a crack that resounded through the empty church like a small firecracker. Timothy's body went limp in Miller's arms. The foreman sniggered and released the boy. Timothy dropped lifelessly to the bloody floor, a puddle of urine darkening the crotch of his jeans.

Miller's grin widened, teeth now black as tar, pointed like daggers. "So then . . . I shall make you give it to me."

Shaking his head in disbelief and horror, Pilazzo backed away, then turned and ran toward the altar. He looked over at the workers near the transept. They were grimacing, glowering at him with their screwdrivers and box cutters and awls drawn. One of them was jabbing a crowbar in the air. Rollo's head was impaled on the end, like a meatball on a toothpick.

Pilazzo stopped at the foot of the altar.

The workers all remained at a watchful distance.

Holding the gently writhing beads close to his body, Pilazzo stepped up onto the altar.

"Your divine inspiration is commendable." Miller's voice carried across the church, deeper and rougher than it had been moments before. He kicked aside Timothy's corpse and stepped down the aisle toward the altar.

The rosary began to grow warm, glowing red. A tiny wave of relief filtered through Pilazzo, despite the hideous circumstances. "I'm safe as long as I remain here on the altar," he murmured, unconvinced of his desperate theory. *But then what of the rest of the world?*

Miller approached the altar, and in the pallid light Pilazzo could see his face had changed even further: the skin appallingly wrinkled, cut deep and sickly green. White gauzy hair sprouted from his previously bald head, like ancient webs. He'd grown larger, round muscles defined beneath his bloody clothes.

"I've visited the altar once before. You remember, don't you? When we first met?"

In Pilazzo's mind, images of the hideous thing he'd seen on the altar returned to him. He remembered how the thing had eaten Larry. Pilazzo clenched his teeth, trying in vain to rid his mind of the horrific images.

Miller laughed so loudly his guffaws nearly shook the weakened beams of the church. He reached out, displaying hands that had morphed into lizard's claws.

"Come to daddy!" the Miller-beast bellowed. "Let's play!" Its voice resonated, sounding like a chorus of many. The workers began to rustle noisily, jostling together like rats in a cage.

Pilazzo stepped up onto the upper platform of the altar and backed into the semicircle of shrouded statues—directly beneath the twelve-foot crucified Jesus. Colored lights fell in from the remaining stained-glass windows above, igniting the altar with ghostly luminescence. Pilazzo gazed up to view its source, but instead of mystical radiance breaking through the night, he saw the spires of flames grabbing the roof of the church.

Oh my God . . .

The roof of the church was on fire.

He began systematically manipulating the rosary, fingers guided by some unseen force. The rosary remained unmoving, its warmth gone. He squeezed it tight, trying desperately to comprehend what was happening, but fear had him too tightly in its grip.

Behind him came a sharp cracking sound. He spun quickly, half expecting a blow from one of the workers . . . but nothing was there.

Nothing . . . except the nailed feet of the great wooden Jesus.

Blood was seeping from its wounds.

CHAPTER THIRTY-NINE

Dear God!

All of a sudden the beads started to move vigorously in his hands. He could see them glowing brighter now, their red warmth spreading over his hands like gloves, just as it had earlier in the rectory. Pilazzo spun away from the great crucifix and saw Miller—no, the *beast* that had replaced Miller—cloaked in moving shadows, dark specters racing over his still-changing form. It stepped to the front of the altar . . . but no further.

Because it can't. . . .

Even in the dim light, Pilazzo could see the hideous transformation of Miller's body, muscular limbs now tearing through clothes, the skin beneath partly reptilian, riddled with patches of hair that swirled and coiled like fire. It jabbed its claws toward the priest, with yellow talons four inches long, sharp as razors.

And then its face: a visage of utter repulsiveness that swam out of the moving darkness. Its forehead was low, covered with thick, flaring scales. Its cheeks, swollen and wet, the eyes glowing white, filled with evil. Its mouth opened impossibly wide, and it roared, beckoning the workers to join it with howls of their own. It shook its newly malformed head and thick foam sprayed from huge bleeding lips. Pilazzo pressed himself back against the wooden Jesus.

Warmth emanated from the hard, carved surface.

Just like the rosary . . .

The workers continued jostling against one another, eager to flee their imprisonment but appearing to be confined. The two workers holding the crate dropped it, producing a loud crack that echoed through the church. They kneeled beside it, rubbing its dusty surface as if searching for something.

Terrified, Pilazzo continued to grip the rosary, searching for an answer in the beads while trying to not want it to become a tool for slaughter. The message reverberated in his mind: *Follow the message that God delivers to you . . . bring down the evil that promises man the end of days. . . .*

But I am no murderer!

He looked at the rosary in his hands. Its red glow had faded. *No!* In a panic, he shook it like a dying radio to keep it functioning.

The voice of Monsignor Sanchez filled his head with a new message: *The beast is afraid of it . . . afraid of what you might do with it.*

Thomas?

"*Give it to me,*" the beast demanded, voice monstrous and booming, barely clinging to its humanity. Pilazzo gasped at the mere sight of the beast. He could feel his very sanity breaking down, his mind overloading with the horror of what Henry Miller had become.

It stood seven feet tall, looking nothing like the man it had been moments earlier—a creature straight from the bowels of Hell, black scaly skin, a muscle-bound torso with a rattle-tipped tail that tore through its pants.

From its head, covered in thick hair, a series of serrated horns surfaced—not just a pair but a cluster of them— each four inches high with a dark rounded end. A few strips of Miller's shirt still dangled from its shoulders. It glared at Pilazzo in threatening silence, eyes glimmering angrily below thick, flaring eyebrows.

Pilazzo shuddered uncontrollably, searching the rosary for guidance. If there were a time when he needed it most, this was it.

"Be gone, foul demon," he whispered weakly, cowering, feeling foolish and afraid. The rosary shifted and curved around his devoted fingers.

The beast bellowed a storm of hellish cries that shook the church.

The rosary shifted again. It began to get hot, a positive sign that help was on the way . . . he hoped and prayed.

And then from out of nowhere, a wave of anger and a want for retribution filled Pilazzo's mind. His muscles twitched and a surge of courage and bravery consumed him until he found himself shouting at the beast, "Do you think I'm such a weakling that I would hand my fate over to you as if it were a child's plaything?"

The beast, standing its ground, turned its huge head toward the priest. It snorted and a craggy black tongue unfurled from its mouth, licking the mucus from its huge lips. Pilazzo recoiled, inhaling the horrid stench of its sulfur breath. Its roar was a chorus of animals: the growl of an angry bear reverberating above an cacophony of squealing pigs and bleating goats.

From above, something cracked loudly. Pilazzo watched the spreading flames beyond the stained-glass windows. His trembling hands and fingers moved about the beads with strange precision. The rosary grew even hotter, calming his racing blood. He beheld violent images of the fires beyond the walls around him, making every hellish attempt to take down the safe haven of the Church of St. Peter.

But something was thwarting the fires, he realized, gazing back up toward the windows. A barrier of some sort around the church.

Its source lay squirming in his hands.

"Please, please," he urged the rosary. The air in the church turned from cold to hot in seconds. Tiny wisps of smoke spiraled from the rosary.

The beast reached its claws toward Pilazzo, only to howl and pull them back quickly, as if scalded.

I am being protected. . . .

In his peripheral vision, Pilazzo could see the workers jostling one another violently. Blood appeared on their faces from the random collisions. They'd dropped their trophy heads and were trampling them underfoot. The worker holding the crowbar with Rollo's head shouted, "Surrender the rosary, priest!"

A loud hiss filled Pilazzo's ears. He saw the beast suddenly distracted, looking up to a point just above its head. Its eyes were wide and wet, and it began swiping a claw through the air like a cat pawing a dangling toy. Its jaws were bared, dripping yellow venom.

It seemed to perceive something in the air . . . something wholly disconcerting.

Something . . . *good.*

Pilazzo continued to work his hands about the sliding, shifting rosary.

Finally, one of the workers—a thin, gray-haired man—broke free from the force that had held him bound. He shuffled haphazardly toward the altar, arms swatting his battered body as though he were on fire. The beast shot the man a wary glance, then let loose a roar that vibrated throughout Pilazzo's body.

If the roar had been meant as a distraction, it didn't work. The worker reached the periphery of the altar . . . and stepped onto it. There was a loud *whump*, followed by a blast of searing hot air. Red flames shot up from the worker's body to a height of nearly fifteen feet. The worker howled like a tortured dog, lurching aimlessly between the altar and first row of pews. Again the air reeked of burning flesh. The worker collapsed beside the front pew, where he curled up, thick plumes of black smoke wafting through the hole in the ceiling.

The beast roared again, jerking its reptilian gaze back and forth, back and forth. The base of the great statue of Jesus grew even hotter against Pilazzo's back, and then he heard a loud sound. Pilazzo cowered, fearful of something dropping on his head.

Despite his proximity to the beast and the terror clawing at his body, he stood his ground, massaging the rosary feverishly and making every attempt to breathe at a controlled pace and calm his laboring heart. His vision faded into a gray blur. Numbness spread through his body. He fought to ignore the din filling the church and the crackling flames eager to make their way inside. Instead he allowed the rosary to guide him to its divine purpose.

Another loud crack came from above, hot dust and the aroma of burning wood trailing in its wake. The priest gazed at the beast. It was reaching through a veil of smoke into the protective domain of the altar, its claw three feet from the priest's hands and the rosary. Pilazzo could see the claw searing, blisters rising. The beast howled in agony, the force of it nearly knocking Pilazzo down. It pulled back, stamping its feet in brutish frustration while snarling in a dozen braying voices.

Pilazzo tugged furiously on the rosary. Hot tears burst from his eyes, irritated by the smoke. The red light emanating from the rosary exploded from his body, igniting the altar like a surge of fire. Heat filled his palms, and then his entire body as the beads seared his skin like embers. Still, he held on, praying, sweating profusely, the words of an unknown language spilling from his lips. He watched with awe as the drop cloths on the statues began to billow beneath the churning blasts of hot air. Then he turned to the beast . . . the beast, now trembling like a sickly dog, barking and coughing up a mess of green vomit. Its piercing eyes darted furiously about the altar, at the drop cloths that one by one flew off the statues like fleeing ghosts.

The beast roared in a panic (the burning man had been reduced to a molten heap of flesh), looking suddenly frail in the storm of wind and smoke slashing through the church. It barked something unintelligible, seemingly using a great deal of its waning strength.

As if a cage door had been opened, the workers spilled forward, many of them tripping over themselves and falling down, free of their invisible bonds. The pair at the front of the group lugged the crate over to the beast and dropped it at its feet.

While the beast used one muscled claw to wrench the crate open, the workers crawled over one another like rats, their faces bleeding and bruised, hands frantically searching the floor for their dropped weapons. Some of them succeeded. Others groped like blind men, deprived of guidance, the heads of their victims rolling about like soccer balls.

Those who were armed stood and awaited their master's command.

The beast reached into the crate and removed the burning chalice, flames and blood dancing across its glossy black-red surface and over the beast's yellow talons.

The beast stepped back and roared with the voices of a thousand burning souls, green vomit still spewing from its mouth. Then it shoved the raised chalice toward the altar: a fearful leader, sending its lambs to the slaughter.

Under the spell of the rosary, Pilazzo hadn't noticed the movement behind him. But he'd sensed something, a thin stretching vibration beating against his eardrums. He realized that something hard was grasping him—something that despite its warmth, felt strikingly artificial.

He turned his face up and beheld a miraculous sight.

The red light had receded. The ceiling was now a dark vista of smoke. Pilazzo wanted to fall to his knees, to cover his eyes and wish away what he was seeing, but he had become a prisoner to a new force.

The statue next to him was holding him by the biceps.

Pure white porcelain, the statue's smooth surface remained inanimate. But its eyes were *moving*.

Pilazzo thought, *It can see me. . . .*

He looked at the solid white arm grasping him, and the other, which remained stiff and lifeless at the statue's side. He made a feeble attempt to pull away, but it was impossible to move. The statue's face had gained a bit of color, the lips showing the slightest tint of pink. The corner of its mouth pulled up into a delicate grin.

Has he come to avenge the death of his mother? he thought crazily.

And then he was being pulled to one side, only the statue's arm moving, creaking hollowly. A hot breeze sprang from the center of the altar, causing Pilazzo's cassock to flap and flutter like sails in a storm. The statue released its grip. Pilazzo shrank down against the rear wall, eyes bulging, arms folded protectively across his chest, holding the glowing rosary close.

By this time, the workers had amassed before the altar, poised for battle, flaunting their weapons. Pilazzo gazed forlornly at them, sapped of all strength behind the moving statue. He felt as if something had sucked all the breath out of him.

And then he heard that scraping sound again, like dry fingers rubbing against plastic, and when he turned he saw that *all* the statues were moving from their positions. St. Peter, St. Michael, St. Thomas, St. Luke, and the Virgin Mary. They bent and flexed ever so slightly, the creaking of their joints amplified, sounding like earth tremors. *They're alive,* Pilazzo thought. Was this Good fighting Evil, or one evil challenging another?

The beast raised its arms high, cockily displaying the burning chalice, tiny flames spilling out and skittering down the length of its massive arm like fleeing roaches. It pulled its lips back, showing teeth and bloodred gums that glinted with fire. It shook its malformed head and bellowed fiercely, pinning Pilazzo with huge black eyes. Pilazzo felt the ground shudder beneath him. The hot stink of the monster's breath washed over him. The beast spun and swung its arms maniacally, its massive claws dividing the air with an unrelenting whisper. Flames spilled from the chalice and burned the floor in oil-slick patches. The beast's free claw struck the nearest pew, carving the polished wood in two, exploding it into a shower of smoldering splinters. The beast's tail, now four feet long, rattled incessantly.

Slowly, the statues plodded forward noisily, descending the steps in uneven totters. Once off the altar, they became targets for attack. The workers—screwdrivers and saws and drills raised high—advanced upon them.

With terror and awe Pilazzo gazed in disbelief at the defending statues, two of them made of white porcelain, the others carved in wood and intricately hand painted in perfect blues and reds and browns. They moved sluggishly, like B-movie zombies, way too slow to provide any defense. The collision of the workers and their tools against them echoed like murderous thunder. This was quickly followed by the earsplitting sounds of metal on porcelain, metal on wood, and the death-grip cries of those beaten workers too weak to challenge the otherworldly presences opposing them.

It seemed to Pilazzo that the five slow-moving statues were not intended to fight in some ultimate battle against Evil—the saints were *not* fighters. No, their purpose was to act as a distraction.

The true adversary of the evil in St. Peter's Church was still rising, a life bigger and more powerful than the five others combined. Pilazzo choked on a small piece of wood that had found its way into his throat, a splinter that had come free from the tearing wood three feet to his right.

The five statues were now completely surrounded. The beast stood back from the fray, flaunting the chalice and watching as its workers stabbed and chopped and sawed at the wood and porcelain figures. The saintly figures, now unmoving, tilted and rocked amid the sea of attacking arms. Their faces did not resemble anything like saints anymore: dark, filthy chips pocked the porcelain pair, and the wooden figures were gouged deeply.

But the most inspiring sight of all was right beside Pilazzo.

The great, crucified Jesus . . . it was . . .

Father Anthony Pilazzo had never been more terrified in his life.

There was a huge crack, like a wooden bat against a baseball, and it nearly deafened him. He prayed that he had imagined it, but then there was another more forceful sound: the ripping shriek of tortured wood. He crawled to his right along the rear wall of the church and gazed at the incredible sight just feet away.

A ghostly red mist rose up from the base of the crucifix in winding tendrils. He followed the vaporous strands up to the face of the wooden Jesus, which was no longer gazing toward the heavens in prayer, but staring at the beast opposing it, eyes showing tinges of life.

Like the painted eyes on my night-light . . .

Yellow smoke swelled from the rear of the Jesus figure's head. The smell of burning wood overpowered the hideous stench of the beast. The floor beneath Pilazzo trembled forcefully.

With a piercing crunch, the statue's head tore away from the crucifix. Splinters of wood rained down on the altar, peppering the battling workers, who were too busy destroying the other statues to notice their *true* threat. Pilazzo covered his face with his arms, shielding his eyes from the storm of wood. A few seconds later, as he uncovered his eyes, another crack of wood boomed through the church, and he saw the wooden Jesus leaning farther away from the cross, its back now free.

Pilazzo looked back at the chaotic battle and saw the beast struggling to rekindle the sputtering fires in the chalice. Pilazzo presumed these fires provided strength to the beast—just as the rosary offered power to the sinless one. The beast's downcast eyes were fixed on the glossy chalice, the beast's arms, legs, and tail flailing in anger and frustration.

With another crack, a cloud of sawdust burst over Pilazzo's head like a blast of gunpowder. The Jesus figure's right arm was now free of the cross, sticking straight out, blood trickling from the wound in its hand and sizzling as it spattered the altar. Then the left arm was freed. It too remained stiff. Like the other, it bled from its wound, the fingers flexing ever so slightly.

The beast finally took notice of what was happening, its black eyes fixed with terror upon the twelve-foot wooden Jesus pulling away from the crucifix, leaning forward, blood seeping from the wounds in its hands and feet. The workers gathered before their dark god, forming a wall of inhuman protection, bloodied from battle but still prepared to defend the beast to the death.

With a creak, the wooden Jesus's tortured eyes shifted to the beast. The beast lowered the burning chalice, the fires within reduced to meager embers.

There was another great wrenching noise as the feet of the Jesus figure tore free of the cross. The massive statue thudded down onto the altar, still standing.

And then . . . it *stepped* forward on the altar, eyes focused on the beast. Pilazzo's mouth gaped as he stared at the statue with its arms spread wide. Its eyes contemplated the enemy standing before it.

The red mist enveloping the Jesus figure parted, leaving it in flickering shadows.

All of a sudden, one of the stained-glass windows shattered and the flames outside finally made their way in. Colorful glass rained down on the altar, onto the standing wooden Jesus, which seemed not to notice or care, and onto the workers and the beast. Pilazzo recoiled and gasped, choking on sawdust and smoke as he spit drily on the floor. Light-headedness washed over him. He felt a gust of hot air and shrunk back even more as powerful flames leaped across the ceiling.

The wooden Jesus, still in its crucified pose, tilted forward.

The beast roared, the flames in the chalice sputtering, rising and falling, clearly unreliable. The beast shook the chalice hard with both hands, but was unable to revive it.

Furious and frustrated, the beast swung the chalice at the minions collected before it.

The bodies of perhaps ten workers went down. Immediate wails filled the church as heads and arms were severed. The beast roared again, stomping its monstrous feet in fury, staggering crookedly over the fallen bodies, crushing them underfoot. The still-standing workers froze and watched in dreadful silence as those fallen minions still alive crawled broken-boned across the floor.

Without hesitation, the beast shrieked and brought the chalice back. Keeping its aim high, it lopped off the heads of more workers. Blood shot up in geysers as their bodies collapsed beside the broken statues and severed body parts. The beast spotted two stunned workers trying to escape. It lunged and snatched them up with one claw and bashed their heads together in a fierce clap before casting their lifeless bodies aside like burlap bags.

Soon there were no workers left standing. Many of them were dead, others too injured to move.

The chalice, now rich with the blood of new sacrifices, began to burn again.

Pilazzo didn't need the rosary to tell him that just as the workers had sacrificed the vagrants to feed the chalice, the beast itself, in desperation, had sacrificed its own minions to gather the power needed to confront the goodness that stood before him.

The great wooden Jesus.

The beast spun in a rambling circle, stomping on the bodies, swinging the chalice back and forth, spilling embers and sparks.

The Jesus figure creaked . . . creaked . . . creaked . . . then slowly began to fall, its arms remaining outstretched.

It fell across the slaughterhouse of workers onto the marauding beast.

Somewhere in the darkness, Pilazzo heard bones crunching, and then a howl of pain and agony in the voices of a thousand creatures shook every beam in the church and shattered every remaining stained-glass window.

The beast arched and thumped below the weight of the fallen statue, sawing into its wooden chest with the talons of its free hand, intending, it seemed, to claw out its heart. The statue, perhaps a thousand pounds or more, didn't budge. But it did bleed, thin streaks that glistened in the moving shadows like tiny rivers. The beast's head twisted sideways, its black, horrible eyes fixing on Pilazzo, almost seeming to plead with him. Again it roared in a chorus of agonized voices, the unbearable stench of which traveled all the way up to the altar, where Pilazzo clutched the rosary and ignored the deep wounds it burned into his hands.

Stigmata . . .

And from somewhere in the darkness ahead, an ethereal voice whispered: *"Drop my chalice, demon, and go back to the hell from where you came."*

Pilazzo saw the startling truth of the matter: The chalice, stolen by some demon in an attempt to harvest its power, in fact belonged to Jesus Christ.

He wondered: *Is this the Holy Grail, used thousands of years ago to absorb the sins of Jesus's followers? Were those sins now being used by the beast to wreak havoc upon the world?*

Still gripping the burning chalice in its right hand, the beast raised its arm and rammed it against the Jesus figure's head. Flames burst from it, charring the wood that made up the sculpture's crown of thorns and hair. The beast continued to pound out its fury, each strike against the statue like thunder in Pilazzo's ears. He shut his eyes tightly, vaguely aware of debris dropping around him.

The Jesus figure remained on top of the beast, arms still spread wide. Tiny bands of fire leaped from its head, meandering five or six feet before withering away. Beneath it, the beast continued thumping and bucking and roaring. Torrential winds swept through the church, sending debris and dust everywhere. Chips of wood brushed by Pilazzo. He coughed and rubbed his eyes furiously, chest rising and falling. When he pulled his hands away from his eyes, he was relieved to see the beast succumbing beneath the oppressive weight of its adversary.

The fires on the wooden Jesus's head had spread across its back, sending dark spirals of smoke up to meet the flames on the roof. The beast brought its heavy fists down on the Jesus figure's burning head, howling so loud that Pilazzo had to clap his hands over his ears. The fire consumed the entire upper half of the statue and was now spreading onto the beast. The beast shrieked in agony. Yellow liquid oozed from its face as the flames took to its thick hair and scales. Still, it struggled for freedom, making every effort to fight back, arms flailing, body bucking. But its efforts were in vain, and soon its face was nothing more than a black and yellow pulp beneath the spreading flames, its movements tapered down to muscle twitching contractions.

Clearly defeated, the beast tossed the chalice aside. The wooden Jesus, now completely on fire and charred black, cracked in half and fell off the beast's body, burning embers writhing across it. The faceless demon rolled over and crawled away, scaly legs kicking up a cloud of dust and blood and glass.

Still on fire, still shrieking, it reached for the chalice.

A shadow emerged from the dark. Pilazzo's heart skipped a beat . . . until he saw the figure's face in the flickering firelight.

Jyro.

The vagrant grabbed the chalice. With a single lunge, he leapt at the beast, and slammed it into its burning head.

An unimaginable chorus of sounds filled the church, of men and women and children screaming for their very souls, of flesh tearing and wood sputtering beneath crackling flames and shaking beams, of terrible animal-istic growls.

When the smoke cleared, Pilazzo saw the beast leap up and shove Jyro back, despite its head having been crushed. Tail rattling, it darted on all fours down the center aisle and leapt at the inner doors of the church. The doors exploded into a violent storm of wood.

Pilazzo scrambled up. He looked at the dead and dying construction workers at the foot of the altar and then beyond to the smoldering heap of wood that used to be a statue of Jesus Christ nailed to the crucifix behind the altar.

He took a deep, painful breath and staggered forward.

The fires above had gone out, leaving only glowing cinders and gray smoke.

He worked his way across the battlefield of severed arms, legs, heads, and torsos, through tacky puddles of blood and glistening organs, shards of stained glass and fragments of porcelain, down the strangely silent aisle.

In a faint, dry whisper, he called, "Jyro?"

From between the pews came a rustle. Then a shadow.

The vagrant stood, gripping a pew for support.

He looked at the priest, face soiled black. "Been a helluva day, eh Father?"

Pilazzo nodded, just once. Then looked past Jyro toward the rear of the church.

The inner doors were destroyed.

The doors leading outside . . . were open.

Pilazzo limped down the aisle, looking again to the ceiling just to confirm that the fires had indeed ceased.

He looked back to the doors. *The open doors.* Daylight filtered into the antechamber.

He looked at Jyro as he walked by, then to the floor where Timothy's lifeless body remained, head askew, blood seeping from his mouth. In silence, Jyro joined Pilazzo and they both headed to the vestibule.

Here they stopped.

Tears filled Pilazzo's eyes at what he saw.

Somewhere in the brief moment between ripping through the inner doors and reaching the large twin doors leading out into the injured world, the beast fled the human body it had possessed. What remained behind, lying motionless on the floor of the vestibule, was a bloody, misshapen lump of human flesh that used to be Henry Miller, foreman for Pale Horse Construction.

A single eye, wet and socketless, looked up at them.

It was moving.

He was still alive. But Pilazzo knew it was only a matter of time.

Two thin flaps of flesh separated in a spot four inches below the horrible staring eye. Pilazzo saw a dime-sized tooth in it. A harsh, faint whisper emerged, followed by a thin line of bloody saliva.

"I'm sorry. . . ."

Pilazzo used the beads to cross himself, then closed his eyes and put Henry Miller out of his misery with a heavy slam of his foot on the foreman's deformed skull.

He nearly slipped down in the spray of blood and gristle. He gagged, paused to take a deep breath, then stumbled to the open front doors of St. Peter's Church.

Father Anthony Pilazzo stepped outside.

He stood on the top step, squinting through the

smoke that filled the street. He raised his head in the early morning sunlight and felt the golden beams on his eyes . . . eyes that had been buried in blood and darkness for the past twenty-four hours.

Jyro stood beside him. "You did it. The fires . . . they're no longer burning."

Pilazzo remained silent for a moment, then looked at Jyro. The vagrant was a bloody mess, beaten and worn, but not seriously injured.

"How did you manage to survive?" Pilazzo asked.

Jyro held up his fist. It was clenched tightly. Pilazzo remembered how Jyro had held his hand out to him in the hallway before being pulled back into the fray in the rectory.

How he seemed to want to show something to him and Timothy.

Jyro opened his hand and showed the priest how he lived through the slaughter.

In his palm was a single bead from the rosary. It was cracked in two. "When you've lived on the streets, Father, you find ways to survive."

And with that, Jyro walked down the steps of St. Peter's Church, turning only once to say, "Thanks, Father," before disappearing around the corner.

CHAPTER FORTY

Two years later

"May the Lord be with you."

"And also with you."

"Go in peace," he instructed the parishioners, who immediately began filing out of the Church of St. Elizabeth. Father Anthony Pilazzo bowed to the assembly and quickly stepped off the altar into the rectory, ignoring those milling about. He raced to his room, feeling tired and not in any particular mood to engage in conversation. He'd been unable to sleep last night. Father Hautala had snored up a hurricane, keeping the rest of the priests—Monsignor Reinhardt included—in the kitchen playing a friendly game of rummy until four A.M.

He entered his room. It was meagerly furnished: an aluminum-framed twin bed alongside a small end table supporting a shaded lamp and telephone. On the opposite wall was an easy chair and small television. Like the rest of the rectory, the floor was carpeted in dull blue, a cotton curtain in a near-matching color over the room's only window.

Sheets of rain slashed the dark pane. He pulled the curtain aside and gazed outside, watching the cars.

Things were much different here in the suburbs. Friendlier. Closer knit. He liked it, but again wondered: *Could it happen here?*

He kneeled beside his bed, folded his hands and recited a prayer, then opened the nightstand drawer, thinking back to the moment he stepped out of St. Peter's Church two years before. The sky had been painted gray by the smoke rising from the fires that had burned throughout Manhattan. The sun's light had eaten its way through a hole in that dark tapestry, helping to guide him to safety. He'd held the ancient wooden rosary in his hands and had used it to thank God for his survival, to say a prayer for those who had perished in the beast's game: Timothy and the others, brave souls who'd seen the threat of evil rising before their jaded eyes; who'd made every last effort to combat it; who'd eventually surrendered their very lives to the cause.

In the days that followed the events at St. Peter's, he'd kept tabs on the news. The fires burning in the city had eventually been extinguished, and all those suffering from rage and hysteria had magically shaken their ills and returned to normal.

The reporters never mentioned that the fires had not been put out by firefighters. The truth was they had simply disappeared, leaving behind thick columns of smoke that lingered in the air for weeks, plus a wicked trail of wreckage that to this day was still being rebuilt.

A month later—after The Calming, as the peaceful days that followed were described—he joined the parish in upstate New York, taking part in the weekly services, but mostly hearing the confessions of those who'd felt tempted by inexplicable evils since the Rise of Fires. Pilazzo explained time and time again that the influence of the beast was not only present, but it was strong, and that as God's children we must make every effort to avoid the beast's ongoing temptations.

He shook away the thoughts. Without looking at the clock, he reached into the drawer and pushed aside a short stack of underwear and balled-up socks. Here was a lockbox, made of gray steel with a small handle on top. He removed it, reached into his pocket, and shook out his key chain—a dozen or so keys ringed together with the brass cross Father SanGiovanni had given him upon his acceptance into the parish.

He fingered the smallest key. Slowly, he slid it into the lock on the box.

He turned it. There was an audible click.

He opened the box.

He reached inside and removed the rosary, now brown and chipped and charred, looking nothing like it had two years earlier. Every day he would repeat this routine, working his fingers about the beads, hoping for another sign from God . . . a sign that everything would be all right in the end.

But nothing came.

And he was beginning to realize why.

He wasn't pure of heart anymore. Devoid of sin.

He was a murderer now.

He'd killed Henry Miller.

And he thought back to how he brought his weighty foot down on the head of the innocent man who was somehow alive in the jumbled mess of his body, how he'd taken away what little time remained of his life— the life of a man who was merely an innocent pawn in some great, diabolical game.

He remembered how, later, after Jyro had left him, he'd gazed at the still-open doors of the church, then ran back up the stairs. He'd paused for a moment at the entrance, then went back into the church, stepping over Miller's lumpy remains, sidestepping small flames and holding his breath, eyeing the burning heap in front of him that used to be the wooden Jesus, looking for . . .

He placed the rosary back in the box.

And removed the chalice.

And realized with equal amounts of dismay and curiosity that as much as the rosary required someone pure of heart to work its magic, so did the chalice need a sinner to realize its evil.

Perhaps, Pilazzo thought, *someone who has committed murder?*

He gazed deeply into the chalice, thinking back to the rush of power and strength he felt while under the influence of the rosary . . . and wondered what level of power he could summon with the chalice.

He looked at the rosary, sitting at the bottom of the steel box like a dead snake.

Then back at the chalice.

He rubbed it gently.

It began glowing bright red. . . .

Somewhere in the city, in a dark, cold, damp hole beneath the streets, a homeless man sleeps. His name is Jyro, and in his dreams he sees fires rising high into the sky. He startles awake, terrified, knowing that somewhere, someplace, it is beginning again. . . .